Bury the Pain

Copyright © 2023 Jane l

Published by The Peapod Press

All rights reserved. No part of this book may be reproduced in any form, or by any electronic or mechanical means – except for the inclusion of brief quotations in articles or reviews – without written permission from the author.

ISBN: 9798375390536
Cover photo © 2022 Jane Phillips
Cover design © 2023 Amy Phillips
First edition 2023

This is a work of fiction. Names, characters, places and events are products of the author's imagination. Any resemblance to actual persons, living or dead, is purely coincidental.

Books in The Burials Series

Bury the Truth

Bury the Lies

Bury the Pain

Mary

Our kid

Resilient, resourceful, a keeper of secrets,

but probably not a spy

Acknowledgements

This is Book Three of a series, so I can thank the same people again! My City University friends, Vicki Bradley, Paul Durston, Vicki Jones and Fraser Massey have been with me for the long haul – reading and re-reading as each of the books developed. The long-prose group at Cambridge Writers has helped by reading drafts. Special thanks must go to Paul Durston, Vicki Jones and Fraser Massey for line-editing and finding all the spelling errors, grammatical howlers and typos that my several readings had missed. My lovely girls, Amy and Sian, have helped me just by being there. Amy stars again as my Very High Priestess of On-line Anything and Glyn continues to make strong dark tea.

About the author

Jane Phillips is a psychologist. This gives her an unhealthy interest in the criminal mind. To counterbalance, she has a husband, two children and four grandchildren. They do their best to keep her on the straight and narrow.

Chapter 1

Sunday 14th April 2013

Ben gazed at Diane's box and wondered if Pandora had felt that same sense of foreboding. Three months now. No, that was a lie. It was more than that. Every day, he'd taken the box from its hiding place and every day, he'd decided that now was not the time. He was too busy. He was not yet strong enough. He was… procrastinating. He couldn't put it off again. Today was his birthday – a big one. So, today was the day that he'd pledged to face his demons.

He listened to the hum coming from below. He could hear his daughters downstairs – the occasional hoot of laughter, the rumble of conversation. Their noise was loud and joyous, in sharp contrast to his protracted silence. Were his daughters, like him, in a state of suspended animation? Of course not. They had closed off the past and moved on.

He remembered buying it for her. Newly-wed, they'd wandered through Camden Market. Diane had fallen for it at once. It had been its intricate opening mechanism that had sold it to her. That had been before the tragedy had begun. But Ben now knew that the tragedy had been in gestation for far longer than he could ever have imagined.

The last time he'd opened it, the catastrophe had been all-embracing. A complete breakdown and, although his stay in hospital had been brief, it had taken him all through Christmas and New Year to get back to any sort of equilibrium. Dr Clare, his guiding light in all things of the head, had told him that he was now at the stage of recovery he'd attained before reading Diane's last letter to him; the letter that had told him he must not pursue her killer. He knew that he was going to countermand that last wish. And, to do that, he had to search through the contents of that box. If he was ever going to understand why she had died and who had killed her, the answer – or at least the beginning of the answer – must lie there. It was all he had. His quandary: if he found something, it could destroy him; if he found nothing, it could destroy him. But, he also knew that, if he failed to pursue this truth, that omission would destroy him in his own estimation.

No contest. He reached for the box.

Chapter 2

Katy's voice. 'Dad, Dad. You coming down to lunch? We're waiting – and we've got a surprise for you.'

Ben withdrew his hand with an intense feeling of relief. The satisfaction of knowing that he had again been granted a reprieve seeped into the recesses of his brain, bringing a rush of guilt. He put the box back in its hiding place. The moment of reckoning had been delayed.

'Coming.'

As he entered the kitchen, a chorus erupted. 'Happy Birthday to you.' The whole song with no rude words, not even from Katy and Sarah. He looked around the assembly. Immediately, he had a tightening in his chest and a pricking behind his eyelids. All the people he felt close to were here; his daughters, of course, plus Sarah's best friend, Pam. Michael, a stalwart in the running of the business, had his arm round Pam's shoulders. His Uncle Mo had his arm round Agnes's shoulders – now there was something to celebrate. And Josephine, looking as beautiful as the day he'd met her, and, with Dr Clare's help, near to being a whole human being at last. Then there was Dr Clare, his saviour, with her fiancé, Professor Hallfield – but that relationship was still under wraps as his wife had only recently died. And lastly, his newest friends, Mary – long a neighbour – now his most trusted friend and confidante and Professor Walpole, who had promised to help him to find the truth. Yes, he loved them all and he knew that each would be devastated if the stones he was about to unturn, released the monsters he feared were waiting to devour him. He pushed that thought away and smiled. 'Thank you, my friends. Thank you so much.'

'Yeah. Dad. Look. Me an' Sarah made you a cake.' Katy looked at Pam. 'Well, it was Pam really but we helped. Here, have some fizz and I'll light the candles.' She giggled. 'We didn't have a big enough cake so we put one for every ten years.'

He looked at the five candles and sighed. Suddenly he felt old.

Henry Walpole slowly eased himself to his feet and held up his glass. 'As the oldest person here...' He glanced round the room and waved his stick in the air. 'Oldest by far, by the look of things.' He gently poked Mo with his stick. 'Even you, young man, I reckon I've got at least ten years on you. I think it behoves me to propose a toast. "To advancing years – may they bring wisdom and peace."' They raised their glasses and repeated the mantra.

'Yeah, Dad. You've got to blow out your candles – then we can have some cake.'

More food was brought and Ben mingled with his guests. He noticed that Sarah was looking jittery so he talked to his daughters first. Katy pushed her sister forward. 'Sarah's got something she wants to tell you.' Katy grinned. 'She thinks, now you're officially ancient…' She nudged Sarah who looked over at Mary. Ben could see them exchange a miniscule nod. He wondered if he should let Sarah tell him her secret or should he pre-empt her. He decided to keep quiet.

When it came, it was blunt and to the point. 'Dad, I'm gay.' Then she added. 'You've been having such a dreadful time that I didn't want to add to your worries. But now that things are sorted...'

He hugged her to him and whispered in her ear, 'Congratulations. Does this mean you've found the woman of your dreams?'

As he released her, he saw the tears in her eyes as she nodded. 'I think so.'

'Good. When can I meet her?'

She was about to answer when he was dragged away by his Uncle Mo. 'She's told you then? Took her a bit of time to get it off her chest. But I saw you. You knew, didn't you. How long've you known?'

'About seven years – ever since she brought home that school friend and I could see the attraction.' He laughed. 'This must be the biggest open secret ever. How's Agnes with it – Catholic and all?'

'No problem. She just wants everyone to be happy. And it looks like better times're coming. We're all moving on.'

Ben talked with all his guests and listened to their news, then at last, he came to Henry Walpole who was in animated conversation with Mary.

Walpole turned to greet him. 'Ah, dear boy, we were just discussing your next steps. I've been talking to your delightful friends and family and earwigging all the time. Sort of thing I used to love doing in my Service days – feeling the room, getting information, sniffing the way the wind was blowing – quite made me nostalgic for the Cold War. Happy days.' He sighed and wiped his eyes. 'The consensus is that you've solved three murders and now you'll settle back down to embalming and the like. Snug and safe and boring. Except that nice Dr Clare. She is something special. Totally professional and, if I hadn't been a spy all my life, I'd have missed the signals. She knows what you're about to embark on. The rest are in blissful ignorance, or are trying very hard to persuade themselves that you are destined to settle back into peaceful obscurity and stop causing them to be terrified on your behalf. Am I right?'

Ben nodded. 'Fraid so. I know my family and, yes, they are indulging in wishful thinking. They're trying very hard to deceive themselves into thinking it's over, and they're almost succeeding. I'll have to break it to them. I've been putting it off, just as I've been putting off looking through Diane's things. But I know the time has come. Yes, it's time.'

'Right,' said Mary. 'How about you do that hobbit thing? Announce it at your party. They'll be expecting a speech and that will get it over with and you won't have time to think too deeply. But first, are you absolutely certain you want to look for Diane's killer?'

Ben breathed in deeply and nodded again. Mary looked questioningly at him. He stood up to his full height and tapped on his glass with a spoon. The room was immediately silent as the company turned towards him.

'Thank you, my friends. Thank you for coming and sharing this milestone birthday with me. You all know that I'm not one for long speeches...' This brought a round of applause and expert – and very piercing – whistles from Katy and Sarah. 'Now, I know you young people think that, as of today, I'm officially ancient.'

Calls of, 'No way!'

Ben held up a hand and silence descended once more. He took in a gulp of air. 'It seems to me that this is a good time, with all the people I am most fond of around me, to tell you that I'm not yet ready to settle for a quiet life.' More whoops from the younger members of the company. Ben waited for the noise to die down before continuing. 'You all know that the past few months have been extremely difficult for me and I have to thank you for the magnificent ways in which you have supported me. Thank you, one and all.' Ben raised his glass to them, then put it down and gave them a round of applause. They joined in – in true celebratory fashion.

He breathed in a deep, deep breath. This was so hard. Why couldn't he just wrap himself in this comfort blanket and let those sleeping dogs snore on? That would be the easy option. There would be no repercussions, except to his own self-belief. Of all his friends, only Mary and Dr Clare knew the agonies of indecision that had racked him over these last three months. But, all through, he had known that he would eventually have to detach himself from this protective swathe of love. If he was ever going to still those nagging doubts, to escape from this monochrome world and move back into the sunlight, he was going to have to face his demons – head-on.

When the applause had died down, he continued in a quieter voice. 'But now is the time for me to move forward, moving from small steps to giant leaps. If I'm ever going to fully recover from Diane's death and be able to lead some sort of normal life, I'm going to have to search out the reason for her death. This will take me away from Cambridge for a time.' He smiled. 'I'm not going to put a ring on my finger and disappear, but I do have a quest to fulfil and I will be going away from you for a while. I'm hoping you'll continue to support me and cover for me while I follow my heart in the hope that I can lay Diane's ghost to rest once and for all.'

He'd been looking down as he'd spoken the last sentence. When he looked up, he could see tissues wiping several eyes. There was silence. Katy was the first to recover. With tears in her eyes, she started clapping. 'Go for it, Dad!' Then the others joined in.

Ben marvelled at this amazing group of family and friends. They all knew – some more than others – the potential for danger and even death. Yet they all seemed to know that this was his only way out of the half-life he had been living for the last seventeen years. Looking around, he could see that they would each travel with him in their own way.

Agnes summed it up when she came over to speak to him. She even made him laugh. 'Ye're a brave man, Ben Burton. There's no mistaking that. Mo and me, we'll do what we can.' She rummaged in her capacious handbag and brought out a packet of tea. 'Here y'are. Real Irish tea – strong as you like – that'll keep your spirits up.'

Chapter 3

He had to admit it, the box was beautiful. Its inlaid lid had an intricate design carved with middle-eastern sigils. The marquetry on each of the four sides showed a different dragon picture. The box was exquisite, yet it filled him with dread. He had prepared himself as best he could. He'd done his yoga exercises and had felt the tension dissipate as he'd prepared himself for the ordeal ahead. Now he had three hours on his own until the family returned and normal life resumed. He might need all of that time and more in order to extract and analyse any clues Diane had left, either purposely or inadvertently. He turned the key twice one way, then once the other and then pressed the tiny button above the lock. The box opened with a soft click. He looked at the pile of papers within, then carefully extracted them all, keeping them in the correct order.

On top was the letter that had caused his breakdown when he had first read it in November. He nearly decided to put it to one side but he knew that it might contain a clue. If he was going to be thorough, he would have to read it again. It was dated 20th September 1996 – just two weeks before she died.

My dearest love

If you are reading this, it means that I am dead and being dead releases me from promises I have made and oaths I have taken. Now I am free to tell you the truth and I hope you can forgive me for the lies I have told – the deceit I have lived.

Never doubt that I loved you from the moment I first saw you and that you and our two beautiful girls are the centre of my world. But I also inhabit another world – and this other world has surely caused my death.

I know you refused Dobson when he approached you, but I was not so circumspect. He recruited me and I worked in a small way in that shady world until our daughters were born.

That should have been the end of it. But when you were posted to Belfast, they had one last job for me. I was persuaded. I insisted on coming with you. You resisted, I insisted. If I'd listened to you, I'd probably be with you now and you would not have had to read this.

I did what was required of me. Through my source, I found evidence for them about a truly evil man and the truths that he held which could rock the nation. To protect my contact, I won't tell you his name – or the name of the villain I uncovered. You might be tempted to go after him. Please don't try to find him. He got me. I don't want our girls to lose both their parents.

I am so very sorry for the lies and the hurt and for leaving you and Sarah and Katy.

Love always
Diane

It told him nothing new.

He quickly put it to one side and picked up a pile of letters tied with ribbon. A quick glance told him they were from him to her when his job had briefly parted them prior to his deployment in Northern Ireland. He knew that he had kept hers but hadn't seen them since his repatriation after the bomb. He would have to ask Mo.

Next came pictures and scribblings by Katy and Sarah. Sarah had tried to write her name and it was just decipherable. Since he'd begun to talk to them about their mother, he'd learnt that Sarah could just remember her but Katy had been barely two when Diane had died and had no recollection of her, only the tales that he and Mo had told her. He smiled as the memories flooded in of a nuclear family – two adults, two children – and how happy they had seemed. He questioned the validity of these memories, as now he questioned every aspect of his marriage.

There were three photos. All were of the family. In the first, he and Diane looked young and carefree. The next was a family threesome, when Sarah was a baby. That one had been taken at their flat in London. He remembered Diane's mother coming to stay to help out when Sarah had been born and she had taken the picture in their back garden. The last photo was of the four of them together, Katy's tiny face just visible peeping from her hoodie. She must have been about eighteen months, a toddler anyway. He remembered that one being taken. There had been a caller at the house in Belfast. For security reasons, they hadn't had many visitors and suddenly remembering who had taken the picture seemed to be important. He knew that it had been a man – a man he didn't know – but someone that Diane had known. Irish definitely, but Ben could not picture him. As he looked at the photo, he remembered that Diane had been flustered by the man's sudden appearance at their door. He looked at the photos again and compared them. In the first two, Diane looked untroubled. The last was different. Was she looking wary? Or was he just reading more than was there? He turned the photo over – nothing on the back. It was probably the last picture before her death. He put the photos to one side. He would have to come back to them, especially that last one.

He sighed. What had he been expecting? Revelations and confessions? No, but something concrete to take him further. So far, there had been nothing of substance to help him.

He picked up the remaining papers and sorted through them. All were from the time before they'd moved to Ireland, little scraps from their life together, a card from their favourite restaurant, tickets from the May Ball they had gone to, the receipt from the hotel where they'd spent their honeymoon – fragments of a life. This was a life that, on the surface, had been simple and carefree. But, he now knew, there had been secrets from the beginning. These fragments showed only the wife who had been open and honest – the one he no longer knew – and they brought him no closer to knowing who had cut that life short.

Chapter 4

'So you've found nothing in the box. You have no leads, but you're still determined to do it?'

Ben was half reclining in his usual chair in Dr Clare's consulting room. He looked at the bare walls. What was that colour? A sort of greyish beige, the sort of colour that no-one could take exception to. He decided that when he returned – if he returned – he'd paint his house in bright colours. Yellows and reds, warm colours everywhere. He could almost smell the fresh paint in his nostrils. Something to come back to. He smiled. He realised that she was waiting in silence for his reply. 'Yes, I've come to that phoenix moment. I'll either rise from the ashes or crash and burn.'

'Well, at least you know the risk you're taking. What do you need me to do?'

'If I succeed, I may need someone to catch the phoenix. Make sure it doesn't do an Icarus. Metaphor mix, but you know what I mean. If I fail mentally, I'll need you to pick up the pieces as best you can.' He paused for a moment. 'If I fail physically, come to my funeral and give me a good send-off.'

He waited for her reply. It was a long time coming. 'That's pretty much the options I was expecting – but not the last.' She produced a short bark of a laugh. It had no humour in it. 'I'm not very good at funerals so I'd appreciate it if you could spare my feelings and stay alive.' He heard her take a sharp in-breath, then she continued in a low voice, 'Ben, for the past three months, I've been concerned about the effect this quest would have on you mentally. And, yes, it could go either way. Whatever you discover, or fail to discover, will have an effect on your mental well-being, and that could be either positive or negative. But physically? Surely your life won't be in danger? Not after all this time...'

He broke in. 'Alison, I served in Northern Ireland and I met some serious fanatics there. I have no illusions. I am about to revisit a crime that people have buried and they would rather it stayed buried. Dangerous people would rather it never again saw the light of day. It was seventeen years ago but I'll be digging into the past of Stanley Murdock and his associates. He was an evil man and I'm damn sure he mixed with evil men.' He too took a sharp intake of breath. 'I don't think Murdock was a fanatic, just a psychopath / sociopath – some sort of path – you'll know which. But he worked with fanatics, killed with fanatics, and even old fanatics are dangerous. They just hide it better. I know Murdock was involved in some way. If I succeed in finding why Diane was killed, I'll be in danger. They've hidden the truth all these years, they won't want it coming out now. So, on balance, if I succeed, the physical danger will far outweigh the mental. If I fail, I'll still have unsettled the natives, so they might still want me silenced. Those are my options.'

He could hear her slap her notebook down on her desk. She came to face him and leaned over him. He'd never before seen her angry. 'Ben Burton, we've been talking about your options for three months. We've discussed all the possible mental outcomes and you never even hinted that you could be in physical danger. Why didn't you tell me?'

'Because I knew you'd try to dissuade me. Right?'

'Damn right! What, in God's name, do you think you're doing?'

Chapter 5

Ben carefully placed the box on the kitchen table. 'Nothing. No clues. Just ephemera from her life.'

He'd gathered together the family, Katy and Sarah, his Uncle Mo and Michael, who now counted as one of the family. They'd closed the shop at the end of the day and he'd made them all a cup of what Agnes would call 'good strong Irish tea'. He noticed with amusement that Mo, whose former preference had been for tea like dishwater, had been converted by Agnes to drinking tea with body.

They all stared at the box. Katy said, 'Can we have a look?'

He nodded. Katy opened the unlocked box and spread the contents on the table. They all stared at the papers in front of them. After a moment he said, 'You can touch them. But I'd rather you didn't read the ones tied in ribbon.' He felt himself blushing – ridiculous at his age! 'They're letters from me to Diane when I was posted away.'

Sarah carefully placed the bundle in his hands. 'Keep these safe.' Then she gave his arm a gentle squeeze.

Mo, Michael and Sarah started sorting through the papers but Katy was untypically silent and still. She was staring intently at the box. When the others had finished looking at the papers and had oohed and aahed over the family photos, she finally spoke. 'Dad, do you remember when you bought the box? What happened?'

One of the side effects of Ben's head injury from the bomb blast had been the ability for near total recall of some incidents. Dr Clare had called it 'acquired savant syndrome' and was using him as a guinea pig in her research. So, as Ben closed his eyes, he had a good chance of taking himself right back to that happy day. He just wished the syndrome was perfect and he could remember the picture-taker in Belfast. 'It was a really small stall in Camden Market. The man was Middle Eastern. Diane asked him about the box and he did this sales patter about the box being made just for her. You know the sort of thing. He did say something strange. I didn't think anything of it at the time. He said it would keep her secrets safe. Then he took her to one side and showed her the box. They kept looking over to me and laughing. Then they haggled

17

about the price and honour was satisfied when she got him to take five pounds off.'

As he finished speaking, Katy beamed. 'Yes!' She reached for the box. She turned it round several times. She turned it upside down, then examined each of its sides and the lid. She pushed and pulled at the intricate designs. 'It's a puzzle box. Could be Japanese – they're really good at complicated puzzles to open boxes – and sometimes there's a secret compartment. Sooo clever. With this one, I think the box opens pretty easily as a screen to take you away from the real hiding place. Now, all we have to do is work out where the secret place is and how to get into it.' As she was talking she held the box to her ear and tapped all round it.

Mo slapped her on the back nearly knocking the box out of her hands. 'Go to it, girl. Want help from an old man who knows nothing?'

Katy shook her head emphatically. 'No way – this is my puzzle. I'm going to solve it and it's going to be hard.'

Michael's brows came together as he looked at the box in Katy's hands. 'How d'ye know there's a hidey-hole? It's beautiful, to be sure. But it just looks like any auld jewel box to me.'

'It was Dad's story. And there's loads on Youtube – tutorials. I've been watching them. Something to do when business is slow. I think I can see how it might work.' She handed the box to Michael. 'Hold it to your ear and tap each side. Hear any difference?'

They all watched as Michael concentrated. He tapped round the box three times. Suddenly his face broke into a grin. 'Yeah.' He pointed to the back of the box. 'This one sounds different.'

Michael passed the box on to Sarah who repeated the process then beamed at her sister. 'Kate, you're a gem.'

Mo tried, then shook his head and passed it on to Ben. 'One of the problems of old age. Hearing gets a bit ropey.' He turned to Katy. 'Well, girlee. P'raps you'd be better off without my help after all. Here if you need someone good with a hammer or screwdriver.' He scratched his head. 'It's a wee bit smaller than a coffin…' He buffed his fingernails on his collar. 'But I've got years of practice. Mind you, I'm better at closing boxes than opening 'em!'

Ben left them tapping the box – all except Katy, who was already glued to Youtube. He gave them strict instructions that on no account were they to break into it. As he left the house, his spirits sank lower. He needed something, anything, to set him off on the right track. He had nothing. Maybe Henry Walpole would have something for him.

Chapter 6

As he rounded the corner and entered Front Court, he stood in the shadows and studied the scenery. Yes, it must be the artist, seated near the Porters' Lodge and ostensibly sketching the Wren Chapel – that would be the watcher. With its view of the main entrance, it was the place he would have chosen. He wondered if 'Chris' had people placed by the three other entrances to this college. He decided to investigate. As he ambled round the college gardens, he looked around, and, yes, each of the entrances was covered. He wandered over to the young man by the back gate and glanced down at the papers on his lap. 'Hello.' The boy jumped. Ben estimated that he could hardly have been eighteen. They were recruiting younger these days. 'Lovely day. What are you reading here?'

The boy hastily covered his papers. Ben pointed to them. 'Looks like Stokes's Theorem. I always had trouble with vector calculus. How are you getting on?'

The young man blushed. 'Not too bad really. It's harder than I thought but it's sort of coming together. I've got a new tutor who's really good – really helpful – doesn't call you out if you don't understand. He's doing wonderful stuff with the medics. I want to do a doctorate with him, so I've got to do well.'

Ben took a gamble. 'Better than Dobson then?'

The boy grinned. 'Oh yes, much better.' Then he added in a sombre tone, 'Sorry. That sounded wrong. Terrible time when he was killed.'

'Let me guess. Now you have Professor O'Connor?'

'Yes. He's really good – I'm learning a lot. You know him, then?'

Ben wondered who was doing the recruiting now Dobson was dead, but then he realised he didn't want to know.

'Yes, and I bet it wasn't Prof O'Connor who set you here to watch the back gate. Who are you looking for?'

The young man jumped up, dropping all his papers as he did so. Ben stooped and picked them up. He shuffled them until a time sheet was on top. 'Slow morning. No-one in or out. So maybe you got some vector work done.'

The boy looked glum. 'I've failed the first test, haven't I?'

'Not necessarily, but let me give you some advice. It's a murky world you'd be entering. Maybe you'd be more suited to medical research with Prof O'Connor. Think about it.'

Too garrulous, thought Ben, as he walked away. He hoped he'd set that young man on a road more in keeping with his talents, and less likely to cause him grief.

* * *

The first thing Ben noticed on entering Walpole's study was that he could see a large portion of the floor. Of the piles of papers that had previously littered the carpet, half had disappeared, leaving brighter patches. Ben waved his arm at the new semi-tidiness. 'What's up? A new broom?'

'Ah, dear boy. Welcome to my new era. Decided that I needed a clear-up before I got too gaga to remember where I'd put things.' He turned to Ben with a rueful smile. 'Brain's OK. It's just the legs that are giving out.' He pointed to a pile of papers in the far corner. 'Pass me those, will you? I've got things to tell you. Not much, I grant you. But it might give you pause for thought.'

'So what have you found out?'

'Hold on, young man. I'll tell you in my own good time. Put those papers on my desk, will you. They're being very tight-arsed at the front end.'

Ben wondered how papers could be tight-arsed, then realised it was spy-central at Millbank he was talking about.

'Even the people I know well wouldn't tell me anything about your wife or Stanley Murdock. They did tell me, in extraordinarily polite terms, to keep my nose out; that people at the highest level would be very unhappy if I didn't let this lie.'

'So that tells us that there *is* something to hide.'

'Oh, undoubtedly. I'm afraid I'm going to bowl you a googly. Now, in any half decent organisation, there are official channels and then there are unofficial groupings where you get your gossip.' He looked sadly at Ben. 'Of course, most of mine have died. AIDS got a lot of them. But I still have contacts who remember that time. All long left the Service, and they're all as doddery as I am, but they all still have contacts to draw on. I asked about Diane, both in her single and married names. A couple of them recognised Diane Scott.'

'Is that the googly?'

'No. Three of them filled in different aspects of a story that has implications for you today. Here comes the googly. There was a rumour circulating at the time of Diane's death that there was a mole in London feeding information to protestant paramilitaries in Belfast. London note – not Belfast. I think it might be related to her death. That all happened in '96 and there was no investigation. My friends would have known if there had been any consequences, any investigation. At least they'd have got a sniff of it. But, Ничто, nada, nothing.' He chuckled. 'Not a whiff of an investigation, so we can assume that there wasn't one.' He wagged his finger at Ben. 'And how can I be sure? Because the Secret Services are very bad at keeping secrets within – and that's because the Secret Servants are very good at winkling them out.'

'So, you're saying that someone in Millbank was feeding intel to the UVF and that person could still be there.'

'And in a very influential position.'

'I see. So it's likely that they've risen to a level where they have the clout to warn you off?'

'Yes, dear boy. Seen the watchers out there? I'll have to be circumspect. So will you. I have just one bit of advice for you – two actually. The first, don't go to Northern Ireland. You'll ignore that, of course. So the second…' He waved a bony finger at Ben. 'Promise me this. When you do go, be sure to take Mary with you. She's rather good in a scrape.'

* * *

As he walked back to work, Ben smiled to himself. His thoughts were on Professor Walpole – one of the old school. He'd grown to love that old man and vowed that, when this was over, he would spend more time with him. A mole. That had piqued his interest; but more interesting was that he'd insisted Ben should include Mary in his quest. That one, he couldn't fathom. Mary had been his neighbour for five years and had been invaluable in looking after him and his family during his meltdown. They'd been out to dinner a few times and she was good company. He'd talked to her about his agonies of indecision and she had listened. And she had offered him no advice. Walpole had known her as the University Librarian, and had been her friend for years. That's what he'd been led to believe. So why had Walpole chosen Mary to be his companion? He would have to ask her. And the fact that Walpole was being watched, however inexpertly; Ben had no doubt that the watcher at the front had been a professional and had clocked his presence. He hadn't seen Chris since the shoot-out where Neville-Taylor had been killed. He'd slunk back into the shadows after clearing up the mess. He wondered how long before Chris would be back with him.

Chapter 7

Ben's walk back to work did not help in his decision-making. When he arrived, he was still ruminating about the pros and cons of his continued search for answers. An hour later, over coffee with Katy, Michael and Mo, he brought them up to date with his visit to Walpole, and his encounter with the undergrad in the garden.

Mo was sceptical. 'You sure they was staking him out? Seems OTT if the old gent was only asking questions about a murder seventeen years ago. Even if it was the murder of a spook – beggin' your pardon – but that's what Diane was.'

Katy patted her great-uncle's arm. Her eyes were gleaming. 'But this means there *is* something to investigate. Why would a bomb in a barracks in 1996 cause this reaction? Yes, Mum was killed and it devastated all our lives but heh, that wasn't unusual.' She looked sadly at her father. 'Loads of people's lives were ruined in the Troubles. So, they must be hiding something. I've been reading up on it. OK, so there were some things like Bloody Sunday and the killings in Gibraltar that shouldn't have happened. What if there's something big that we still don't know about?'

In the past, Ben had dismissed Katy's ideas as fanciful – and he'd been wrong. What if this was a cover-up? What if he was getting into something much deeper and darker than the murder of his wife? What if…? But what-ifs could be never-ending. What he needed were facts.

Michael's contribution broke into his thoughts. 'Sure, I can believe it. I was there, don't forget, and they were lawless times. We didn't trust the law makers and we didn't trust the law breakers. Another barracks bomb wouldn't have been big news for more than a day or so. This smells – no doubting that.'

Ben thanked them. He had a lot to assimilate. 'We'll see if Chris shows himself. That'll clinch it.' Then he took a new tack. He turned to Katy. 'Any further with the puzzle box?'

She pulled out a diagram from her shoulder bag. 'It's taking time but I'm making progress.' She pointed to the picture. 'I've found similar ones on the net with solutions so I'm trying to work out the entire sequence before trying it. That way, I'll make sure I don't jam it. I think I'm nearly there so I reckon maybe tomorrow –

if I'm lucky.' She looked sideways at her dad in a way that he knew preceded a request. He waited for it.

'Dad, you know I was going to do gap-year-travelling?' Ben nodded. Then it came in a rush. 'Well, how about I include Northern Ireland in my travels? I could help you find out what happened to Mum. I can't remember Ireland at all and I sooo want to see where I was born.' Ben shook his head vehemently. She looked disappointed but still added, 'I really wouldn't be any trouble, and I could be a load of help.'

Ben was adamant. 'No way. If MI5 are sniffing round – then it's probably above my pay grade and definitely above yours. Henry Walpole suggested I take Mary with me as cover. I'm not so sure that's…?

Before he could go further, Katy chimed in. 'Dad, that'd be awesome! You need someone to look after you and she's so good at that. And we all love her. Would she go? Stupid question. Course she would.'

And that was the dilemma for Ben. He too thought that, of course she would. But casting his mind back to Stanley Murdock's funeral where he'd been warned off by a pack of Northern Irish heavies, he knew there would be danger. He also knew that he didn't want to go alone. Could he ask her to go? The ping of the door chime in their front office meant he didn't have to answer that. 'A customer, I think. Back to work.'

But it wasn't a grieving relative wanting to lay their loved one to rest. Ben replaced his undertaker face with a cheery smile. 'Hello, Chris. Long time no see. So, what brings you to my door?'

'You know damn well what brings me here. You and that geriatric friend of yours are meddling in things you shouldn't be. You've been warned. You've been told keep your nose out. You've been fucking told not to go there. But, no, you have to barge right in where you have no right to be.'

That was too much for Ben. He interrupted this tirade with one of his own. 'Hold it right there! Remember – it was my wife who was killed. Hear that – *my wife*. You tell me I have no right to know why she died?' He pointed his finger at Chris. 'You talk about rights. OK, what right have you to come in here and tell me what I can and can't do? Eh?' Ben stopped when he realised he was poking Chris in the chest.

Chris stepped back and held up his hands. 'Look, sorry mate. I'm only trying to protect you. It's my job, look after my people. Keep 'em safe.' He gave a rueful laugh. 'So they live to do the next job. That's what I want for you. You're a valuable asset. You come up with the goods. I've given you more than enough rope to hang yourself and that is just what you seem desperate to do. I gave you a friendly warning but you didn't listen. So now I'm telling you straight. Don't pursue this. If you do, you'll be on your own. I won't be able to help you.'

Ben was cogitating. If Chris thought that calling him a valuable asset would bring him onside, he was seriously mistaken. 'Give me one good reason why I should leave it.'

'I've had orders from above.' Chris stretched his arm way above his head. 'This high above. That's all. I don't know why. And even if I did, you know I can't tell you. It's come from way up – and that's all I know.'

Ben thought about the slip. Can't not couldn't. 'Not good enough. You know more than you're telling me. Now, tell me what you know or I'll blow the gaff on some of the things you've done that you'd rather were kept secret.'

Chris looked surprised. 'You're bluffing. I know you're bluffing. I know you and I know your attachment to your precious moral code. You're too straight-laced to do anything so underhand.'

Ben gave a hollow laugh. 'You talk about *my* moral code. My moral code doesn't include killing a suspect in cold blood, no matter what crimes he's committed. It doesn't include spiriting away another suspect whose crimes against children would have landed him a life sentence. I've bent the rules in the past and it's caused me grief. Bending the rules now would give me no angst at all. You think I'm bluffing. Then call my bluff.'

Chris sat down heavily. 'Bloody Hell, Ben. I'm only trying to keep you out of deep shit. I was told to warn you off so you'd stay off. For your own good.'

As Ben's anger subsided, he decided to change tack. 'So what is it you're not telling me? Could be I'll listen to reason if I know what the reason is. This is your one chance of stopping me, so tell me what you know.'

'All I know is this. There's people at the highest level – you know what that means – the *highest* level, who want this to go away. And because people at the highest level want this swept back under the carpet, you'll put yourself in serious difficulty if you don't let it drop. Comprenez?'

'And what was Murdock's part in all of this?'

Chris, who had been holding Ben's gaze, let it flicker for a fraction of a second. That was enough for Ben. He waited for the lie. 'Nothing. I told you at the beginning that Murdock wasn't implicated. It was the UVF who planted that bomb. Murdock was a shitbag and we're all glad he's dead but he had nothing to do with your wife's death. For everybody's sake – especially your family's, can't you let this lie?'

By Ben's reckoning, that was way below the belt. If Chris thought the implied threat to his family was going to persuade him, he really didn't know him. If anything, it further alienated Ben. He knew he'd put his daughters in danger in the past few months. He didn't need reminding. 'So Dobson was lying?'

'Of course he was. You knew him. You hated him. Why would you trust him?'

Ben had evidence in his possession that Chris knew nothing about: a letter from Diane, a letter from Dobson, a note from Murdock threatening retribution to an unknown associate. He would have to look through it all before he could formulate a plan. But first he had to placate both Chris and the gods he was working for.

He spoke in language that he knew Chris would understand. 'OK. What can you do for me if I drop it?'

Chris looked relieved. 'That's better. Tell me what you want.'

'Financial support for Josephine Finlay until she no longer needs it. No approaches to Katy or Sarah to get them into the Services. And for you to stop calling Henry Walpole geriatric. He has more wisdom in his little finger than you have in your entire body.'

'That all? No problem.'

'Good. Now get out of here before I have to throw you out.' Ben turned and walked briskly into the back office leaving Chris to see himself out. This precluded his having to 'shake on it'. So, to Ben's mind, no bargain had been struck – but he was tempted, sorely tempted, to go for that bargain and to let those sleeping wolves slumber on.

Chapter 8

Ben's exit from their front office was accompanied by a squeal from Katy coming from way back in the bowels of their capacious establishment. He must tell her that she could be heard throughout the building and that, if he had been comforting grieving relatives, that noise would certainly not be appropriate. But he didn't tell her that because she came rushing towards him. His heart leapt. He thought she looked terrified.

He was wrong.

'I've cracked it, Dad.' And she held the box aloft. 'It was sooo clever. There's something in there but I didn't think it right to take it out. That's for you.'

Ben looked at the box in her hands and found he was shaking. 'Let's go up to the staff room and sit down.'

As they proceeded through the building, he found that they had acquired an entourage. Mo and Michael had downed tools and followed them. They ascended the stairs as in a procession – following the box – the icon held aloft by Katy.

He beckoned them all in and they sat in silence, a silence that contained, for Ben, and he suspected, for all of them, a degree of trepidation. He took several deep breaths to slow his heartbeat, then said, 'OK Katy. Show us what you've got.'

Katy twisted and turned the box and eventually a door in the back panel sprang open. She slid the box across the table to her father. Ben carefully removed a folded sheet of paper. Slowly, he unfolded it and spread it on the table. Its message was short. It was dated 7th October 1996 – the day she died. He read it aloud:

I knew you wouldn't, couldn't let it go. That's the sort of man you are. But I'm not going to make it easy for you. If you succeed, I fear that you will meet the same fate as me. Find Moira, then find Kevin's cousin. You'll know him when you see him.

There was a palpable silence as they all digested the message.

Chapter 9

At Ethel's, the Head Porter had obviously been surprised by Ben's request but had agreed without demur. Yes, the artist was still in Front Court painting the chapel and yes, if Ben came dressed as a delivery man, Fisher would point him to other rooms in the general direction of Professor Walpole's. When Ben had contacted Walpole to agree a meeting, Walpole had insisted that Mary should also be present. Mary had been instructed to arrive at the Porter's Lodge and to converse with Fisher, in tones loud enough to be overheard, about her purpose in delivering some books to the college library.

Ben had duly arrived at the Porters Lodge with a laden parcel trolley, a cap pulled down over his forehead, a brown overall and workman's gloves. Fisher carried out his part of the plan, loudly pointing Ben towards Staircase C. The artist had looked up briefly and then gone back to his painting. Ben reckoned he'd got away with it.

When Ben arrived in Walpole's rooms, Mary was busy sorting papers and there was even more floor showing than on his last visit. Ben reckoned about two-thirds were done. As she turned to greet him, she burst out laughing. 'Hallo Gov. Got somefink for me to sign?' Her hair was awry and there was a smudge of dust on her nose. She stood with her hands on her hips and he realised that she was a very attractive woman. How hadn't he noticed that before? He removed his gloves, cap and overall and threw them on to the nearest chair. She pointed to the trolley. 'What's in the boxes?'

'Five very important papers. Where's the Prof?'

'Loo visit. He won't be long.' She pointed to the cleared spaces. 'Impressive huh?'

'Where have they all gone?'

'I'm helping him to sort, catalogue and archive them.'

'You mean you're sorting, cataloguing and archiving while he drinks g and t.'

She smiled. 'Something like that. He's got some very important ephemera from the cold war. It's worth preserving – but finding it in the piles of detritus is time-consuming. Still I'm enjoying his company.'

A voice came from the door. 'Of course you are, young lady.' Walpole turned to Ben. 'I've still got it you know. I'm falling to bits but I can still be devastatingly charming. Now, tell me Ben, what do you want of us?' Ben noticed the difficulty with which the old man was walking but was pleased to hear that his voice was as stentorian as ever. Walpole continued, 'I think we should all have a drink and sit round my perfectly clear desk. Mary, can you do the honours?'

Ben pulled a sheaf of papers from the box on his barrow. 'I've got some papers for you to peruse. I want your input – to try to make some sense of them.' He could see the old man's eyes sparkle.

'Of course, dear boy. Happy to help. You've chosen well – a redundant spy and a very clever librarian. A match made in Heaven. And she still won't marry me, more's the pity. Now, let's get on.'

'I'll show you them in the order I received them. The first came from Stanley Murdock's safe and was accompanied by a large wodge of bank notes. Chris told me to bury everything with Murdock, but I kept a few things: his blackmail list, this note and a small key. Katy worked out where the key fitted and we found Stanley's blackmail evidence in a lock-up on the east side of Cambridge. I gave some of it to Chris, but kept back a few things to repatriate to some of the victims.' He turned to Mary. 'Henry knows all this but I'm not sure you do?'

'Henry has been a bit indiscreet but tell me anyway. That way I'll know I have the full picture.'

'OK. This is the first – written by Stanley – not sure when.' He handed over the note and Henry Walpole read it aloud.

5th issue Swiss francs. Worthless. I'll get the bastard sure as eggs is eggs. Margaret won't be so pretty after this.

Ben continued, 'We weren't sure if he was referring to his second wife. Her name was Margaret and she had a tough life with Stanley, coercive control big time.'

Walpole was looking contemplative. 'I knew Murdock years ago – the nastiest man I've ever had the misfortune to work with.

That "eggs is eggs" rankles. It doesn't sound like him. He was a stickler for correct usage.'

Ben's ears pricked up. 'Ah, I thought it might be a metaphor. All his blackmail notes were in riddles so we had to decipher them. Could be we'll need to work out what he meant by "eggs" and make out who Margaret was. I'll get Katy on to it. She loves doing these. Must admit, she did most of the spade work last time.'

'I have a thought,' said Walpole. 'Old friend in the English Department, knows about metaphor, slang, not quite saying what you *are* saying and expecting people to deduce content. Mind you, that's what we all do here all the time. I'll call to see him.' He chuckled. 'And he likes a snifter too. So, what else have you got for us?'

Ben put that page to the back and showed them two more pages. 'I think these two are linked – they're both from Professor Dobson. I received both soon after his murder.' He flourished one of them. 'I got this from Dobson's solicitor. He left it to be delivered to me immediately after his death and he left his entire estate to me; he told the solicitor that he owed me.' Shall I read them to you?' They nodded. He started to read.

Benedict,
Please forgive me for allowing your most precious gift to be stolen from you. She was mine before she was yours. I loved her very much. They found out, and then she died. You blame Stanley Murdock but I blame myself.
Graham

'At the time, I thought he'd had an affair with Diane. That was hurtful enough but later I found that he had recruited her to MI5 when she was a student here. She confirmed it in a letter I found later. It seems Dobson felt responsible for her death.' He waved them to silence. 'Henry, you found the next one when you were clearing Dobson's things. It was dated October 1996, just a few days before Diane's death. It was from Dobson and addressed to Stanley Murdock but it was never sent.' He read it aloud.

Stanley

31

You are mistaken. Diane has no evidence and Ben doesn't suspect her or you. She told me yesterday. Relax – your secret is safe Graham

Again, Ben waved them to silence. He flicked the page in his hand. 'I think the secret is that Murdock had led a gang rape when he was a student here. What if Diane had found out? We all know that Murdock was a dangerous man. Could that have prompted him to kill Diane to keep his dirty secret? Maybe...'

Mary interrupted him. Her tone was sympathetic but determined. 'Ben – stop a moment. I can see this could be a motive for killing Diane, a strong motive. But what I can't get my head round is why that would cause such a commotion in Millbank now – seventeen years later. There must be a different explanation. They are determined to stop you. But, if the rape had been his secret, they could have washed their hands of it by declaring that he'd raped a woman before he'd been recruited. They could have shoved all blame on to him and say they were revisiting the vetting process. He's been dead over a year and you can't libel the dead so no come-back. Job done. There must be more to this. He must have had another secret; an important secret that Diane discovered. They're afraid. But what are they afraid of?'

Ben had a sudden rush of understanding, but it had nothing to do with the problem in hand. The inspiring flash came because Mary's words suggested that she knew how Millbank operated. Clever woman. Oh, what a clever woman. She'd very quickly sussed that he had spook connections but had managed to keep quiet about her own background. No wonder Henry Walpole was insisting he took her with him to Ireland. What was it he'd said? She was 'rather good in a scrape'. He smiled inwardly as he turned his attention back to the paperwork, and his dead wife.

'I don't know what the secret is, but you're right. It's big, and it seems Diane had found something but had no proof. Anyway, next one. Mary, you've seen this one. Henry, this is the one that sent me doolally last autumn. Meltdown, breakdown, call it what you like, but my world fell apart. I found it in Diane's puzzle box and it confirms that she was the target. For years I'd thought her death was collateral damage and it had been me they were after, me and all those soldiers at the barracks.'

Henry looked concerned. 'Shall I read it to myself? Save you the effort.'

Ben smiled. 'Not necessary. My sessions with Alison Clare have shown me the positive aspects. I've been carrying around guilt for Diane's death for years. Now I know I wasn't the guilty one, it's taken *that* load off my shoulders.' His smile became rueful, 'Doesn't mean the shoulders are empty. I've just acquired another load for them; finding out who killed her and precisely why she had to die.'

He started to read.

My dearest love

If you are reading this it means that I am dead and being dead releases me from promises I have made and oaths I have taken. Now I am free to tell you the truth and I hope you can forgive me for the lies I have told – the deceit I have lived.

Never doubt that I loved you from the moment I first saw you and that you and our two beautiful girls are the centre of my world. But I also inhabit another world – and this other world has surely caused my death.

I know you refused Dobson when he approached you, but I was not so circumspect. He recruited me and I worked in a small way in that shady world until our daughters were born.

That should have been the end of it. But when you were posted to Belfast, they had one last job for me. I was persuaded. I insisted on coming with you. You resisted, I insisted. If I'd listened to you, I'd probably be with you now and you would not have had to read this.

I did what was required of me. Through my source, I found evidence for them about a truly evil man and the truths that he held which could rock the nation. To protect my contact, I won't tell you his name – or the name of the villain I've uncovered. You might be tempted to go after him. Please don't try to find him. He got me. I don't want our girls to lose both their parents.

I am so very sorry for the lies and the hurt and for leaving you and Sarah and Katy.

Love always
Diane

Ben could see Henry Walpole surreptitiously wipe his eyes. Then he cleared his throat. 'I can see why that would have affected you so badly; turned your world upside down. Glad, dear boy, to hear there's a smidgeon of a silver lining to this.'

'In between then and now I've had another wobble – several wobbles. Even after declaring at the party that I was going to pursue this, I was still ambivalent. And I was veering towards leaving well enough alone when Katy extracted this from a secret compartment in Diane's puzzle box.' He showed them his last bit of paper. 'This decided me once and for all. I must do it.' He cleared his throat, took a deep breath, and began to read.

I knew you wouldn't, couldn't let it go. That's the sort of man you are. But I'm not going to make it easy for you. If you succeed, I fear that you will meet the same fate as me. Find Moira then find Kevin's cousin. You'll know him when you see him.

Mary pointed to the last two sentences. 'Well, that sure is needle-in-haystack stuff. Who on earth are Moira and Kevin?'

Ben responded, 'Moira – not who but where. I only know this because I've talked to Stanley Murdock's children. In the nineties, the Murdock family lived in a small town called Moira – about twenty miles from Belfast. So, if that's the right Moira, and I think it is, then it's a link between Diane and Stanley Murdock.' He settled back in his chair and started to relay the history – or some of it. 'Stanley Murdock had three children, one by his first wife and two with his second, Margaret. They're all in their thirties now. The eldest one's disappeared since Murdock's death. Took his vast inheritance and went God knows where. The other two have decamped to Brighton. I've been to see them since they moved there. Nice people – so unlike Murdock.'

He didn't add that DNA tests had revealed that Murdock had not been their biological father, a fact only known to Chris and himself. Chris had decided that the two offspring should remain unaware. Ben had seen the sense in this after all they had suffered at Stanley Murdock's hands. He felt they deserved peace and their share of the large fortune that Murdock had accumulated. Ben knew that Chris had his own reasons for keeping anything Murdock under the radar. At the time, Ben had thought that his rationale and Chris's were vaguely congruent. Now, he was becoming convinced that their values and motives were divergent. 'I'll have to go and see them again, find out if they remember a Kevin from their time there.' He looked from Mary to Henry. 'Anyone fancy a trip to Brighton?'

Chapter 10

Virginia and Alistair Murdock had been delighted to invite Ben and 'his mysterious lady friend' – Alistair's description – to Sunday lunch. This brought memories of trying to teach them the rudiments of cooking. With this in mind, he had alerted Mary to the possibility of an interesting meal – and maybe not in a good way. He was looking forward to seeing them again. He'd visited them twice since their move and had been delighted by the change in them since their father's death. He marvelled at the resilience of youth and just hoped that same resilience extended to middle-aged undertakers.

Knowing how difficult the journey to Brighton could be on a Sunday, even in April, they'd set out early with a plan to be tourists. High on the list was a visit to the Old Police Cells Museum and a wander through the Lanes. Neither of them fancied the Royal Pavilion. Ben felt this was a good omen for two reasons. One, they wouldn't have time and two, it made it quite obvious that Mary was a woman of taste, preferring a dank and dismal underground prison to the opulence of a Prince's folly.

* * *

Alistair opened the door with a flourish. Ben had decided, the last time he'd visited, that the house they had bought was ideal for their needs but he knew he would hate living there. The only redeeming feature, in his view, was that they had access to the Kemp Town Enclosures. The house was about half the size of the one they'd sold in Grantchester, but was still more than adequate for their needs. Regency, beautifully proportioned, parking a nightmare, the area busy day and night.

Ben and Mary had arrived early in Brighton, so they'd had no difficulty in parking at Black Rock and the bracing walks around the town had whetted Ben's appetite. He sincerely hoped the pair's cooking had improved, so the first smell that greeted his nose surprised him. It was the delicious aroma of the Mediterranean – the scent of herbs, tomatoes, a hint of garlic. Alistair ushered them in and kissed them both on both cheeks. He called his sister to come and greet their 'two beautiful guests'. It took Ben a long time to disentangle himself from first, Alistair's effusive embrace then Virginia's. This was evidently much to the amusement of Mary, who managed to raise a quizzical eyebrow while laughing.

Alistair gathered the two of them and led the way to the kitchen. 'Let me introduce you to Gavin. Gav, come and meet one of our dearest friends – and his mysterious other. Ben and Mary.' He turned to Ben. 'Gav's moved in with us.' And he gave a stage wink. 'He cooks like a dream. Ginny won't let him leave, will you Gin?'

Gavin came and shook hands. The first thing that Ben noticed was that Gavin moved with supreme grace. The second was that he had a wide and very infectious smile. He looked to be in his thirties, about the same age as Alistair and Virginia. Now, the question; was he a tenant or was he attached to one of the siblings, and, if so, which one? He wouldn't ask but maybe he would find out.

Lunch was delightful. Gavin certainly could cook and Ben had learnt something new – spaghetti bolognese with chicken livers – a recipe from Gavin's Italian grandmother. Gav's tiramisu was lip-smackingly good and everyone had second helpings. They talked inconsequentially about Alistair's Emporium and Ginny's studies. The Emporium was going well. Alistair had found someone to sew drag dresses, and that was a real bonus. Business was buzzing. And so was Alistair. Virginia had started her course at Sussex Uni and was loving it. And here was the connection to Gavin. He lectured there and they immediately insisted that he was not teaching Virginia. This tempted Ben to ask, 'You an item, then?' And he was delighted with an answer in the affirmative.

Ben asked about their older brother, Lucien, the one who had disappeared. Virginia had good news. It seemed he'd kicked his gambling habit and had taken up competitive sailing. Alistair took up the tale. 'He's bought a yacht from the widow of one of Father's friends – and at a good price.' He grinned. 'He'd have liked that, even though he's got more money than sense. We had a postcard. He's in the Caribbean.'

Ben felt a tingling in his fingers – itching to remember why this might be important – and not managing to bring anything to mind.

His thoughts were interrupted by Gavin, who was asking Mary about her name. His voice was as fluid as his movements. Ben thought he would make a good interrogator. 'Mary – that's a good Irish name, but I noticed your name on the bookmark you were carrying. Your family name is Hungarian?'

'Russian, actually. My husband was Russian. He died aeons ago. My maiden name was O'Shaughnessy. I hated it and no-one could spell it so I kept Amelina. People have difficulty with that too, but at least it's at the beginning of the alphabet.'

So, Ben thought, not only a good interrogator but he picks up clues too. He had to ask him, 'Gavin, tell me, what subject do you teach?'

Gavin laughed. 'Rumbled! Forensic Science. I lecture part-time and do the real work the rest of the week. But I'm fascinated by what people's names say about them.'

Ben had been wondering how to raise the subject that had brought them there. These two Murdocks seemed so happy now. He was loath to bring back memories that might cause them pain. He liked them, they trusted him and he didn't want to hurt them, so this was an opening he couldn't allow to pass. He waved an arm towards Virginia and Alistair and asked, 'I have a question for you about names. Mary and I have been doing some research and we've come across Moira and Kevin. I told her Moira might be a place not a girl. And to prove it, I showed her Moira on a map of Northern Ireland. So the question is, did you know any Kevins when you lived in Moira?'

Alistair's eyes twinkled. 'So you're still after our father, are you? Good for you. The old sod doesn't deserve to rest in peace.' He turned to his sister. 'Ginny, there was a Kevin in school, wasn't there?' Then back to Ben, 'Any particular age you're looking for?'

'I think adult – late teens and upwards. Someone who would have known your father.'

Virginia shook her head. 'We knew nothing about his friends. He kept his two lives separate. Only that time he took Allie to Belfast. Allie, any Kevins there?'

Alistair grinned. 'What? The time he found out the hard man he so admired was a kiddy-fiddler. Jacko liked little boys. I didn't mind him touching my dick but Father was incandescent.' Then he giggled. 'That was a great day!'

Alistair screwed up his face in thought. 'Give me a minute.'

They sat in silent contemplation of their coffee cups and Gavin proffered the pot to offer them a refill.

'Can't think that I found out any of their names. It was Jacko he'd gone to see. They all looked hard – you know – heavy-set and butch. They didn't talk. Him and Jacko did all the talking. Jacko sent everyone away, but I could tell they were trying to listen in. And then we upped and left when Father found that Jacko was touching me up.'

'Do you know Jacko's surname?'

'No, but he was big, big, big in the UVF. Must've been – you know – the others all deferred to him like he was the boss. They were like the kids who hang round with the bullies in school, all scared of him but wanting to be with him. S'pose it was better than being against him.'

'Remember anything of what was said?'

Alistair scoffed. 'Now you're asking! It was nearly twenty years ago.' He paused, 'Tell you what, I'm going to a brilliant new counsellor. She does hypnotism. We've talked about it. I'll ask if it would be a good idea.'

Ben broke in. 'Alistair, please don't do anything that would make things worse for you. You're doing great. I really don't want to be the one to set you back. I couldn't bear it.'

Alistair laughed. 'Yes, I am. We both are – doing great. Spending the old sod's money like it was going out of fashion and still not making a dent in it. I promise I'll do what she says, if she thinks it would help me, I'll ask her to take me back to that pub. If not, I won't. Whatever. But now you've made me curious, I'd like to know what my bastard father was talking about!'

Ben looked at his watch. 'God, is that the time? Sorry to break up the party but it's time we were going. It's been great to see you again, and, Gavin, good to meet you. Will you excuse me. I said I'd ring Katy before we left. She worries about me.' He walked into the hall and took out his phone. Then walked back into the dining room. 'Sorry – dead battery. Can I use someone's phone?'

Virginia leaned over and handed him a phone. 'Here, use this. And tell Katy it's about time she visited again. And to bring Michael too.'

As they were leaving, Virginia took Ben to one side. 'She's lovely. You kept that quiet. You look after her. Don't let her get away.' And she gave him a hug. 'And thank you for everything. You'll never know how much we owe you. Let us know if there's anything we can do. And be very careful.'

Chapter 11

They were making good time when it happened. They'd left the M11 and were taking Ben's usual route on the A11 to the east side of Cambridge. The road was nearly empty. Ben said casually, 'I may be paranoid but could it be that we're being followed.'

Mary lowered her visor so she could look in the mirror. 'Big, black SUV with tinted windows – two cars back?'

'Yep. It's certainly been behind us since we joined the M11. I slowed down on the last stretch of the motorway and so did they. Am I being paranoid?'

'Don't think so. Try speeding up. See what they do. I've noted the number plate.'

Ben revved up and shot forward. The black car overtook the car behind them and then kept pace at a safe distance. The other car behind turned off towards Hinxton so there were just the two of them on the straight stretch of road. The SUV accelerated and drew level. Ben eased his foot onto the brake and decelerated to let it pass but so did the other. They kept pace side by side on the dual carriageway for some seconds. Ben glanced sideways but the front windows were also tinted – something Ben knew to be illegal. He knew then that they were in real trouble.

He shouted, 'Brace yourself,' and saw Mary grab the handle above her door with one hand and put her other out onto the dashboard. Then a side-swipe. The crunching sound was thunderous. Ben's first thought was, My New Car! His second, how incongruous to be worrying about a box of metal. He kept control of the car – just. They were still on the road. He looked ahead to where the verge widened. Another side-swipe and Ben still managed to keep the car on the road. The third hit sent him careening off across the wide grass verge and juddering to a halt in a hedge. The black car drove on.

After a few seconds, he said, 'You OK?'

'Yes. You?'

'I'll have a few bruises, no doubt. Better get out of the car.'

They emerged and tested their limbs. Mary looked at Ben then at the car. 'You did well.' Then in a lighter tone, 'Had practice at being driven off the road?'

He laughed a bitter laugh. 'Well, yes, actually. Last time it happened I got beaten to a pulp – but that was a warning and they'd been told not to kill me. I'm sure this is another warning, otherwise we wouldn't be standing here with a damaged car but both still in one piece.' He shivered. 'Last time it was a couple of amateur heavies. This time, I think they were professionals.'

'How come you think they were pro's?'

'Big expensive car and they weren't worried about damage. This lot are serious. They knew precisely what they were doing.' He looked at his new, and very expensive, car. 'Good job I decided to buy a quality motor. It's sort of kept its shape. Anyway, it doesn't seem to be about to explode. I'll see if I can back it out of the hedge and assess the damage. If we're very lucky, it will be drivable and we can limp home.'

They were lucky. The damage to the bodywork was extensive but the doors still closed, the engine and brakes still worked and the steering hadn't been affected. As they drove on at a sedate pace, Mary voiced her thoughts. 'Of course, you're wondering how they knew where we were. I can't believe they were following us all day so it's likely to have been a tip-off after we'd left Brighton. What d'you think?'

'Sounds the most likely. What a bummer. Can't believe it was Alistair or Virginia. That only leaves Gavin. But I don't want it to be Gavin! Virginia obviously adores him and she deserves some happiness.'

'You're right. They do look good together. It is a pity. I can get his surname from the university website. Can we find out about him – his background outside academe?'

'Could do. Sarah's too lowly, Pam's a sergeant – still too lowly. One of Mo's mates might be able to but it's dicey if they get caught. I don't want to but I'm going to have to ask Vin. I remember when you two met. Didn't like each other, did you?' He didn't wait for a reply. 'She's now a DCI with the Met. We parted not on the best of terms – not my doing, but she was unhappy with the outcome of her big investigation in Cambridge. She had to have someone to blame. She might not want to help me.'

'Want to tell me what happened?'

'I think it's probably covered by Official Secrets.'

It really didn't surprise him when Mary replied, 'I've signed.'

He thought he ought to sound surprised. 'Oh! Well! Mary Amelina, you're full of surprises. You'll be the first person I've told this whole sorry tale to. Here's what I know. Vin was closing in on Dobson's killer, had him in the bag and then the police were ordered to stand down. My handler, Chris, intervened to ensure there was no trial. I was the bait to bring him out of hiding. Chris killed him and disposed of the body. His accomplice has been spirited off to Thailand – courtesy of Chris. They were paedophiles and Dobson was blackmailing them. Vin's two bent coppers got off scot-free. She got no collars and she blames me.'

'Ben Burton, for a man who calls himself an ordinary undertaker – you certainly live a colourful life.'

'Mary Amelina, for a University Librarian, I believe you too have led a colourful life. Perhaps, one day, you'll confide in me?'

'One day.'

Chapter 12

Katy was dancing round the kitchen like a woman possessed. 'Look, I know you've had lunch, but I also know what lousy cooks they are so I'm cooking supper for you both.' As Ben opened his mouth, she stopped him. 'No argument. I've been preparing it all afternoon.'

Mary stepped in. 'Katy, we'd love to join you for supper, and Ben can get us a nice bottle of wine to go with it.' As Ben went off to the cellar to retrieve the wine, he heard Mary say, 'Katy, have we got a tale to tell you.'

Katy beamed. 'I want to hear all about it. I thought you'd be home earlier – but the supper hasn't spoiled.' Katy busied herself serving out her version of moussaka. As she slopped it onto the plates, Ben came back in with a bottle of Merlot. Katy turned. 'I hope it's all right. When you phoned, I had all my timings worked out.'

Ben was in the process of removing the cork and he whirled round. 'Say that again, Katy.'

'What? I hope it's not spoiled?'

But Ben was smiling broadly. Mary laughed and said, 'Of course. You used their landline to call.'

Katy was now looking from one to the other and shaking her head. She put her hands on her hips and, sounded more like a parent than a daughter, 'Will you two stop grinning like a pair of Cheshire cats and tell me what's so funny!'

Ben was conciliatory. 'I'm sorry, pet. We'd better start at the beginning. Virginia has a man. His name is Gavin and they look like they're made for each other.'

As he spoke Katy's face softened. 'Aw Dad, that's great. She deserves to be happy after what that bastard put her through. Has Alistair...'

'Not yet – I don't think so – he didn't say. But he is so together these days, confident in his sexuality and his shop – sorry, his Emporium. It's doing really well. He has a business partner and they're making drag outfits. Apparently it's big business in Brighton.'

'Whoohee! I must go and see them.'

'Virginia said that. I think she wants you to meet Gavin, and she said to bring Michael.' Before Katy could respond, Ben continued. 'Anyway, someone forced us off the road on our way home – that's why we're a bit late. Don't look like that. We're fine. And you can serve up that supper before it gets cold.' Katy did as she was told and Ben poured them all a large glass of wine. Ben took a mouthful of the very wet moussaka. 'Katy, this tastes delightful. Do you think we could have some bread for mopping?'

'Dad, are you really OK? Some drivers! Did you get their number?'

This was serious but he didn't want to alarm Katy. He decided he'd have to play it down. When he'd eaten three mouthfuls, he continued, 'This is really nice, Katy. Anyway, it was deliberate.' He held up his hands as Katy was about to interrupt. 'It was a warning and we've been trying to work out how whoever it was knew where we'd been. We suspected Gavin. I was going to have to ask Vin to investigate him, and was feeling bloody awful about it – what with Virginia being so obviously in love with him. But, when you said about ringing you, it rang a bell. Sorry! Dad joke. It must have been the phone. I called you from their landline. I remember saying we'd learnt some more about Stanley's past. So, even after all this time, I think their phone's being tapped.'

Just as he'd wanted, he'd managed to divert Katy from the car crash. 'But that's awful! It's… It's invasion of privacy. I've seen those things on TV where they put bugs on the phone, but why them? Their dad's been dead a year now. We know Stanley Murdock was a bigwig criminal but they had nothing to do with that! Have you told them? Of course you haven't yet. You must!'

He'd never told Katy – or anyone except Mary and Walpole – what else he knew about Stanley Murdock. For, not only had Murdock been a 'bigwig criminal', but he had also been an MI5 operative in deep cover in Northern Ireland; an operative who had gone rogue and who, until his death, had had some sort of hold over the Services. And it seemed that the Services were still trying to break that hold. Ben didn't know what that hold was but he was damned sure it had something to do with Diane's death.

Chapter 13

As he walked Mary home after supper – a short walk as she lived only three doors away – he did his usual perusal of the street and the likely places for watchers to secrete themselves. Nothing. Good.

He was loath to say what he had to say, but say it, he must. 'Look, Mary, this is getting serious. I know Henry wants you to help me, but I think I'd better do what I have to do on my own.'

They'd arrived at her front door. She put her key in the lock then turned and smiled, 'Come in. I have something to tell you. I owe you an explanation.'

She pointed him towards her study. 'Sit down. I'll get you a glass of wine. You may need it.' He stood in her book-lined study and marvelled again at the number of books she possessed – but then, she would – she was the University Librarian. It was an eclectic mix and, this time, he noticed a whole shelf of Russian history and politics. Some were in Russian – and he wondered if she was the reader or had it been her dead husband. He realised that Mary knew a great deal more about him than he did about her. He hoped they were about to redress the balance.

She came quietly back into the room and handed him a large glass of wine. He pointed to the Russian books. 'Never noticed those before. Important?'

'Mm. Part of my history. A painful part of my history. He was a Russian diplomat. I met him at an embassy do. I was there to keep my eyes and ears open. My cover was as a translator for one of our lot – a Cabinet Minister so inept I could have wept – but at least it kept the Russians amused.' She smiled. 'Sergei asked me out and I was hooked. We were married within a month, secretly, of course.' She sighed and picked out one of the books, then retrieved a photo from behind the flyleaf. 'See, he was a handsome man.'

Ben looked at the picture of a young man smiling into the camera. He handed it back and said quietly, 'What happened to him?'

'MI6 tried to turn him. The KGB got wind of it. Sergei found out and told the MI6 agent, but they did nothing. He was murdered in Knightsbridge a week later. The Soviets were very understanding when it was reported as a mugging. They made no fuss. And then his body was returned to Moscow for a hero's burial.'

Ben put his arms around her and held her close. He could smell the faint perfume of her hair – like freshly mown hay. He breathed in deeply. She rested against him for a few seconds, then gently pulled away. 'So you see, I have a motive. I can't right that wrong; it's been twenty years and I know I'll never have redress. But maybe I can help you to get some justice for what was done to Diane.'

They sat in silence while he took it all in. Eventually he broke the silence. 'I'm sorry. I've been so selfish. Henry insisted I ask you to help but I never thought to ask why. You seem to be so sane. Your life so ordered.' He smiled a rueful smile. 'It appears that you're coping with your trauma much better than I am.'

'Now, I am. You should have seen me in those first few years. And don't forget, I wasn't witness to my husband's death. That must make a huge difference. Henry helped me to get myself back together. He's been a good friend to me.'

'How much does Henry know – from the inside, I mean?'

'More than he's willing to tell me. I think he's trying to protect me.'

'You're sure the Soviets killed him; it wasn't a mugging?'

'Oh, yes! I found that out at the time but everyone was tight-lipped. Nobody knew I was married to him, otherwise I wouldn't have known of the Service involvement. Our lot just said it was a Soviet problem and we weren't to get involved. End of.'

'The KGB got wind of it. Any idea how?'

'No. I was a lowly clerk who was only at the embassy because I could speak Russian. Henry might have a better idea.'

'And twenty years, you say – so '93?' She nodded and he continued his train of thought. 'So Litvinenko wasn't the first and undoubtedly he won't be the last. Your husband was killed on British soil. If our people had called it out at the time, who knows? History might have been different.' He frowned. '1993 – Yeltsin was weak – and he didn't have Putin propping him up till '98. If we'd made a stand at the time and insisted on keeping the body for analysis, I bet Yeltsin wouldn't have argued. God knows why our

47

side didn't make a fuss – didn't get involved? If they had, we might have been living in a very different world.'

Mary shook herself. 'That spilt milk dried up long ago. But now you see why I need to be involved. Henry reckons it will be part of my recovery too.' She held up her glass and tapped Ben's. 'Partners in crime?'

A feeling of intense relief washed over him. For the first time in seventeen years he felt he was entering an equal partnership. In this room, he wasn't Katy and Sarah's dad, he wasn't Michael, Katy and Mo's boss, he wasn't Josephine's protector, he wasn't Vin's informant, he wasn't Chris's underling. He raised his glass. 'Yes,' he said, 'Partners in crime.'

She smiled and stared into her glass for a long time, then stood up and paced the room. 'Well, I think we'd better get started. We've got to tell those lovely young people in Brighton that we think their landline has been tapped. Probably their mobiles too. An old-fashioned, first class letter should be the safest.' She put her glass down and resumed her pacing. 'When you were talking to Katy on their phone, I was earwigging.' She smiled and shrugged. 'Old habits. I remember you mentioning Stanley but I'm pretty sure you didn't mention Moira or Kevin's relative. Your phone'll probably be tapped now – even if it wasn't before. So we'll need a supply of burner phones. I'll look up electoral rolls for Moira in the nineties and the surrounding censuses, '91 and 2001; see how many Kevins I can find. I'll do that from the University – can get into all sorts of databases from there. It might take some time. How big is Moira? D'you know?' Ben shook his head. She continued, 'Can you find out the owner of the SUV?' She handed him the note she'd written of the number plate.

'I'll try Sarah but I may have to go to Vin. Pretty sure they'll draw a blank. But thinking of it, if it's MI5 it won't register, just kick up more dust. Maybe safer just to let that one go for the time being. But at least I know Vin's sort of forgiven me, partially anyway. Don't know if she's up to doing me a favour but she's invited me to her wedding with a plus one. Care to come?'

'That was quick. Well done her! I'd be delighted to be your plus one. When is it?'

'Not till the autumn, September sometime. I'll dig out the date for you. In the meantime, what we need is a nice short holiday in Northern Ireland. We won't need passports so that's one less problem to overcome.'

'Yes, but, if MI5 is on to us, how do we get there without being spotted?'

'Easy. I know someone with a plane – a six seater. We'll have to take a coffin with us but that's no problem.'

Chapter 14

Early next morning, Ben was in his back office carefully preparing false paperwork for the collection of a body from Rathfriland – the closest airstrip to Moira – when the expected visit from Chris occurred. Chris burst in and slammed the door behind him. His voice was low – which made him sound all the more menacing. 'What the fuck do you think you're doing?'

Ben looked up, then carefully slid the offending documents out of sight. 'Hello Chris. Heard about my little accident, have you?'

Chris ignored this response and stood face to face with Ben. 'We agreed that you'd keep that long nose of yours out of this. You didn't and a warning shot was fired. Next time it might not be a warning. You really don't know what you're getting into.'

'No, you're right. I don't. There's something behind all this that your lot just don't want me to know. But what I do know is that there's been a mole in your organisation for at least twenty years and you still haven't been able to nail the bastard.' Ben didn't know this but felt it was a pretty good guess. And the brief lift of Chris's eyebrows before his reply gave lie to his denial.

'Absolute rubbish. I know where that one came from. Look Ben, Henry Walpole is way past his sell-by date. He's always been a bit of a conspiracy theorist and he's got worse. His mind's going. For your own sake, don't listen to him.'

Ben didn't follow that line but took a tack of his own. 'Tell me. Why are you tapping the Murdocks' phones?'

Chris looked slightly uncomfortable and Ben decided that the pause before his reply was just enough time for Chris to fabricate an answer. 'Look, we're still trying to protect them. You and I know that Stanley was into criminality both sides of the Irish Sea. Those thugs from Belfast haven't disbanded just cos there's a Peace Process. But it could equally be some someone from organised crime over here that might want some of Murdock's dosh. Thought you were well enough away from the action that you'd be safe. My advice is that you keep it that way.'

The explanation sounded feasible, but Ben had the feeling there was more that Chris wasn't saying.

When Ben remained silent, Chris added, 'You're going to get yourself killed, you know that? Another word of warning, and this time not so friendly. If you go on with this, you'll have enemies on all sides – and I mean, all sides, and I won't be able to protect you.' He handed Ben a card, a plain white card just like the ones he'd had before from Chris. 'Phone this number if you're in grave danger. And only if you're in grave danger. Then I'll see what I can do, but no promises. My hands might be tied.'

And he walked out closing the door quietly behind him.

* * *

Two hours later, in Dr Clare's consulting room, Ben was adamant. 'Yes, I'm absolutely sure this is what I want to do. I've listened to all the possible downsides and I'm prepared to sign to say I take full responsibility for the outcome.'

'Ben, it's not only that. I've given you my considered opinion that there is a distinct possibility that this could cause a relapse. In your case, the odds are quite high that this will take you backwards, not forwards. Do you still want to take that risk?'

'I think I have to.' He held out the photograph to Dr Clare. 'Alison, I need to know who took this picture. She kept it in that box so it must be important.'

Dr Clare took the photo and studied it for a long time. She looked so sad that Ben had to ask if she was all right.

'Yes, yes, I'm fine but you all look so happy there; you and Diane and Sarah and that little bundle which must be Katy. It was taken while you were in Belfast?'

'Yes, Katy was only a toddler. I don't remember much about that day but we didn't have many visitors so whoever took that photo might be important. Of course, they might not be but it's a risk I'm prepared to take. Not only prepared to take – need to take.'

'OK. I'll need as much background as you can give me so I can pinpoint precisely and focus on what questions to ask. Tell me as much as you remember.'

'I know it was in our back garden; I recognise the house. Security meant that we were extremely careful so the person who took it must have been someone we knew and trusted. I can't think of anyone outside the army who fitted that category. That's all really.'

'OK. This is how it will work. When I take you back there, I'm only going to keep you there for a very short time. I want you to focus absolutely on the questions I ask and not to stray into anything other than the questions. Is that clear?'

He nodded.

* * *

'You're looking straight at the camera. What do you see?'

'It's a Nikon – great big hefty thing – we've just put in a new roll of film to take pictures of the family.'

'And the person behind the camera?'

'The man taking the photo – I don't know him. But Diane does. She says she got to know him at the library. He says he wanted to come to say hello to our daughters. Diane isn't pleased – don't know why – he seems a nice enough sort of person.'

'Are you sure you haven't seen him before?'

'Certain. He only stays a few minutes but it's long enough for me to know. Diane sort of hustles him out. I ask her why she's in such a hurry. She says she wants this time with just the four of us – that it's a special time that we won't have again.' He paused.

Alison interjected, 'Describe the man for me.'

'He's tall for an Irishman. Has that Celtic colouring – dark hair, bright blue eyes. Yes, it's his eyes that make him stand out. Almost turquoise. They dance.'

'How old is he?'

'About the same as us.'

'Would you recognise him again?'

'Oh yes. I've got a picture of him now.'

'When you wake up you'll remember the man but you'll forget again the feelings you had on that day. Understand?'

'Yes.'

* * *

'How do you feel?'

'Absolutely fine. I have a picture – no a video – in my head of the man who took this photo. It's very clear and this thing I've got with my scrambled brain...'

'Acquired savant syndrome.'

'That should make sure that it stays in my head and won't get corrupted?'

'From my study of your new abilities, I'd say that is the case.'

'Seems he knew Diane. I took it as gospel when she said she knew him from the library. Now, I have to doubt that. I know what he looked like in 1996, but I'm still no nearer finding out who he was, or hopefully, still is.'

Chapter 15

'That's easy. How many do you want? Oh, and you'll need a dongle and pay-as-you-go sim. And you'll need to pay cash.'

Ben looked hard at his daughter. 'Katy, how do you know all this?'

'Heh, Dad. Suddenly you look worried. No need. Remember I told you about Jodie and his big brother?'

Ben shook his head sadly. 'You mean those two in the blackmail photos with Alistair?'

'They're the ones. Well, they were into all sorts. Fake ID – had one of those – but you'll be pleased to know I avoided all their other enterprises. They did soft drugs. But I wouldn't buy from them – didn't trust their suppliers.'

Ben had got diverted. 'So, you…?'

'Don't get worried, Dad. Of course I tried weed but don't forget I was doing chemistry – didn't trust any pills. You never know what they've bulked them with. Anyway, I'm past that phase now. I survived, so you don't have to worry. End of.'

And, with that, Ben had to be content. 'Right. And the burner phones?'

'You need to go to one of the small independent shops selling second-hand. Some of them are so keen for a sale, they don't ask questions. I know a couple.'

At this point, Mo walked in with Michael in tow. For a moment Mo looked curious. 'Coupla what?' Without stopping for an answer he continued, 'Ben, me an' Michael done that embalming. She looks lovely. Think she must've been a nice old duck. Coupla what?'

'Dad's going under cover so he needs some burner phones. I know where to get them.' She tapped the side of her nose. 'And no questions asked.'

Michael joined in. 'I know a fella from jail – a forger. Any use?' Michael looked wistful. 'One of the few gentlemen in there. Led the art classes. Even the screws were impressed.'

'D'you know, Michael, that could be an answer to our prayers. We've been thinking up a cover story for when we talk to the Kevins. We've decided that we would have a will with bequests for people from Moira and we're trying to track them down. The thought of unexpected money should loosen some tongues. We were trying to work out how to do it. We could do with ID for a solicitor and her clerk plus driving licences for them. Could your mate do those?'

Michael nodded. 'Should be a doddle for him.'

Ben turned to Katy. 'Thought you'd approve of this bit of role reversal. Mary will be the solicitor and I'll be her clerk.' Katy gave him a double thumbs-up as he continued, 'Michael, can you talk to your man – best to be careful. We all need to consider ourselves under observation. Josephine says she'll help so can you go to see her to find out what we'll need? And Mo can you go with him to occupy Agnes while Michael gets the info?'

Mo beamed. 'Good idea. We could have a dance lesson. I'm teaching her to jive. But I don't bend like I used to, that's for sure.'

* * *

Preparations were well under way and Ben knew that detailed preparation was the key to success. He'd never been on 'the other side' before, with the weight of the establishment working against him. He was scared, for himself, but also for Mary. It was true that she had turned out to be a resilient and resourceful woman, more so than him, but he still had no idea just how resourceful they would have to be. He thought back to the 'heavies' who had made veiled threats at Stanley Murdock's funeral. He was sure that they would suffer no remorse if they felt the need to carry out their threats. And then there was MI5. He had no hard evidence, but he was pretty sure that one of the people pulling the strings high up in there had something to hide – and it was related to Diane's death. He did not know to what lengths that person would go to keep that secret. He'd seen Chris's extra-judicial disposal of two paedophiles so he had no illusions. He too could disappear.

This was his third day taking money out of the hole in the wall. If they had him on camera, it would prove that he was in Cambridge. Mary was doing similarly and they'd decided six days each would suffice. With Katy's help, eight burner phones plus a dongle and sim had been bought for ready money. He was growing a beard to change his appearance, although he doubted there would be much CCTV coverage where they were going. They had enlarged a photo of Stanley Murdock and one of Diane. The photo of Stanley had, at first, been problematic as the Murdock offspring had systematically and ceremonially destroyed all photos of their father, and they had been thorough. Ben had had to resort to the photos he had taken of the dead man after embalming, and after he'd readjusted Stanley's mouth to remove the smile in the light of Alistair's derogatory comments.

They'd ummed and aaahed about the content of the letter they would send in advance to the Kevins. With advice from Josephine, Mary had drafted a letter which was both professional and enticing, purporting to come from Josephine Finlay and suggesting that it could be to their financial advantage for the Kevins and their cousins to accept a visit from the solicitor and her clerk. No more details were given. Josephine, with Agnes egging her on, had been delighted to be able to help. As she had said, she was never going to practise again, so it was not going to hurt her reputation. It seemed that Mary and Josephine were planning further meetings 'when this is all over'. Ben was surprised and delighted.

Mary had found the names and addresses of all the Kevins and their cousins living in Moira by trawling census data, ancestry sites and other databases accessible to the University. She should not have been using University links but, as she told Ben, there was no-one who would check up on a University Librarian. She had hand-written all their details on a spreadsheet so as to leave no trail. Fortunately, all of the Kevins and most of the cousins still lived in the vicinity of Moira – just three cousins had moved away and luckily all three had moved to England. Ben and Mary decided to see these three first – in Birmingham, Paddington and Liverpool. Diane's cryptic note had told them the cousin was male but, to make their cover story ring true, they'd decided to see all the cousins, male and female. Luckily, they'd had a positive response from all three cousins in England.

In order to stay under the radar of MI5 they concluded that they should hire a car and take in both Birmingham and Liverpool in the same trip. Mo knew of a small-time garage that operated just this side of the law. They still owed him a favour from his time in the Force so he would hire a car, pay cash and with no questions asked. Mo had also booked, by Airbnb, a small flat in Wavertree very near to the Liverpool Kevin-cousin. They would take Mo's phone and send a few texts while they were there while Mo kept a low profile in Cambridge.

* * *

The first Kevin-cousin, in King's Heath, was easy to find – not so easy to park, but they managed to squeeze into a space in York Road. A short walk brought them to a prim Victorian house with a small and tidy front garden. The door was opened by a tall man with classic Celtic colouring. He ushered them in and offered them tea. They refused the tea and were shown into a tidy dining room with black and white photos all around of a young man holding a hurling stick.

John Shea pointed to the pictures. 'Me when I was young and fit. Played for the County, you know. Course, it marked you as Catholic but I left all that behind when I moved to England. Well now, this is quite fascinating. Made me think back on my time in Moira. What can I do for you?'

Mary took out a folder marked 'Legacy – Kevins' Cousins'. She retrieved two photos from the folder and put them face down on the table. 'We have a client who has made a very unusual bequest. The will states that a cousin of a Kevin, name unknown, who lived in Moira, had been kind to the benefactor and was to be left a sizeable sum in the benefactor's will. As executor, it is my duty to find the right person. I'd like to show you photographs of two people. I must warn you, one was alive when the photo was taken but the other was taken after the person had died. I'd like you to tell me if you know either of these – and, if you do, to tell me what you know of them. Is that OK?'

'Perfectly.'

Mary turned over the two photos. Ben thought it was a bit like a game show, or that long lost family programme. Still, there wouldn't be any happy reunions here as both the people in the photos were definitely dead.

John Shea studied both. 'Knew him. Couldn't stand him so, if it's him, I'm not your man. I can't place her at all. No, don't know her. Looks nice though.' He prodded the picture of Stanley

Murdock. 'He was a snake. Not sorry he's dead.' He smiled. 'Ah, well. Looks like I'm outa luck with the money. Are you sure you'll not be wanting a cup of tea?'

They politely declined and left soon after, having told John Shea they'd be in touch.

* * *

Their visits to Liverpool and Paddington were equally disappointing, though Anthony Maguire and Siobhan O'Donoghue were rather more polite about Stanley Murdock than John Shea had been. But neither had any idea who Diane was.

So, next stop, Ulster. Ben had made a note of the name of a local undertaker in Moira in case he was asked. The driving licences and photo ID for Mary in the name of Josephine Finlay and her clerk, Adam Morris, had arrived from Michael's artistic associate. The plane was booked in their real names – there was no way round that – but the van at the other end was booked in their assumed names to carry Ben, Mary and the coffin to Moira. Rooms had been booked at a local B&B. Although they expected to be away only a few days, they'd arranged for Katy to text from both of their own phones in Cambridge every day while they were away.

Chapter 16

'Soon you'll be able to do this yourself. I can give you advice if you want to buy your own plane.'

'Maybe.' Ben replied. 'I'm not planning on doing this on a regular basis. But for fun maybe. How long before I'm ready to try for my licence?'

'A couple more lessons should do it. Then you'll be able to fly dead dudes all over.' Richard laughed and turned to Mary. 'What are you doing in this reprobate's company anyway?'

They were sitting snugly in the six-seater taxiing for take-off. The pilot, who Ben had introduced to Mary as Richard, had installed Mary in the co-pilot's seat. Ben was in the back beside the coffin. They were cleared for take-off and, as they rose, Cambridge spread out below them. Richard pointed out various landmarks to Mary.

The flight was largely uneventful with Richard doing nearly all the talking. Barely an hour after leaving Cambridge, they were touching down at Rathfriland Airstrip and unloading the empty coffin. The only sticky moment had come when Richard had asked why it was going to take three or four days to pick up 'a stiff'. Ben had quickly explained that the undertakers who were storing the body were embalming it so they had given themselves extra time as they were unsure as to when it would be ready. When Richard had looked as though he was going to ask more, Mary had added that they were also making this a short holiday 'away from family and prying eyes.' Richard's raucous laugh and elbow dig into Ben's ribs had sealed the conversation.

'Paperwork seems to be in order.' The airport security man pointed to the other side of the yard. 'Your van has been delivered.' He looked at a separate piece of paper. 'Different name though.'

Mary smiled up at him. 'Oh, that's no problem. It was another member of the firm that organised it. D'you want to check with them?' She rooted round in her handbag. 'I had it. It must be here somewhere. Oh dear, I'm not sure where I put it. It might be in the overnight case. Can you wait while I find it?'

59

'No worries,' replied the security man. 'You look honest.' He handed Ben the keys. 'Just drive it over here and I'll help you load the coffin. We'll dragoon that pilot of yours to help when you get back. Is it a heavy fella you'll be picking up?'

Ben's turn to lie. 'No, he's old and I believe he has been frail for some time so he shouldn't be too heavy.'

Ben drove over and they slid the empty coffin into the van.

'Grand,' said the man. 'See you in a few days.' And he waved them off.

* * *

The landlady at the B&B pointed them to 'the only place in town to eat.' And indeed it was the only place in town to eat – the only one that was open, anyway. Ben already knew that Pretty Mary's was the new incarnation of Norman's Bar, the hostelry that Stanley Murdock had been used to frequenting when in Moira, though he doubted that they would find out anything useful there. In that, he was wrong.

Pretty Mary's was warm and cosy. As they walked in, all heads turned to see who was arriving. Ben estimated that there were about twenty customers, all nursing pints of dark liquid. It was obvious, from the curious looks that went on too long, that there were not many visitors in this part of the world. Mary walked straight up to the bar, thrust out her hand and proclaimed to the barman, 'Hello. I'm Josephine Finlay. What a lovely place you have here. A hidden treasure. Any chance of food?'

As they sat at a table with menus in their hands, a small man sidled up. 'Sorry ma'am. Josephine Finlay, you say.'

She smiled broadly. 'Yes. And you are...?'

'Patrick Sheehy, at your service ma'am.' He took off his cap and bowed. 'Well, there's a thing. So you're real. See, I thought me cousin Kevin was codding me. He said there might be some money in it for me. There's never been any money in it for me so I didn't believe him. See, our Kevin's a cute hoor so I'm sorry, ma'am, but I told our other cousins that he was taking the piss – beggin' your pardon ma'am. Shall I tell them that you're real after all?'

'Yes please, Mr Sheehy. That would help me a lot. Can I ask you to help me a bit more?'

'Why sure, ma'am.'

'After we've eaten, can I talk to you about your Kevin and any other Kevins in Moira?'

'Yes, ma'am. Anything I can do to help.'

'And can I buy you a drink to keep you occupied until we've finished eating.'

'Well, ma'am, that would be grand. Indeed it would.'

At that, Mary got up and went to the bar. 'A round of drinks for everyone.' She pointed towards Patrick Sheehy. 'And two for my friend here.' Ben smiled. She certainly knew how to play the crowd.

Their dinner had been quick and delicious. As the plates were being cleared away, Mary motioned for Patrick to come and join them. He brought an almost empty glass with him and Mary motioned the barman to bring a refill. She drew a sheaf of papers out of her handbag and extracted her list of contacts and the photos of Diane and Stanley.

She held the two photos so Patrick couldn't see them and explained, 'I've got photos here of two people. The one of the woman was taken when she was alive, the man after he'd died. I want you to tell me if you recognise either of them. I'm afraid I can't tell you any more than that at the moment. Is that OK?'

Patrick nodded. Mary put the photos down in front of him. He picked up the picture of Diane and studied it, then repeated the performance with the photo of Stanley. 'Never seen her. Remember him though. Used to come in here mebbe twenty years ago.' He laughed. 'He used to buy drinks all round too. And he wanted information in exchange. You're not related, are you?'

The thought that Mary was being compared to Stanley Murdock made Ben's stomach heave but he kept silent.

Mary ignored the remark. 'Know anything else about him?'

'Nothin. He had a wife and three wains here. He lived in Belfast, I think.'

Mary put the photos away and brought out her list of names. 'Look, there you are on my list of people to see. All I can tell you is that someone has written in their will that they want to give money to a cousin of a man called Kevin who lived in Moira in the nineties.' She smiled brightly at Patrick. 'This is just the sort of needle in haystack job that solicitors hate. See this list – thirty names. These are the Kevins we've come up with. You could help by looking through the list to see if we've got all the Kevins and all their cousins – as far as you know.'

'Billy'd know more than me. He's been here for donkeys years – used to work in the Post Office. Knows everyone. Will I call him over?'

'That would be so helpful.' she grinned at Patrick. 'Or should I say, that would be grand!'

Billy was a mine of information. He knew all the Kevins and all their families. Grand people, one and all. Ben suspected that all people would be described to them as 'grand people' so he took that with a pinch of salt. Billy was fascinated by the concept of the unusual legacy and they thankfully accepted his offer to gather the Kevins and cousins in Pretty Mary's the following day. He thought he could get them all to come. Ben smiled at the thought of the bar bill.

* * *

The Kevins with their cousins in tow started arriving when the bar opened at eleven. All accepted a drink with alacrity and settled down to wait their turn. Ben's aside to Mary that it was like a doctor's surgery brought her retort that she'd never been offered even a coffee at her doctor's. They came, they looked at the two photos and they ticked their addresses as correct on Mary's list. Almost all recognised Stanley Murdock's photo and could add details about his life in Moira. All those who had known him gave favourable accounts of his character. But as Ben said afterwards, 'They're expecting a legacy – why wouldn't they?'

No-one recognised Diane.

Billy came over when the queue had subsided. 'Well, Miss. I counted all the Kevins and sixteen cousins. A grand haul. That just leaves the seven here and three in England – am I right?'

Mary nodded.

'Gimme another look at that list.' He prodded the unchecked entries. 'They all work away in Lisburn or Portadown. I'll make sure they're in here tonight. That suit you?'

Mary gave him a dazzling smile. 'Billy, you are wonderful. You've made this so much easier. Thank you so much.'

'D'you know, Miss Finlay, I have to thank you. I haven't had the craic like this since I retired. I've been chatting to auld customers – got invited to a baptism – so that'll be grand. And I've got me an invite to join the unofficial bowls team in the park. I'm going.' He looked round the bar and lowered his voice. 'I've been spending too much time in here. You've done me a good turn.'

Mary looked delighted. 'I'm so pleased.'

Billy waved as he left. 'I'll send those others here. I'll say from six, will I?'

Ben didn't know what Billy had said to the remaining Kevin-cousins, but all seven were lined up at the bar on the dot of six. The performance was repeated and, again, some recognised Stanley Murdock and a few could put a name to him. No-one recognised Diane. As the last one left, Mary sighed.

Ben said, 'Well, that's all of them, and easier than I thought. And I'm supposed to know him when I see him but I didn't recognise any of them. Let's have a drink. What would you like?'

Mary looked towards the bar. 'It's got to be a Guinness mix. Ask the man if I'd like a snakebite. If not that, then his recommendation. Tell him I don't want anything sweet.'

Ben came back with two drinks. 'A snakebite for you and straight Guinness for me – with a shamrock on top. Cheers!'

They both took a swig and Mary laughed at Ben with his Guinness moustache on top of his recently grown one. 'You're right. It has been easier than we thought. And I've discovered snakebite so a fruitful couple of days.'

'Yeah, fruitful except we're no further forward. Surely, the cousin must have known Diane, otherwise the clue doesn't make sense. Maybe it was too obvious – looking for the Kevins and their cousins. But I can't see what else we could do.'

'How's your Guinness? My snakebite's delicious. I could get used to this.'

'Well, you'll need your energy; we've got a coffin to pack.'

They paid yet another enormous bar bill, counting out several twenty pound notes. They were waved a fond farewell by the barman, and started for their B&B. The plan was to phone Richard to ask him to collect them sometime the following day, then to leave early, stop at a garden centre and pack the coffin with some bags of compost and drive directly to the airstrip.

When they arrived at the B&B, they found their bags piled neatly on the doorstep.

'What the...?' Ben looked at the pile of luggage. He rang the bell.

A head appeared at an upstairs window and a voice said in a stage whisper, 'Go round the back.' Then the window closed.

The landlady was waiting for them at the back door. She was wringing her hands. 'I'm so sorry. You'll have to go. I've been told you're not to stay here.'

'Who told you?' Ben asked but he was sure he knew the answer – it was either MI5 or Stanley's erstwhile UVF friends. 'Don't tell me – some heavies arrived and warned you off. Did they search our room or our van?'

'They searched nothing. Told me you were asking questions and I was to have nothing to do with you. Told me to tell you to go back where you came from and not to come back. You're not welcome here. I'm sorry.'

Ben took out his wallet and counted out the cost of three night's stay. 'We're sorry to have caused you bother. Of course we'll go. Will you be all right?'

The landlady looked apologetic. 'I'll be fine if I do as they say. See, we still have hard men from the Troubles who have secrets to hide. They don't like people asking questions and you've been asking questions. We won't be free till they all die. God forgive me, but I wish they would.'

'Could you tell if they were local?'

'They had balaclavas but I know who they are. They're local, all right. I can tell you no more but I wish you well.'

'One last question – did they know our names?'

She pointed to Mary. 'They knew you. Said "Get that Finlay woman out of our town." Sorry.' And with that she closed the door.

Chapter 17

After phoning Mo from one of their burner phones and disposing of the phone and the sim in different wheelie bins, they felt relatively sure that Josephine would be safe in Cambridge. The men who had run them out of town were local and low level, so it seemed likely that they would be satisfied that they'd done enough to ensure that their secrets, whatever they were, were safe. Ben had phoned Richard and they were to be picked up at 10am at the airstrip. He'd then disposed of the second phone in the same way as the first. They'd spent an uncomfortable night in the van, parked hidden in a wooded area – having deciding that was the safest place for their last night in Ulster. The trip to the garden centre had been uneventful and they now had a coffin stacked with bags of compost with its lid screwed down.

    Ben was driving, making sure they stayed within the speed limit and looked totally unattractive to the constabulary. 'We screwed up with Josephine.'

    Mary squeezed his arm. 'I'm sure she'll be OK. Don't beat yourself up. As you said, they're local villains so their reach won't be far. What we need to do now is send a letter to all of the Kevins and their cousins with a share of the "legacy" for each of them. That should sweeten the atmosphere in Moira. I'll cobble something together as soon as we get back and send each of them a letter with some money in it. It'll have to be cash – which doesn't look the most professional – but won't be traceable. I'll send to the English cousins too. I can send them using the PO box I set up for the first round of letters.'

    Ben looked troubled.

    'What's wrong? Have I missed something?'

    'Mary, you are a wonder and I appreciate all you've done but, listen – this is getting serious. We seem to have managed to stay under MI5's radar but we've already ruffled dangerous feathers in Moira. I really shouldn't have let you get involved.'

    Mary chuckled. 'Ben, look at me. No, don't look at me – look at the road. Just imagine my smiling face. Do you think I didn't enjoy my performance in Pretty Mary's? Don't you know

I'm having the time of my life? Don't you dare try to cut me out of this. I'd never forgive you! Now, we'd better get a move on. We don't want to miss our plane!'

* * *

Richard was waiting for them. Ben, Richard and the man from the airstrip hefted and manoeuvred the rather heavy coffin into the small plane. Ben decided they'd been a bit enthusiastic with the compost when airstrip-man commented, 'Thought you said he'd wasted away. You sure you got the right stiff in there?'

Ben's riposte seemed to satisfy him. 'They told us he'd weighed 19 stone in his day. Then we'd've had problems. Anyway, thanks for your help.' Ben was sure that the tip he passed over would also help ease matters.

Back at Cambridge airport, Mo and Michael helped Ben unload the compost-filled coffin and stow it in their body wagon. The official at Cambridge airport greeted Ben like a long lost friend and asked how the lessons were going. He took a cursory look at the paperwork and waved them on their way. Mo drove with Mary chatting beside him. Michael and Ben sat hunched on the coffin in the back – something Ben would never have allowed had the contents been human.

It was no surprise to Ben when Mo suggested, 'a nice cuppa and then you can tell us what you found out.' Ben was relieved by Mo's next utterance and could see that Mary was too. 'By the by, I sorted Josephine. She's having a holiday with Agnes at her place in Hunstanton. Just in case, like. Drove em up there last night. Me and Michael helped 'em settle in. Nice little bungalow – that.'

Michael was looking nostalgic. 'How was the auld place? I've been thinking of going back for a holiday. Taking Pam to see my roots.' He grinned. 'Bet it was raining. Did you get a good Irish welcome – apart from being warned off, of course?'

Ben sighed. 'Disappointing. A good welcome – yes. But no rain and no-one knew Diane. Moira's not a big place and the local ex-postmaster told us we'd got all the Kevins and all the Kevin-cousins. None of them recognised Diane. Loads recognised your uncle Stanley. They were polite, of course. There was the possibility of a windfall but I think we can be certain that he was not well-liked.'

Michael grinned. 'Sound like sensible folk. But my uncle was still important enough to some people for them to run you out of town.'

'And, as well as that, we got precisely nowhere. We're at a dead end.'

Mary squeezed his arm. 'Let's go and see Henry. Maybe he'll have something for us.'

Chapter 18

'By the look on your faces, I gather your trip was not a success?' Henry Walpole patted Ben on the arm. Ben knew it was an excuse to lean on him while Walpole shuffled across to the other side of his study.

'Dead end. They remembered Murdock – but no-one knew Diane.'

While Mary poured them all a gin and tonic, Ben studied the quad from Walpole's window. 'I see your painter watchers have gone. I asked Mr Fisher before we came. D'you think they've given up on you, us?'

'Well, dear boy, I've been a bit more circumspect in the people I've been talking to. Concentrated on the old school – the ones that aren't dead, anyway.'

Ben wondered if he meant 'old school' as in school attended, or in the wider terms of people of his era. He decided they might be precisely the same group.

Walpole smiled but there was a sadness there. 'I've been asking about the time your wife was killed. Now here's a thing. I was on the periphery in '96 but it seems that Service personnel were in full scale panic for most of that year and some of the next.'

'So what was bothering them?'

'My confidantes couldn't say. There was a lot happening, so they were certainly being kept busy. Nasty goings-on. Your barracks bomb was only one of the atrocities that year. There were two mainland bombings – Docklands and Manchester. Then there was Dunblane. Terrible, that was.' Ben could see immense sadness in Henry's eyes as he sat in silence for a moment. Ben and Mary waited and, after a pause, he rallied himself and continued, 'They came to the conclusion that Dunblane wasn't terror related. Other things though, the Maxwell trials brought up their father's Israeli links. That would have caused consternation in case anything came out. Then there were two royal divorces. That sort of thing always gets the services twitchy. They like stability. Then the following year, Hong Kong in July and poor Diana's tragic death in France. Those would have had both services on tiptoes. But this is the thing, it all seemed to calm down after the general election in May '97. Remember that? Landslide Labour victory.'

Ben could see that Henry was settling back into his chair so he awaited the reminiscences. They came. 'I remember, I was sitting quietly in this very room, celebrating that result – my tipple then was whisky – can't drink it now.' He patted his rotund stomach. 'Upsets the innards. Anyway, I was sitting and quietly enjoying the country's euphoria when I had a visitor. He burst in. It was my handler and he'd come hot-foot from London to see me and asked if I was "all right" with the result. Of course I knew what that meant. Would I cause trouble at the prospect of a Labour government? Then, I think he remembered I was an old Commie so he asked if New Labour was left enough for me. I seem to remember telling him I was ecstatic that we'd kicked out the Tories. That was all he wanted to know. Would I accept a Labour government and not make waves. They had a majority of 179, so I told him I thought that was pretty decisive and why would I question it. He seemed satisfied, he finished his drink and went. Odd, that. Didn't think anything of it at the time.' Henry looked from his empty glass to Mary.

'Fill it up, Henry?'

'Yes please. Doctor says I should cut down, but he's a mere child, so what does he know?' Henry's brow furrowed into a frown. 'Didn't question it at the time but now I'm thinking, why would an officer of reasonable rank in MI5 come all the way to Cambridge to ask me my reaction to a Labour victory? Doesn't make sense.'

Ben clarified. 'So you're saying that whatever was causing all the hullabaloo was sorted by May '97.' He counted on his fingers. 'Whatever it was, it was big – otherwise why would they still be making such efforts to keep it buried. And it must have been to do with Stanley Murdock because he's the link to us being forced off the road. And we have evidence from Dobson that Murdock was worried that Diane had found out his secret.' He stopped for a moment and slapped his hand to his head. 'What an idiot! The secret can't have been about the gang rape when he was an undergrad here. Way back, when I told Chris about it, it was clear that the Service knew nothing about the rape. I got the impression that Murdock had been too useful for them to have cared anyway. Stanley Murdock must have had a bigger secret – and one they do care about. Diane knew it and she was killed. And the powers that be really, really want to stop us finding out what it was.'

Mary added, 'Oh! So all we have to do is find out Stanley Murdock's secret – a secret closely guarded by MI5 and kept hidden for more than fifteen years. Anyone know where to start?'

Chapter 19

Ben ignored the phone. Katy or Michael would answer it. He was at a delicate part of the embalming process and needed to concentrate. And concentration wasn't coming easy these days. They'd come to a dead halt with what he now saw as his obsession to find out who had killed his wife. He'd talked it over with Dr Clare in a couple of sessions and was working through the process of coming to terms with never knowing. It was hard. His consolation for the failure of his quest was threefold; they'd tried their best, he'd gained a firm friend in Mary and, in addition, his family had been thoroughly supportive. They'd all done what they could to cushion his return to the world of the mundane.

Katy was cooking for him – a dubious pleasure but one he appreciated. Mo had relieved him of some of Katy's meals by taking him out to the pub to eat. He could tell that Mo was missing Agnes, but they both knew it was safer if she and Josephine stayed in Hunstanton for the time being. He was delighted by the way that pairing was progressing. Mo had a spring in his step and Ben thought that, these days, Mo was younger than he was. Michael, Pam, Sarah and her new girlfriend Dani had made a standing invitation for him to join them at the pub. And they'd suggested he bring Mary.

Then there was Mary. He didn't know what to do about Mary. It was only a week but now that their joint enterprise had ground to a halt, a gulf seemed to have appeared between them. He wanted to bridge the gap but was unsure how. As he was musing, Katy burst in. 'Dad, it's the receptionist at Josephine's old firm. She says she needs to speak to you. Says it's urgent.'

'OK. Can you take over here?'

Katy nodded and Ben hurriedly removed his gloves and went to the phone. 'Hello, Ben Burton.'

The voice of the indiscreet receptionist at the offices of Marriott, Henson and Finlay, greeted him. She spoke at a pace and sounded out of breath 'Hello, Mr Burton. I hope I'm not bothering you. I didn't know what to do or who to tell and then I thought of you.'

'Hello, Dot. It's no trouble. What can I do for you?'

'Well, it's like this. We had this phone call yesterday. I answered it. I told the boss about it and he said to ignore it but I can't get it out of my head. It's got me worried.'

'And…'

'See, it was this Irishman and he was asking for Miss Finlay. When I told him she didn't work here anymore, he got really angry. Said I must be lying. Wouldn't take no for an answer. He wanted me to give him her address. Well, of course I told him I couldn't do that. That's when he started shouting. Said it was urgent and he had to speak to her.'

Now Ben sounded urgent. 'Did you tell him anything?'

'No. When Josephine left us, Mr Marriott said she'd had a breakdown and, on no account was she to be contacted. So then I thought of you. See, if it is urgent, maybe she needs to be informed?'

'Did he say anything else?'

'Well, he mentioned a woman called Moira. Yeah, said he was from Moira. Said she'd been somewhere and had caused trouble. I didn't know who'd caused the trouble, Miss Finlay or this Moira woman. He was so angry, I didn't dare ask. That's all. When I wouldn't give him any information, he swore and slammed the phone down. Quite shook me up, I can tell you.'

'I'm sure it did. Are you sure you didn't tell him anything? Didn't give him any clues about where she was?'

'Mr Burton, I couldn't even if I'd wanted to. I know her flat's empty and she's moved out. And I don't know where she's gone. I was hoping you would and you'd be able to sort it all out. I'm hoping Miss Finlay is OK but no-one talks about her here.'

'Thanks Dot. Yes, I can sort it. This man, did he talk to anyone else?'

'Only me. I was going to transfer him to Mr Marriott but he put the phone down before I could suggest that.'

'Thank you, Dot. You did exactly the right thing. And Miss Finlay is doing well. I'll pass on your best wishes to her. If he phones again, don't bother Mr Marriott. Give him my number. I can sort it from here, so don't you worry.'

'Thanks Mr Burton. I always thought you were a gentleman.' And, with that, the phone went dead.

Ben smiled a rueful smile. The man from Moira post office had assured them they had picked up all the Kevin-cousins. They'd thought their problems with the old paramilitaries had stayed in Northern Ireland but, it seemed, they'd followed them back to Cambridge. They'd thought it would be a good idea to use a real solicitor's name and Josephine had been keen. But it had been a mistake. That they couldn't change, but at least they could keep Josephine safely hidden in Hunstanton until they could think of a long-term solution. Tricky. They might have to call on Chris. But he now had an excuse to visit Mary.

* * *

'I'd love to come. The Who – d'you remember "Boris, the spider" and "My Generation". That *was* my generation – well, nearly. But I didn't get Quadrophenia at all. Totally baffling. Let's see, I can do tonight or tomorrow.'

And so it was agreed. A trip to the Arts Cinema that evening. They'd faced the threat of paramilitaries together, he'd taken her out to dinner to thank her for all her help but this was the cinema – a breakthrough to what Ben definitely thought of as a date. He'd surprised himself by asking her to come to the cinema with him, and had been delighted when she had been so enthusiastic. Diane had also been a fan of The Who. Was this a good omen or bad? Neither, he decided.

He'd explained about the phone call to the solicitors where Josephine had worked. Mary had been both sympathetic and practical, and optimistic that they could keep Josephine out of danger. Mary had told him that following the bank transfer of £30,000 from Ben, she'd posted the 'legacies' to all the Kevins and cousins explaining that the will had specified this as a backstop if the right cousin couldn't be found. The hope was now that the paramilitaries would lose interest in them. Mary suggested that he come for a drink before they walked to the cinema together. He'd agreed with alacrity. Suddenly, having a drink with an attractive woman and then going to the pictures seemed so normal and ordinary and safe.

He pondered the last time he'd taken a woman to the cinema. Not Vin. Theirs had been primarily a physical relationship, an affair in the normal sense of the word. No, it had been Josephine and he'd taken her to see 'The Man Who Fell to Earth' and she had described it as truly sad – the story of a family breakdown. Knowing her past as he did now, he could understand her take on it. But, with the help of Dr Clare, she was healing herself and building a relationship with her mother. Ben knew that, whatever they did now, Josephine's well-being had to be sacrosanct.

They'd had a pleasant glass of wine. Mary preferred red so, in deference to Ben's usual preference for white, she'd produced a fine Freurie. She'd laughed when she'd said she was educating his palate – starting with soft and gentle – and they'd move on to higher tannin at a later date. That sounded promising to Ben who was beginning to relish Mary's company. She was an intelligent companion and fun to be with. He thought he would happily suffer tannic wines for the promise of more meetings with Mary.

At the cinema, they bought salty popcorn, and he felt like a teenager again. He smiled to himself. Perhaps he'd learn to live with not knowing the truth and relax into this new normal. They settled down to watch the film. It had been remastered so the fact that it was nearly forty years old mattered not a bit. The sound was excellent. They sat in cosy silence for half an hour.

Thirty minutes in, Ben leapt out of his seat and shouted, 'Christ Almighty. I'm such a fool!'

He started shuffling sideways out of his seat beckoning Mary to follow. 'Scuse me, sorry, got to get out. Sorry. Sorry.'

Once back in the foyer, Mary looked at him. 'You OK? You look as though you've seen a ghost. Sit down. Take deep breaths. What happened in there?'

'I'm sorry, Mary. But I've been such a fool. Of course that's who she meant. It's probably the same man. Suddenly, it begins to make some sense.'

'Well, it might make sense to you but I'm completely in the dark.'

After several deep breaths he smiled up at her. 'If you haven't worked it out by the time we get to your house for another glass of red, I'll tell you.'

They walked back, each deep in thought. Mary poured two glasses of wine and Ben asked, 'Any ideas?'

'One question first. Was Diane a Who fan?'

Ben nodded.

'Easy then, when you can make that link. Kevin's cousin Tommy – the pinball wizard. So now we have to find a Tommy in Moira. Can't use the same process, so we need to think how to go about it.'

'Mary, you are undoubtedly a genius and, I'm sure you could think of a way. But I believe I may have a short-cut. Hope so. Virginia Murdock told me that, when they lived in Moira, their next door neighbour was called Tommy. He was a good friend to Margaret Murdock and helped out when Stanley was away in Belfast – which was most of the time. We need to go back to Brighton and talk again to Virginia and Alistair.'

Chapter 20

The next day they hired a car from Mo's dodgy acquaintance. Mary had thought that they might get fuller information – and be less likely to be overheard – if they met the Murdocks in person rather than asking questions about Moira over the phone, even a burner. Following the car incident, they decided not to phone in advance but hoped Virginia would be home. If not, they would call on Alistair at his Emporium and, as a last resort, go to see Gavin at the University. If all else failed, they would post a note for Virginia through the front door.

They rang the bell and waited. They rang the bell a second time and waited. 'We could try Alistair's shop.'

Then they heard a voice from on high. They stepped back and saw Virginia leaning out of an upstairs window. 'Hello. What a surprise! Hang on, I'll be down in a minute.'

As the window closed, they heard a man's voice asking sleepily, 'Who is it?

'Ooops!' said Mary. 'I think we've disturbed the lovers.'

Ben looked at his watch. 'Eleven o'clock. Young people, huh!'

Mary replied, 'Those were the days. Jealous? Me? Oh, yes!'

Before Ben could respond, Virginia opened the door. Ben apologised for disturbing them.

'Nonsense. Come in, come in. If I'd known you were coming, I'd have baked a cake. Or got Gav to do one – safer all round.'

She led them to the kitchen and put the coffee on while they settled themselves. Ben said, 'Really sorry to have disturbed you, but we thought, after last time, it would be safer just to arrive. We have some more questions for you and Alistair. Is he here?'

'No probs.' Virginia looked at her watch. 'You're in luck. He's due back in about ten minutes. He was expecting a parcel and it's arrived.'

Gavin appeared looking not at all sleepy but still unshaven. 'Hi. Good to see you guys. Thanks for the tip-off. Ginny's told me about her dad and his dodgy dealings. So someone's still chasing him? Anyway, after your letter we've all bought burners and we've been very careful with the old phones – using them for innocuous stuff. But there's always the mischievous desire to talk to the listeners. You know, say "Hello, you nasty police officers. How's it going?" Won't, of course.'

'I know,' said Mary. 'When you know they're there, you just want to let them know that you know.'

'And,' added Gavin, 'We've had the house swept for bugs. Clean. Seems we weren't high enough up the pecking order to merit those.'

Virginia handed round the coffees. 'Allie's got some news for you. He had that hypnosis yesterday and he's full of it. He wanted to phone but I said it was better to write to you. He'll be so pleased to tell you all about it. But what brought you down here today – telepathy?'

'I wanted to ask you some more about Tommy – your neighbour in Moira. We think he might be able to help us.' Ben hated dissembling but he and Mary had decided that it was safer for the Murdock family if they were kept in the dark about the abortive visit to Moira. 'We're thinking of going there – but we're not sure if it would be worthwhile. If you could give us his address and surname, that would help enormously.'

'Oh, God, it was years ago. It was Glebe something. Glebe what? I remember the houses were all new when we moved in – we were in 54. Tommy, he was such a lovely man. But, I suppose anyone would seem like that when we had a father like we did. God, I hope Allie can be more help. Tommy – I think it began with a C and we used to laugh because he was tall. I remember we called him Tommy Tallman and he laughed at that. Thinking about it, he laughed a lot – not like our miserable father. Glebe what though? That doesn't help you, does it?'

'If it gets us there, it helps.'

While Virginia had been talking, Gavin had brought up Moira on Google maps. 'OK, so there's Glebe Park, Glebe Avenue, Glebe Crescent, Glebe Way, Gardens, Drive and Place. You get the picture? There are a lot of Glebes in Moira.'

'Let me look,' said Virginia. 'I might be able to picture it.' She looked at the map. 'Glebe Park, Glebe Park – we were at the end of that road.' She pointed. 'There. See. Father always complained. Said that, in an emergency, we wouldn't be able to get out.'

For Ben, this fitted. His considered view was that Stanley Murdock had been thinking of his own skin, as he was the one whose lifestyle might have led to his being cornered. 'So 54 Glebe Park.'

'Not sure. I was little. These things weren't important to me. He was definitely next door and we were definitely at 54. Ask Allie.'

As if by magic, the front door opened and slammed shut again.

Alistair's greeting was delivered from the hallway. 'Hi, sis. Got any first class stamps – got to post that letter to Ben.' Then he rounded the doorway. 'Good God, you must be psychic. Well, Ben. Hello! Have I got a tale to tell you! I won't keep you in suspense any longer than I have to. Got to have a pee – back soon.'

Ginny grinned at them. 'It's worth hearing, though I think it raises more questions than it answers.'

Alistair came back and flung himself on to the nearest chair. 'Aren't hypnotists amazing. Love a coffee, sis. I didn't remember anything much until she put me under. I must admit I told a little fib. Said it was an incident in my childhood that I wanted to come to terms with. I wanted to know what my father and Jacko were hatching and if it concerned me. I told her about Jacko feeling me up, and that it didn't really bother me but I thought it might have something to do with my relationship with the old sod.' He stopped and laughed. 'Oops! Probably the wrong word to use for my father in this context. She asked if she could record it so I asked her if it might help us to hear what I'd said afterwards. She recorded it so nothing got lost. Nothing on it to harm me so she gave me a memory stick. I'll give it to you afterwards. Anyway, she agreed to take me back there – on the understanding that she would bring me straight back if I was showing any signs of distress. So, off we went.'

Ben found that both he and Mary were leaning forward. 'And?'

'Well, a little suspense is good for the soul.' Then Alistair lapsed into silence again.

Ben glared at Alistair. 'Out with it. You know you've got us on tenterhooks.'

Alistair laughed. 'OK. So we went to this bar in Belfast. I can't remember the exact name but I know it was a dog's name; not the Rover's Return, that's for sure. Anyway, we waited for Jacko, and like I said before, the waves parted to let him through. He was obviously the top man there. He sat down beside me with my father on the other side of the table. Jacko waved his hand and a drink appeared. Then he waved it again and all the other drinkers moved away down to the other end of the bar. He motioned them to turn away and then all we could see were lots of backs, but I could tell they were trying to hear what they were saying. Jacko and my father were talking in low voices so, I'm pretty sure the listeners were too far away and couldn't overhear. The table was sticky with beer. I touched it and wiped my hands on my shorts. Funny – it was all in the present – like I was really there. Anyway, my father passed over an envelope and Jacko looked inside and just pulled out a stash of money, just far enough to see it – there was loads. Then he stuffed it into his inside pocket. He kept needling my father, asking him who the bigwigs were.'

Ben interrupted. 'Did he say "bigwigs"?'

'Think so. Jacko said he wanted to shake their hands after the war was over. Said he'd always wanted to mix with "the upper echelons". That was the hypnotism doing good things. I'd never have remembered "echelons" if she hadn't put me back at that table – didn't know what it meant at the time. He said he'd have to get my father to introduce him.

'Father said that he might get an introduction when the job was finally done and there would be the same bounty on each head. He said he'd been promised a seat in the House of Lords after the job was done so Jacko might get an invite there.'

Ben interrupted, 'He definitely said "bounty"?'

Alistair nodded and Ben continued, 'He was promised… Never got to the House of Lords. Right?'

Virginia joined in. 'Right. So we assume the job – whatever it was – was never finished.'

Gavin's turn. 'Or the bigwigs reneged on the deal with your father.'

Mary. 'Or your father was lying about the House of Lords.'

Alistair. 'Or Jacko was lying about the job.'

Ben. 'Or something else happened. You were right, Ginny, it raises far more questions than it answers. One thing we do know from this, your father was plotting with the UVF to kill people, and paying them to do it.'

Alistair looked deflated. 'And we've got his genes. That's what keeps me awake at night.'

'Me too,' said Virginia. 'There was evil in him. I just hope we haven't inherited any of it.'

Ben was trying to decide if now was the time to tell these two about their DNA test results. The tests that were taken to eliminate them from enquiries into their father's death; those tests that had shown that their half-brother Lucien was indeed the biological offspring of Stanley Murdock – but that neither of these two were. They were full siblings but it was certain that their father had not been Stanley Murdock. As he thought of the best way to tell them, the moment passed.

Alistair was grinning again. 'But this is the best bit. Father stood up to get more drinks and he saw where Jacko's hand was. He leaned over the table right up to Jacko's face and said in that low snarl of his, "Get your filthy hand out of there and finish this job or, as God is my witness, I'll tell all your friends in here what you are." Then he turned to me. "Out!" he said, and we left.'

Mary was looking thoughtful. 'A promise of a seat in the Lords – who could offer that?'

Gavin asked, 'This was when? 1996?' Ben nodded and Gavin continued, 'The Labour Party manifesto for the election in '97 promised to reform the Lords. They got in, so maybe he got caught up in that?'

Ben kept his counsel about Henry Walpole's revelation that the panic at MI5 had calmed down after the election in '97. Could it just be relief that Murdock hadn't managed to wangle ennoblement? But here was evidence of Stanley Murdock soliciting murder – and the offer of a peerage suggested the involvement of at least one high-ranking politician. He turned to the Murdocks, 'You remember that picture of your father shaking hands with a Cabinet Minister? I don't suppose it escaped the bonfire of his belongings, did it?'

Ginny answered, 'Sorry, no. We were thorough. All the pictures went but I remember that one. He said they'd been at Ethel's together. Does that help?'

'Oh yes. Indeed it does.'

Before they took their leave they asked Alistair if he could remember anything else about their neighbour in Ireland. He had nothing to add except that he'd been a really kind man. He'd been the only one to help their mother. He'd done 'all sorts' for her even though they were on opposite sides of the divide. Then Ben had a sudden hunch. 'Were you two born in Moira?'

'Yeah – both of us – why?'

'No reason. Listen. I think I'll have some good news for you. I've got to work it out in my head. I'll write and I think you'll be pleased. Could be some weeks – need to make some more enquiries. Can we leave it like that for now?'

'Oooh!' said Alistair. 'Now you've got us all agog. Write soon.'

'I will,' said Ben, but he was not at all sure what precisely he would be able to tell them about their paternity.

Chapter 21

Ben searched through his fireproof box. Everything that he had pertaining to Stanley Murdock's life and Diane's murder was in there. For safety, he'd made two copies of every paper and they now resided with Mary and Henry. He'd taken the key to Stanley Murdock's lock-up to a locksmith in Mill Road, and copies had gone with the paperwork. As he'd handed over the key, he'd thought it had been sloppy of Stanley. If Ben had been doing it, he would have provided a lock with a restricted key.

'Ah, here it is.' He pulled out a scrap of paper with three names on it – the names of the co-conspirators in the rape of Agnes Barrett when they were undergrads at Ethel's. Old Mr Fisher had told him that the four had been 'as thick as thieves' while they had been students and, to Ben's mind, that was an appropriate epithet. One had become a Cabinet Minister, one a senior Civil Servant and the third a merchant banker – and Murdock had become a spy and a crook. If one of them had been in cahoots with Murdock and had offered him a peerage, it was probably the first of these three but could possibly be the second; the third seemed unlikely but couldn't be ruled out. He had no idea if pursuing information about these three rapists was going down a dead end but he had little else to go on. Chris had told him that one had died in a boating accident. Ben had no recollection of any Minister dying on a boat but then, in the early years after Diane's death, he hadn't been in any fit state to take in much at all. He'd go for the Cabinet Minister first. Better still, ask Mary to do it. She seemed to be able to get access to information in a way that was beyond his capabilities. He was cogitating about the precise nature of his relationship with Mary, and coming to no conclusion, when one of his remaining burner phones rang. It was Henry Walpole and he had news so he declared that he had less inclination than usual for pleasantries. However, that did not mean that he came straight to the point.

'Well, dear boy, Bill Bradshaw, that colleague of mine in the English Department, we've just spent a very pleasant afternoon reminiscing. We had a tincture or two and we're going to make it a regular occurrence, so thank you for getting me up off my derriere to go to see him. Do you know, he actually taught Murdock. It passed me by but, apparently, there was a move to make Cambridge mathematicians more literate. The idea, they said, was to fit them for a life in the civil service, diplomatic corps and all that. We agreed, of course, that it was to fit them better for a life of espionage.'

Ben wondered, was it still like that at Ethel's? Then, he remembered that first year undergrad sitting by the back gate and supposed that it was. Maybe the 'open recruitment' to spookdom was still being supplemented by the back door. Not his problem.

Henry continued. 'The upshot was that they included an English module in the Maths degree. Obviously didn't work; they dropped it soon after. But he shares my view of Murdock's character. Thought he was going to make millions or enter a life of crime. Of course, as we now know, he did both.'

Ben thought of trying to get a word in but the old man was happy, so why should he interrupt? He didn't need to.

Henry Walpole was ready to move towards divulging his nugget of information. 'And he agrees, it's a strange thing for Murdock to write.'

'You mean "sure as eggs is eggs"?'

'Precisely. He was quite clear. Murdock was a stickler for correct usage. But here's the interesting bit; they did a lecture on World War Two slang. I have no idea why. He couldn't remember either, probably took his fancy at the time. We were allowed to work like that then.'

Walpole sighed. 'Happy days, happy days. Anyway, back to the point. Murdock was very taken with it. Asked lots of questions especially about bombs. Now this is it, my boy. This is it! In World War Two, "eggs" was a slang term for bombs. Murdock passed the module way ahead of his peers. Bill said he was a natural, said he was the cleverest and most unpleasant undergraduate he had ever had the misfortune to meet.'

'So you think he took it into his vocabulary as a cover? Bombs became eggs.'

'Seems feasible.'

'It certainly does. I don't suppose you mentioned Margaret – who wouldn't be so beautiful?'

'Well, young man, you underestimate me. Of course I did, but he couldn't help me there.'

'So you had a good session?'

'Wonderful. We both decided we should write our memoirs before our brains shrivel into peanuts or the grim reaper manifests himself before us.'

'The reaper could be female.'

'Lord, yes. Now, that *would* be interesting.'

'Surely, they'd never let you publish?'

The old man laughed. 'Probably not – but have I got some tales to tell! A nom de plume. That would do it.'

* * *

He had no evidence – only hunches – and Ben realised that hunches can send you down all sorts of rabbit holes and you still wouldn't find the rabbit. He decided to go to see Mary at the University Library. He hadn't been back there since he'd been a student – and was intrigued to know if the piles of books at the entrance still turned. The library itself had always awed him with the vastness of knowledge held within. He phoned Mary, burner to burner, and arranged to meet her in front of the building.

The good news was that the books still turned. Mary got him a lanyard and took him through security then along a maze of corridors. On the way, he told her about the egg / bomb relationship. After five minutes brisk walk including three flights of stairs, they arrived at a large oak door. She keyed in a code and then took out a key for a second lock. Ben knew that this building contained priceless objects – with huge historical if not monetary value. But, as they had had to go through strict security to get this far, with Ben's photo being taken and his pockets searched, he wondered why the added security for Mary's office.

When they entered the room, he realised why. Her office was opulent in an understated way. The furniture was modern and stylish, the walls covered with modern paintings. Ben's jaw dropped. He pointed. 'Is that what I think it is?'

'Well, if you think it's a Banksy – then, yes. I bought it early in his career. He needed money then.'

Ben turned to another. 'A Hockney?'

She nodded.

He pointed to a third. 'Is that an original? He's been copied so much.'

'Authenticated long ago. It's not mine. It's Henry's. His father went to the first Lowry exhibition in 1939. Bought that. I love it. I love all the paintings here – that's why I have them.'

'Insurance?'

'That's why I keep them here. The insurance is so much less in this secure environment. Added to that, I'm here more than I'm at home so I can enjoy them.'

'Aren't you worried about losing them?'

'Of course. That's why everyone else thinks they're copies. See how much I trust you? I don't bring many people in here; we have meeting rooms. Other visitors to this room, I just lie to them.'

Ben smiled. He realised how very much he wanted to be in the circle of people that Mary trusted. He wondered how large that circle was.

She walked over to her enormous desk. 'I've made progress in the search for Tommy, but first, I'm intrigued. What can I do for you?'

'I've got some names I want you to investigate for me.' He handed her the scrap of paper.

'Um. These three. When I looked through the papers you left with me, I wondered about these – how they fitted in. Care to enlighten me?'

'It's shocking. The four were a group of Ethel students who gang raped Agnes Barrett. Stanley Murdock was the leader. They followed.'

Mary sat down suddenly. 'That's diabolical.' She looked deep in thought for a moment. 'Obviously, they got away with it.' Then she turned to Ben. 'And Josephine was the result?'

'Yes. And I think that the initial shared crime might have led to complicity in other ways. Of course, it might have done the opposite and spread them asunder. I'm most interested in the one who became a Cabinet Minister.' He pointed to the first name on the list. Then he pointed to the second. 'A Senior Civil Servant and the other one became a merchant banker.'

She drew up a second office chair and turned her screen so he could see it. She typed furiously for several seconds bringing up sites so quickly that Ben couldn't keep up. Then she began to search each one. Ben still couldn't keep up. At last, a page appeared. 'There, that's the life story of your man.'

Ben recoiled. 'He's not my man!'

She scrolled through the page and said, 'Edited version – rose quickly in politics. Worked his way round the Ministries – forever rising. Had consultancies on the side – made lots of money and died on a boat in the West Indies. All that's in the public domain.'

Ben's fingers began to tingle. Lucien had bought a boat from a friend of his father's and was sailing in the West Indies. 'Find out more about the boat.'

Mary's fingers danced on the keys again. 'Let's see if I can get a date. Ah – here it is.' Ben could see a newspaper page with a smiling man standing on the deck of a large yacht. Mary's eyes were flickering across the screen. 'Ah, this is interesting. The boat was damaged and taken into dock in Barbados.' Her finger went deftly down the words on the screen. This was speed reading at a pace way beyond Ben's. She continued, 'He died in hospital there. The boat was damaged – suspected engine malfunction blowing a hole in the side. The coroner returned an open verdict. His body was repatriated but the boat stayed out there. But, here's the good bit.' She covered a part of the screen. 'Want to guess what the boat was called?'

Ben looked questioningly at her. Then his brow cleared. 'Margaret!'

'Yep. Sure as eggs is eggs.'

'So, wow! Now, it could be that Stanley murdered his co-rapist because he'd swindled him out of a whole lot of money. That worthless money is now sitting in a grave with Stanley Murdock's body. But we still don't know what the payment was for. Could have been for any underhand deal between Stanley and this Cabinet Minister. Could have been blackmail – we know Stanley went in for that.'

Mary looked sceptical. 'Surely, they were equally culpable for the rape. I would have thought that was a secret they would all want to keep.'

'Let's look at the others.'

The whizzing fingers brought up several pages which Mary scrolled through. 'Civil Servant, pretty boring. Seems he had an uneventful career – rose slowly, did little to get himself noticed. Got a knighthood when he retired. Died of a heart attack. No questions asked. Ah – but...'

Mary scrolled through several more pages. 'Did a stint working in the Northern Ireland Office. Moved from there in '96. Asked for a transfer.'

'Could be something, could be nothing. And the banker?'

'Let's look for an FT obit. They usually come up with the goods. Yes – made lots of money, never married, and while he was alive, gave it all away. Let's see who he gave it to.' She searched another site. 'Well, well. Rape crisis centres and support for young single mothers. Looks like he was trying to make amends.'

'And, so far, the banker is the only one coming out of this with any semblance of repentance, but we'll have to keep him on our radar. Now, you say you have news of Tommy.'

'He was easy to find. Still lives there – same house. Well, he did at the last census. No record of him dying and he's unlikely he'd have moved since. I think the problem will come in trying to visit him. I can't see that we can pull the same trick as last time.'

Ben smiled. Things were moving forward. If this Tommy was the right Tommy – and that was a big if – they were near to solving Diane's murder. He knew that could bring its own problems and new forms of distress but he felt sure that he had the support he needed to face them. He hoped so, anyway. But first, they had to ensure they stayed under the radar of both MI5 and the Ulster paramilitaries.

He thought for a moment. 'I have a cunning plan. Fancy a holiday in the Republic? We go across to Dublin, stay in some out-of-the-way place in the South and drive to Moira. No border checks with us all in the EU so we can easily do a day trip to the North.'

'That should work. We'll have to look different. You'll need to be clean shaven, though I thought that beard did suit you. I think I'll dye my hair. I'd love to go red but we have to be inconspicuous. Different style, different colour, then a quick trip to Glebe whatever under cover of darkness. That should do it. How long before you want to go?'

Ben looked at his phone. 'I've got three funerals this week. Got to be there. Michael, Mo and Katy could really do it all, but I'm the face that mourners like to see, and it's not fair to lumber them. They're great, but I feel guilty. I know I've not been pulling my weight. I want to get this done but I have responsibilities.'

'That's fine. A bit of normal life will be good for both of us. My time is flexible. Nobody keeps tabs on me.'

'Good. I'll organise another car and the ferry from Fishguard. That OK with you?'

'Tell me when you're ready and I'll fit in. But I must warn you – I'm a terrible sailor. I get sick just getting on a boat.'

Ben found he was glad – not because Mary would be sick – but because it proved she wasn't perfect. And he realised that the anticipation of having to look after her was rather pleasant.

Chapter 22

Ben found that he was whistling while he worked, and not because the job, in itself, was pleasurable. It was the challenge that was making him happy. This embalming was proving trickier than he'd anticipated. The girl in question had been a mainlining addict so he'd expected problems. Her parents so wanted her to look as she had before her habit had taken hold. He had a photo. In early teens, she'd been pretty and plump. Just five years later, her body was wasted. He could do little about the weight loss but he could make her look somewhat like the girl in the photo. Her parents needed that. However, Lisa's veins were proving resistant.

A voice came from the doorway, jogging Ben out of his reverie. 'Hi Dad, want any help?' Katy came in and looked at the body of a girl no older than herself. 'At least she now looks at peace. And way better than when she came in. Know what happened to her?'

'She got in with the wrong crowd. Her mum says they tried to help her but she just needed the drug more than she needed them. It got her in the end.' Ben sighed and stood up straight. 'Help? Yes please. The dress they brought in for her to wear, it needs a bit of an iron.' He pointed across the room. 'I've put up the board. Can you make it look pristine? Especially the top half. That's the bit they'll see. I'm going to plump out her cheeks.'

They worked in silence for a while then Ben broached the subject he'd been thinking about for weeks. 'Katy?' He stopped work. This was so important.

'Yes, Dad. God, this is a fiddly dress. Bet she hasn't worn anything like it in years. Still, I suppose they want to remember her as their little girl. Sorry, Dad? What were you going to say?'

He came at it at a rush. 'What would you say if said I wanted to get married again?'

Katy stopped ironing and slowly placed the iron upright on the board. Ben waited and realised he'd stopped breathing. He took a deep breath in. Katy came over to her father and put her arms around him. 'I'd say it was bloody lovely – but only if it was Mary you wanted to marry!'

He was quiet. Katy looked concerned. 'It is Mary, isn't it?'

'Oh, yes. But you should keep back.' He pointed to his full PPE then to Lisa's body. 'Could have any number of infections. As for Mary, I haven't said anything to her and I really don't know what she'd say.'

Katy went to the sink and washed her hands and arms. She turned back to her father and gave a big grin. 'Well, you won't know if you don't ask. And you were made for each other – anyone can see that.' Ben continued with his embalming and Katy with her ironing. A companionable silence ensued. Then Katy broke it. 'You know, Dad, we've been thinking about you – me and Sarah. We've been talking and we think you've changed.'

'How so? And is it a good change?'

'Oh yeah. Deffo good. You still want to find out why Mum died, that's for sure. But her death isn't eating away at you like it used to. That's what's different. Like your head is leading your heart and not the other way round. Makes sense, eh?'

Ben stopped working and thought for a moment. 'I have two very clever daughters. I hadn't thought about it in those terms, but, yes, I think I've turned a corner.'

'So when are you going to ask her?'

'Not yet. The time's not right.' And he thought, I know she likes me and I know she trusts me but I haven't even tried to kiss her. And I haven't a clue what her reaction would be.

While Ben was cogitating, Mo came bustling through. 'Ben, you got a visitor. Says he needs to talk to you. It's that Chris – terrible taste in clothes – and too smarmy by half. Want to talk to him or shall I say you're busy?'

Ben looked at the corpse of Lisa, eighteen and dead, and sighed. 'I think I've done as much as I can here. Mo, will you finish off for me. I'll go and see what "that Chris" wants.'

'That Chris' was sitting comfortably in the low armchair in their front office. He turned as Ben entered the room. 'Well, you have been busy – and kept yourselves under the radar – impressive. Not under my radar though. I've been keeping a close eye on you.'

Ben was immediately worried. He really didn't want spies gumming up the works or, worse still, maiming or killing him or Mary. He decided to play it cool. 'OK, so what have we been up to?'

'Let me ask you something. What did you find out in Moira? You splashed the cash so you must have come up with something.'

Now Ben was getting seriously concerned. This was not just about him. Mary was in danger too. MI5 operatives were so much more dangerous than ancient Irish heavies. 'Zilch. We've got no further.'

'Sad that. Any more leads?'

'We've come to a dead end.'

'Real pity that. I was counting on you.'

Ben was sceptical. 'So, if you know so much, how come there haven't been any more "little accidents"? We've not been forced off the road or fallen down a lift shaft or got beaten up by muggers. All in all, it's been a quiet life.'

'Ah. That's because I've been putting in false reports. My superiors think you and that lovely lady of yours are being model citizens. They believe you've been frightened off. See, I know you and I knew that, whatever I forbade you to do, you'd go ahead and do it. But a dead end. That's not good news.'

'So you've been playing us?' Ben had to laugh. This was something he hadn't expected. 'Tell me,' he said

Chris wriggled further into the chair. 'For a long time I've suspected there was something stinking at the top. Got confirmed when you were forced off the road. I did some very careful digging. Couldn't find out anything cos it's all tucked away from spying eyes – even spying eyes from within. There's something big the high-ups are hiding, and it's all way above my pay grade. Got a few minutes? I want to tell you the story I've been told. And I don't want you to believe a word of it.'

Ben nodded.

Chris settled down further in the chair. 'It's a bit of a once upon a time story. There was this spy. He was under cover in Northern Ireland and had to be brought out pronto when his cover was blown. This was 1996. The UVF people who suspected him were neutralised and he was considered safe. But he had to be protected. Just before he left Ireland there was a bomb in a barracks and a woman was killed. She just happened to be on a mission in Ulster too. Caught in the cross-fire was the story – UVF – Shankill Butchers. Years later, when the spy was murdered, the story was that the UVF had caught up with him. Still feasible. Then the woman's husband wakes up and starts digging. Appropriate, as he's an undertaker. And he comes up with things that don't add up. Finds out that what I've been told from on high is a loads of bollocks. You can believe that last bit.' Chris shifted in his chair. 'Got a beer?'

Ben nodded and went to the fridge in the back room. He thought Chris would be a cold beer man. In this, he was right.

'Great. Thanks. Icy. You having one?'

Ben shook his head. Chris continued. 'So then I begin to ask around and get told straight out that I'm to leave it alone. Nothing to see – I'm told. Red rag to a bull. I know there's something to see but I don't know what it is and I don't know how to find out. Then this undertaker keeps coming up with the goods. Bloody useless trying to tell him what to do – he's working for himself not for me – but it's my job to keep him safe. He's my man.' He crossed his fingers. 'So far, so good.'

Ben looked at his watch; five o'clock. He turned the sign round and locked the door. 'Go on.'

'So I tell him to stop. I know he won't but I tell the high-ups he has. They relax but I don't. Been bloody difficult keeping an eye on him, I can tell you! So that's my story. Get my drift?'

'No. That's *my* story. What about your organisation? What's the story there? I haven't a hope of getting to the bottom of this if you don't tell me all you know.'

'Remember when you said we had a mole – well, we don't have a mole. We have an animal but it's not a mole – it's a rat. No, it's not a rat. It's a tiger with sharp claws and long fangs. We have someone high up who is playing his own game and has been for years. And it's tied up with Stanley Murdock's work in Belfast and your wife's murder seventeen years ago. He's covered his tracks. That's all I know and I want you to find out who it is.'

Ben's laugh was mirthless. 'No pressure, then. You say "he". Not a woman?'

'Possible, but women're thin on the ground up there.'

'So, the big question. Are you working on your own in this? Any back-up from within?'

'My immediate boss – she's in. That's all. See, we don't know who we can trust. She was reporting upwards until your accident. We don't know who ordered it but they must have clout.

When that happened, she stopped. Since then we've been reporting no action on your part. They think you've given up.'

For the first time, Ben was feeling admiration for this young man. He'd put him down as a pushy, brash, uncouth individual with no moral compass. He had to ask, 'Why are you doing this?'

'Funny. I've been asking myself exactly that question. Always thought of myself as a company man. Would do anything for the Service. Thought they knew best. Now I know that there is corruption there and I don't like it. So decided to stand up and be counted.' He smiled. 'Well, I decided that you'd stand up and be counted and I'd stand right behind you.'

He took a swig of his beer. 'You've managed to unearth evidence about Stanley Murdock that we could never find. We need a name and we need evidence of their collusion. Then we can nail the bastard before he does even more damage to the Service.'

'We may have an avenue to pursue.'

'Ahah! Thought you might. You make a good team – you and Mary Amelina. You might just be able to root out the corruption in the Service.'

'No pressure then!'

Chapter 23

The sea was a deep dirty grey, the seagulls were noisy and the air smelled of ozone and seaweed. The drive down to Fishguard had been long but uneventful. Mary had kept a wary eye out for followers and they were sure that there had been none. The small twisty roads towards the end of the journey had allowed them to stop, several times, and let the following traffic overtake them. There had been no pattern to be discerned. The crossing had been mercifully calm but Mary had still suffered, and so Ben had suffered with her.

As they docked, she breathed in deeply and let out a sigh. 'How long before we have to do this again?'

'Four days. Just enough time to recover. Then the Herculean task of getting back across the Irish sea.'

'OK. And you can stop taking the piss. Just think how much I must...' and she stopped. 'Anyway, the pills helped and I've survived – just.'

It was Ben's turn to drive. They drove in silence for a while, then Mary said, 'We need to talk; to get some things clear. Our cover is a holiday for two middle-aged, star crossed lovers. I told the hotel that our families don't approve so we're on a secret holiday and we don't want anyone to know. I can play that part. You saw my acting skills last time in Moira.' She paused until he responded with a nod. Then she lurched on. 'We'll be sharing a room but I made sure we had twin beds. It's a posh hotel so they're queen sized. I hope you're OK with that.'

'Perfectly. We're both adults and we are both middle-aged. As for clarity, well I'm not quite sure what you're saying.'

'I'm saying that you don't have to pretend when we're not being observed – that's what I'm saying.'

Ben was beginning to enjoy this conversation. 'Ah! But what if I'm a "method actor"? I'd have to immerse myself in the part, observed or not.'

'You're really enjoying this aren't you? My discomfiture. Well, I'll be straight. I haven't been alone in a bedroom with a man for five years and that was a complete disaster. That's what I'm telling you.'

Ben was immediately contrite. 'Mary, I'm sorry for teasing you. I'm not a monster and I promise you, I'm not a method actor. I'll be led by you. You set the rules and I'll follow them to the letter. Happy now?'

'God, yes. Thank you. Glad I got that off my chest.'

He added under his breath. 'Would be nice, though.' He didn't think she'd heard.

* * *

The hotel in Donegal was stunning – a castle, no less – and Ben felt they should do this more often. They'd decided to spend two days in their acquired roles and then travel to Moira on the second evening. They arrived at the hotel in the afternoon, swam in the pool, walked hand in hand in the grounds, dined sumptuously in the grand restaurant and kept strictly to Mary's rules in the bedroom. They took turns to undress in the bathroom and took themselves chastely to their separate beds. To Ben's chagrin, Mary fell instantly asleep and he had to listen to her gentle breathing. He took a long time to doze off.

The second day, they needed to fill the morning and afternoon. Ben wanted to see the wild Atlantic coast and Mary, the Belleek Pottery, so they did both. Then they spent the rest of the day wandering around Donegal Town. And, for Ben, it all felt so comfortable. He hoped Mary felt the same. The journey to Moira would take about two hours and they wanted to get there under cover of darkness. They had no idea what they would find, if anything. They knew that Tommy had lived there since 1996 and up until the previous census. But there was the chance that he'd moved away. He might still live there but not be in or he might be on holiday. Or he might be dead. Or he could be the wrong Tommy, not the one alluded to in Diane's note. They would have to hope to be lucky and deal with the consequences if not.

As they drove into Glebe Park, they could see that the road was empty – no people out, just parked cars. Lights were on in several houses as they drove quietly to the road's dead end. Alistair had been pretty sure Tommy had lived in 52 but, as he said, he'd been young and could be mistaken. Mary had checked and Alistair had been right. They looked at number 54, the house where the Murdock's had lived. It had a for sale sign outside and looked empty. They parked outside it. It was ominously dark. Ben led the way up the path of 52 and rang the bell. He heard it reverberate through the house. They waited – nothing.

'Try again,' said Mary. 'But we'll probably have to come back tomorrow.'

'God, let's hope this isn't another fool's errand in Northern Ireland.'

As Ben was about to ring again, the neighbour from number 50 popped her head out of her front door. 'Youse looking for Tommy?'

'Yes, we are.'

'He'll be round the back. He's probably in his shed. I'll give him a call, shall I?'

'Thanks.' Ben turned to Mary. 'At least we know he still lives here.'

They followed the neighbour round to the back garden. The shed was nearly as big as the house and light shone out from every window. Ben thanked the neighbour, who departed with seeming reluctance. He knocked on the door.

A tall man opened it. He had his back to the light so Ben could not see his face but his greeting came as a shock. 'Well, youse took your time. I expected you sixteen years ago. Ye'd better come into the house.'

He led them to the back door and into a spotless kitchen. As he turned, Ben let out a cry. The piercing blue eyes gave it away. 'It was you! You took the picture! She said she'd met you at the library.'

'Not true. And my belated condolences for your loss. She was a grand woman – so brave.' He turned to Mary. 'And this grand woman? She's not Josephine Finlay by any chance?'

'Mary Smith – a good friend.'

'The Mary, I believe and the Smith is a good choice. Over here, it would be Murphy. May I call you Mary?' She nodded.

Tommy continued, 'But I do believe you are also Josephine Finlay?'

Mary nodded again.

'That's grand. I tried to phone you but the receptionist said you'd left the firm. I thought I'd missed you. I shouted at the poor woman. Apologise to her when you see her, will you?'

Ben let out a long sigh. 'So that was you! You've no idea how relieved that makes me feel. We thought the UVF were following us. But you are the man who came to see us and took our picture in Belfast. Diane was not happy. Why did you come?'

'Cup of tea? Yeah – then I'll tell you the whole stinking story. I'll close the curtains first.'

With mugs of strong tea in their hands, they sat round the kitchen table. Tommy started his tale. 'Your wife was my handler. I was IRA and not happy with their tactics so I was informing. Eejit that I was. More than an eejit. After they'd gone, your wife and Margaret, two beautiful women…' He paused a moment, seeming to be somewhere else, then gave a deep sigh and wiped his eyes with the backs of his hands. 'I still wanted peace so I joined the RUC – a Catholic in the RUC – so I was a pariah to both sides. Thought I could help end the killing, close the divide. Then the police station was bombed so I left. Anyways, that day in Belfast, I had to come and see your wife because I had something urgent to tell her – about Stanley Murdock. You know who he is?'

'Was. I buried him last year. I'm an undertaker now'

Tommy's face hardened then softened again. 'And Margaret?'

'She died the year before.'

Tommy's eyes glistened. He took out a white handkerchief and blew his nose. He said softly, 'I loved her, you know. There was never anyone else.'

Ben knew he would have to talk to Tommy about Virginia and Alistair, but now there were more urgent things to discuss.

He asked, 'Your news about Murdock?'

'It came from Margaret. She'd overheard him talking on the phone about a big new plan he was hatching in London. He saw her and he hit her; told her not to say a word or he'd kill her and the children. He'd never threatened that before so she knew this had to be important.' He wiped his eyes again. 'Another brave woman because that made her determined to find out what it was and to stop him. I told your wife and she said to keep Margaret safe. Those were her words and I didn't do it – may God forgive me because I can't forgive myself. I lost everything.'

Ben put a hand on the other man's arm. He would have to wait for his own gratification; to hear Diane's history. This was more important. Now was the time to tell. 'We have a little good news for you. There is DNA proof that Stanley was not Virginia's or Alistair's father. I think you know who their father is. And I think they would be delighted to know too.'

Tommy gave a watery smile. He blew his nose again, took a deep breath and sat upright in his chair. 'I always thought, suspected… But when they went, she told me that I mustn't try to find them. Their lives might depend on it. So I never did. How are they? They were just wee children when they left. Ginny was growing so fast, like they do at that age. Allie was a sweet boy, not like that brother of his. So, they're mine, are they? Do they know? Would they want to see me?'

'They don't know yet but they soon will and they'll be delighted. They remember you fondly and they hated Stanley Murdock, so they'll be over the moon to know that they have your genes and not his. They loved their mother very much and did their best to protect her. I'll get it sorted when I get back. You'll be hearing from them, I promise you. Now, are you OK to go on with your story?'

'Yes. Of course. That's why you're here. But I'm their father – and they'll want to see me?'

Ben replied, 'I'm certain they will.'

Tommy beamed and his eyes sparkled. 'That's grand news. The best for a long time. Anyways, back to your tale. Margaret had kept me informed but there was nothing really to report for over a year. Then one day he had to rush out and he forgot to close down his computer. Margaret found a file and copied it. Videos of meetings, audio files, emails, Murdock's written report of what they were up to and who was involved. It was called "Operation Fourth Realm". I never understood what that meant.'

Mary gasped, then she spoke. Her voice was cold and measured. 'I do. And it's chilling.' As if to demonstrate, she shivered. 'I think it comes from the German. We know about the third realm, The Third Reich. This would be some kind of successor.'

Tommy looked sombre. 'That makes sense. Their aim was to exterminate the Catholic population in Northern Ireland.'

'What!'

'That's right. The gist of it was that they were going to arm and reinforce the Protestant Paramilitaries in order to wipe out the Catholic population here. Margaret told me the bare bones of it and I told your wife and then she was killed and Margaret whisked off to England.'

Mary was silent but waved her hands to keep the men quiet. Then she spoke. 'But it never happened so some message must have got through. I wonder how they stopped it?'

There was silence while they took this in. Then Ben said, 'Diane was killed on 7th October. How long after that did the Murdock family leave for England?'

'A matter of days, I'd say. It was October definitely and they upped and went so quickly I hardly had time to say goodbye.' He looked at Ben. 'You sure they'll want to see me?'

Ben smiled. 'Yes, I'm sure.'

Mary was still following her line of reasoning. 'So they broke the chain of command by removing Murdock. I wish we knew who was in that chain – who was giving the orders.'

Tommy replied, 'Oh, we do. I have the file. The day before she left, Margaret gave it to me for safe-keeping.'

Chapter 24

After ascertaining that Tommy had not taken a copy and was glad to get the two DVDs out of his house, they waited while he retrieved them from their hiding place. He told them that he hadn't known what to do with them so he'd done nothing. He'd looked at it all when he'd first taken possession of them and had hidden them awaiting Divine Intervention, and that intervention had now come in the form of Ben and Mary. He added that his memory was not so good these days so he could now forget about it completely and leave it in their competent hands. Ben was just hoping that the things still worked.

* * *

By the time they got back over the border, it was past midnight. Mary voiced the unwelcome thought that was uppermost in Ben's mind – and it had nothing to do with Tommy, Margaret or Stanley Murdock. 'Do you think we should pick up our things and drive straight down to the port?'

Ben did not want to cut short his time alone with Mary but was becoming resigned to that outcome. But she hadn't finished. 'There's a lay-by up ahead. Can you pull in.' Once the car had stopped, she turned to Ben. 'I was thinking that it's going to get a whole lot more complicated once we've looked at those DVDs so we should make the most of our ignorance and snuggle up together in one of those nice queen sized beds? What do you think?'

Ben managed to keep his jaw from dropping. He grinned. 'Are you sure?'

Mary nodded. 'I've never been more sure about anything.'

'Well, I think it's the best idea I've heard in a very long time. I have to admit, I brought some condoms in hope.'

'Fancy that,' said Mary. 'So did I!'

* * *

Their first coupling was frantic. On Ben's part it was full of pent-up longing – and he knew that Mary felt the same – because she told him so. Their second was gentle and leisurely, bringing joy and fulfilment to them both.

Afterwards, they lay for some time listening to the night sounds – the creaks and groans of this old castle, the wind and rain attacking the windows, the lonely cry of an owl searching for food or a mate, the sound of their slow breathing and the beating of their hearts. As Ben was about to speak, Mary put a finger to his lips and whispered, 'Hush. Don't say anything you'll regret in the morning.' So he didn't tell her that he loved her and that he wanted to marry her. He wondered if this omission was one he would come to regret.

Chapter 25

After a slow, languorous start of mutual pleasure and a very late breakfast, their journey back had been unremarkable. As soon as they'd arrived in Wales and Mary had recovered from the travails of the boat trip, they'd arranged by burner to go immediately to see Henry Walpole. But first they had to go to Ben's house to pick up his laptop, DVD player and burner dongle – in case they needed internet connection.

They arrived back in Cambridge without incident. It was Ben who first noticed the car – a black SUV similar to the one that had pushed them off the road. It was parked five doors down. There was just one occupant, wearing black gloves while hidden behind a newspaper. Ben had laughed at the hotel when Mary had suggested carrying the discs in her underwear. Maybe the car was just a coincidence but now he was glad that he'd overcome his reluctance and the two discs were sitting, he suspected uncomfortably, in Mary's knickers.

They decided to part company with a brief wave and to meet at Henry's rooms in Ethel's. Ben quickly let himself into his house, hoping that the occupant of the car, if he was what he thought he was, would be more interested in him than in Mary. As he went in, he made sure to double lock the door behind him, then he hurriedly collected the equipment he needed. He looked out of an upstairs window, making sure he couldn't be seen. The occupant of the car was still in place. He thought of going out by the gate in the back fence and along the back lane but decided that would be the risky option. If he were caught in the back lane, there would be no witnesses. If he was going to be followed or attacked, he needed to be in public places. He had reset the new alarm – knowing that Mo would set it off if he let himself in but that couldn't be helped. He let himself out of the front door, making sure to double lock it.

The car and occupant were still in situ and Ben breathed a sigh of relief. His inclination had been right and they were more interested in him than in Mary. Her precious cargo had a chance of escaping detection. He decided to take a circuitous route to Ethel's. As he rounded the corner into Hills Rd, he stepped quickly into

Tesco's. From behind the window display of toilet roll – special offer – three for two, he waited. A man in black gloves passed by, walking quickly. Ben could not see his face but, as he passed, Ben noted his trilby with a long black pony tail poking out beneath. It was the pony tail that made him shiver – and then he realised why. He studied the retreating figure and came to a judgement. This was not a man but a woman.

* * *

All was silent in Henry's study as Ben inserted the first of the discs. Henry had already passed them a note. He was unsure as to whether his rooms were bugged so no names were to be voiced. Ben had no idea what they would find but he knew it would be game-changing. His nascent relationship with Mary had already changed his game. All he wanted was for this to go away so he could settle into the rest of his life. But he knew it wouldn't and he couldn't.

The disc marked Disc 1 contained several files, written, audio, video and photographs. Thankfully, none was password protected nor were they encrypted. Ben turned down the volume on his laptop so that they had to strain to hear it. This, together with the poor quality of the recording, made them certain that if there were any bugs in the room, they would not be able to pick up anything useful. As they watched, listened and read all the files, their mood became, if anything, more charged and infinitely more sombre.

At Henry's suggestion they were stopping at intervals for Mary to write down the names of those they recognised. Henry, as the oldest, had a more encyclopaedic knowledge of the grandees whose names, voices and pictures kept recurring. It was obvious that the videos had been shot surreptitiously. They bounced around and the speakers were often out of shot. But the words were chilling. As they listened, Ben realised that, shocking though these were to those who knew the essence of the plot, the speakers had been circumspect in what they'd said. They alluded to 'the other side' and 'the solution'. So far, Operation Fourth Realm was interesting but probably not incriminating.

They sat back after viewing all of Disc 1. As they relaxed, Ben realised how much his shoulders were aching. He stretched his muscles and could see that Mary was doing the same. He pushed to the back of his mind the thought of her sleepily stretching her naked body.

Henry Walpole was sitting immobile. Ben looked concerned. 'You OK, Henry?'

Henry stirred. 'Yes, dear boy. Fine. Just trying to work out how all this fits together.' He motioned them to follow him. Ben packed up his laptop and the two disks and brought them with him. No way was he going to let them out of his sight until he had copies. When they were out on the quad in Front Court, Henry spoke. 'From what we've seen here, it seems we had a cabal of senior politicians and their acolytes who were plotting genocide. If we look at this list...' He waved his hand and Mary handed him the list of names of the people they had recognised. 'There's a handful that I'd consider to the far right of the Tory party. But you must remember I'm a Commie, so some would just consider them mainstream, leaning right. More worrying for me, there's one here who I thought shared my beliefs and principles.' He slumped on his bench, then sat up sharply. He winced. 'Bloody knees. Giving me gyp today. No matter – get him up on Wiki. I really can't believe he was involved.'

Ben sat on the stone wall, attached the dongle to his laptop and typed in the name. Henry pushed him to one side as soon as the Wiki entry came up. 'There!' Henry read from the screen, 'He died from asphyxiation. The coroner ruled out foul play and ruled that his death had been a bizarre accident. He was found dead in his flat with a plastic bag tightly covering his face.'

Mary asked, 'I vaguely remember that. Big news for a few days. When did this happen?'

Ben scrolled down the page. 'December 1996 – just two months after Diane's death. There's more. *"There was no sign of a struggle and a large amount of alcohol was found in his bloodstream leading the coroner to the conclusion that he had inadvertently taken his own life."* God, yes, I remember it now. He'd been an outspoken advocate of gay rights and his name was dragged through the mud. The gutter press had a field day.'

Henry was openly weeping now. 'I missed all that at the time. Head too far into Soviet plots, no doubt. He was tee-total, you know; brought up in a strict Methodist tradition. He was always spouting about the evils of drink and how it kept the workers down.

I'm certain he would never have touched a drop.' He mopped his eyes again. 'I can only conclude that he was murdered.'

Mary put her arm round Henry's shoulders and gave him a squeeze. 'Was Murdock the assassin, d'you think? He was back in England by then.'

Ben was thoughtful. 'Quite possible – likely, even. I'd lay odds he was murdered, but why? Did he blow the gaff on their plot, I wonder?'

Henry wiped his eyes. 'The man I knew was as straight as a die, in all senses. He wasn't gay but he championed gay rights. And he was honest as the day is long. I think he was spying on this group. The sad thing is, I don't think we'll ever know the truth and his name will continue to be mud. Good God! The more we delve into this, the dirtier it becomes.'

Mary said, 'Have we any idea who he might have told – if he was spying on them?'

'Don't know. He was left wing Labour. Didn't get on with Blair and his lot. We might find out from Disc 2. Have we got the energy to trawl through it?'

With nods from the other two, they went back to the warmth of Henry's rooms. Ben placed the second disc into the player. There were more audio recordings, presumably of phone conversations. No names were mentioned but Henry thought he recognised some of them. He whispered, 'That sibilant voice – just like Hendrick's – but it's not him. If I've got it right, this one's in the Lords now. He was a Minister in '95, '96. His name's gone. That's the scourge of old age. It'll come back.'

They scrolled on, trawling through several videos made with a hidden camera. 'Hang on.' Henry waved his arms wildly and gestured for Ben to go back. 'Stop there.' A fuzzy form at the back of the room was frozen into stillness. He continued in a whisper, 'Well, bugger me. He's new. And do you know who he is?'

The other two shook their heads. There was silence. Ben thought Henry must be enjoying his moment. At last he continued. He mouthed, 'He's MI5.'

Ben immediately covered Henry's mouth with one hand and waved his other hand pointing to the door. He looked alarmed but his voice was light. 'Time for another stroll, I think. Need to keep those knees moving.' And with that he picked up his laptop, the dongle and the two discs and walked to the door. Mary took Henry's arm and they followed him out.

As soon as they were safely outside, Ben told them of Chris's visit and his disclosure of a 'rat' in MI5 – a rat who was now in a position of power. He had been humouring Henry about the bugging of his rooms, but if they had indeed been bugged, it would have been MI5 who had done it.

Mary suggested that they adjourn to the college library to continue their exploration. As soon as they were settled in a quiet corner of the empty library, Henry told them who he had seen. 'Jeremiah Knatchbull. Always thought it a stupid name and he's now second tier MI5. In '96 he was mid-ranking but everyone thought he was destined for the heights. Had the right connections, the right family, right school, the Guards – Coldstream, I think, that sort of thing. Walks like he's got a rod stuck up his arse. Never could stand him.'

Ben was thinking. 'If MI5 was involved in the plot, and it wasn't that they were just keeping tabs but were genuinely involved and they weren't excised at the time… God, we have a lot of ifs. And if they have bugged your room, Henry, they may know what we have found out. Shit!'

Mary said, 'Can you contact Chris and get him to meet us here. While we're waiting, we can look through Disc 2.'

They were near the end of the second disc when they came to a recording of a meeting very different from the rest. This time the camera was steady and its wide-angled lens covered the whole room. Ben reckoned it must have been sited carefully before the meeting. As the recording opened, each member of the group entered the room and sat down. The chairs were so arranged that each person was in view. Ben counted the group members – twelve – and he recognised them all from previous videos. There was one further figure standing at the back with only his chest in view. He was a high ranking army officer in full dress uniform.

Knatchbull was there, together with members of the Commons and the Lords. A speaker held forth, out of shot behind the camera, outlining the part the UVF was going to play. He was persuasive – Ben had to give him that. He spoke in detail about the means and ends, how the arms would get to Northern Ireland and be distributed, how the killings would escalate, starting with IRA command, then known IRA members and sympathisers and then to the general Catholic population, men first then, "the rest".

The three watched silently with horror on their faces. This man was describing, to this select group, the means by which an entire population would be destroyed. And the group was made up of members of the party in government and a high ranking member of military personnel. He was describing genocide within UK borders and the assembled company were nodding. They seemed to Ben to be mesmerised by the speaker's words. Ben realised just how clever this person was at self-preservation when he finished by saying, 'I need to be able to trust you all. So I'll ask each of you in turn if you're in. You just have to answer yes or no. If you say no, you won't betray us because you know what happens to those who do. And it will be a grubby death, I can tell you. Your reputation will be in tatters. Our brother spy is good at organising these things. Right?'

He turned to Knatchbull. 'Right?'

Knatchbull replied, 'Right.' And this was followed by a boast. 'I know all your weak spots. Could be a bag over the face, a dirty story and you and your good name are dead. Easy.'

Ben could see some very frightened faces.

The speaker laughed. 'But don't worry. You can say no and say nothing and there will be no repercussions. You can walk away now and keep quiet and forget you were ever involved. My word on that. So, are you in?'

His hand appeared on camera as he pointed to each man in turn. 'Yes?'

And each one answered, 'Yes.'

The anonymous Army officer remained silent. He was neither asked nor did he answer.

Chapter 26

Ben was kicking himself. He'd thought that Henry was being paranoid about his rooms being bugged. But now that the full extent of Knatchbull's involvement and his present position in MI5 had become apparent, he was becoming as paranoid as his old mentor. Where was bloody Chris. It was two hours since he'd left a message – a very coded message but one which said, 'Come quickly, we need you.'

They had decamped to Mary's office in the university library – that being the most secure place they knew. They had debated whether Mary should look up firms that search for bugging devices and decided that they would wait for Chris. Ben's second phone call to Chris had also gone to voicemail and the lack of response was worrying. In addition, there was the 'follower' from this morning, the one that Ben had shaken off in town.

As they sat in silence waiting for Chris, Ben's mind was racing. Chris had been right the first time. This was big, this was momentous – monstrous. If this got out, it could bring an end to peace in Northern Ireland. The Catholic population would feel vindicated in its distrust of the British establishment, the waning power of the IRA and its newer iterations would be strengthened and all hell would break loose. Tommy had told them that the old enmities had continued to smoulder among the few, even after the Good Friday agreement had heralded power-sharing. As Tommy had said, old habits die hard; the flames would just need a spark to set them running again. And this was just such a spark.

Mary's intercom buzzed. There was a visitor who wouldn't give her name but said she was expected. She said Mary knew her son, Chris. Mary said she'd be down immediately.

When Mary came back with her visitor, Ben recognised his 'follower' instantly. So this had been the woman who'd been shadowing him. She introduced herself as Chris's boss. 'Call me Jane – it'll do.'

She sat down hard. 'Chris has gone into hiding. He picked up on briefings against him and he's taken himself somewhere safe. You've certainly set a hare running and, whoever it is in our organisation, they mean business. I'll probably be next so I'm going underground too. I came to warn you today but you gave me the slip.' She smiled a rueful smile. 'Desk job – I've obviously lost the knack.'

Ben said, 'We have something to show you.'

He found the recording of the incriminating meeting and played it back.

Jane's composure was shattered. 'That fucking bastard. God, he's so smooth, so establishment, so bloody up his own arse.' She screwed up her face. 'So fucking unctuous. So fucking clever. I'd never have guessed he was so bloody devious. Yes, I would. He got up that greasy pole with blood on his hands. He'd have to be one slippery bastard to do that.'

Then she took two deep breaths and carefully poured herself a glass of water. Ben was amazed to see that her hands were perfectly steady. This was someone he wanted on his side, despite the rustiness of her surveillance techniques.

She smiled at Ben. It was a sad smile. 'This is such a good start – precisely what we needed.' Then she waved her hand towards them all. 'You are geniuses, all of you.' She pointed to the computer. 'Can you make a copy of that? Now?'

Mary took a box of disks out of her desk drawer. 'How many do you want?'

While Ben took the six requested copies, Mary and Jane exchanged burner phone numbers.

Jane wrote on each disk including a code that held nothing for Ben. She asked, 'Can you get these posted from here – urgently?'

Mary replied, 'Can have them couriered if you want.'

Jane hand-wrote a covering note for each. Ben noticed that one was addressed to the Prime Minister – at an address other than Downing Street and one to the Leader of Her Majesty's Opposition. The others went to people he did not know but he noticed Henry nodding approvingly. Mary took the packages down to reception with strict instructions that they were to be sent by the speediest and most secure route.

When she returned, Jane outlined her plan. She was going straight to a place where she would be safe. They should do the same. Then they should await further instructions.

Ben had two other priorities. 'My family, Josephine Finlay and the Murdocks in Brighton. Can they be protected?'

Jane made a brief phone call then explained. 'Security company we sometimes use. My brother owns it. No-one in the Service knows that. They'll put someone in each house. Can you contact your people to let them know?' Ben nodded as Jane added, 'Use burners.'

Ben said, 'Also, Henry's rooms at Ethel's – can you get it searched for bugs? Before we realised Knatchbull was involved, we were looking at these disks in there. We were circumspect but we're not sure if we were clever enough. I know we didn't mention any names'

'That's good. Will do.'

She thought for a moment. 'Even with bugs, he won't know precisely what we've got. And what we've got is incriminating but it's not enough. Looks like he was part of the plot but he can argue that the plot was never carried out – and that he was the one to stop it. He could still slip out of this.' Jane paused. 'Why, I wonder? What stopped it happening? It was all organised but it never happened. Anyway, the Service will want to get something more – something that pins his balls to the floor.'

Ben's phone – one of his phones – gave out an insistent ring. He answered it and spoke briefly. Then he turned to the rest. 'It's started. Police at my door with an arrest warrant. GBH. Apparently I beat up the driver of the car that sent us off the road. Katy told them she thought I was in Yorkshire but she wasn't sure. Mo's organised a car from his mate and he'll make sure it comes with more phones and cash and a key to Josephine's place in Hunstanton. He'll tell us when and where to pick it all up. We can all stay at Josephine's – Chris knows where it is.'

Jane said, 'I'll make my own arrangements. But I'll tell Chris and I'll keep in touch.'

Henry had been silent for a while. At last he said, 'I'll stay here. It makes sense. I can't move fast and I'll be a hindrance to you, and if we all disappear, it will give them credence that we're planning something. I can make up a cover if they've bugged my rooms. I'll find something to fit the bill to show that we were three innocents discussing the history of left / right divisions in the nineties.'

110

Mary looked worried. Ben felt worried. He voiced his thoughts. 'This is one desperate bastard. We don't know what stories he's woven, or what he'll do. We've heard him boast about one killing. You could be in danger.'

Henry smiled a beatific smile. 'Wonderful, dear boy. Makes my life worth living. Haven't been in danger for far too many years. And anyway, I can't come with you; I haven't got my pills. So that's an end of it. I've got to go. Need to set up a false trail. Looking forward to it.'

He turned to Mary. 'Look after this young man. Oh, and can you call me a taxi.'

Henry hugged them all – even Jane, who he'd only just met and Ben noted that he left the room walking not shuffling. Then, as he watched the retreating figure, the deepest sadness invaded his soul as he realised he might never see this old man again.

An hour after Henry's and Jane's departures, Mo's next call told them that their car would arrive shortly at the service entrance to the Library. His mate had been thrilled to help especially as 'the rozzers' were involved. Mo said his mate had chosen a popular little silver hatchback as he knew these didn't usually arouse police suspicion. The tank was full and Mo had been to his bank so there was £1000 plus some clothes and food in the car. Katy had taken it all out the back way and they'd made sure the car had not been seen by the officer in the police car sited in front of the house.

Ben and Mary arrived at the service entrance to the library to find a small silver car and three people hopping from foot to foot.

'We couldn't let you go without saying goodbye.'

Katy, Sarah and Mo took it in turns to hug both Ben and Mary. They were all in tears but Sarah was the first to speak. 'You'll be pleased to know that I've moved back home. Pam and Michael have moved in too – so I have an escort to work every day. And Uncle Mo's moved in with Agnes.' She turned to her Great-uncle and did a strangled giggle. 'I bet Josephine's feeling like a gooseberry.'

Katy was still crying but she managed to say between gulps, 'And that man who's come to look after us – he's a dream. Don't come back too soon. I need time to get to know him.'

Ben replied, 'We'll phone you if we need anything, otherwise no contact. It shouldn't be too long. Things outside our

control have been put in train. We just need to hide away and keep ourselves safe until it's all over.'
    He said the words but he didn't believe them.

Chapter 27

They'd been ensconced in Josephine's cliff-top house for three weeks and had heard nothing. There was that feeling of impending action, that something was bound to happen, but, what and when was still a mystery. They'd seen on the local news that two people were being sought in connection with a serious incident near Cambridge. They had shown a very old picture of Ben – one which must have come from his service records. Then other news had taken precedence.

In some ways, Ben was content. If he had to be holed up, he'd already decided that Mary was the ideal companion. He'd laughed when he'd opened his bag of clothes and found a note from Katy with some condoms. He'd laughed even more when Mary had shown him a similar note in her bag of clothes and another pack of condoms. Katy had done her best to kit out Mary with clothes and Ben rather liked the 'new' Mary, but Mary's comment of 'Mutton!' had ensured that she had immediately gone out and bought herself some clothes that she felt more comfortable in. She'd also bought him a tweed cap, saying it would help him fit in. Next time out, he'd looked around. Clever Mary. It did seem that Norfolk men of his age were cap wearers.

Mo had posted a second tranche of money to them, wrapped up in a pair of socks. With it had been a cryptic note – with no names – which they had deciphered as telling them that the police had been back but, as they were the local force, and they knew him and Sarah, it had been low key. The note had also told them that their oldest friend at college had been in touch with Mo to say that there was a rumour going round that 'their young friend' had run off with his boss and the 'big cheese' was livid. And the friend had said that the rest of the gossip about the supposed lovers was too fruity to pass on. There had been no other news.

They were living frugally so money wasn't a problem. They'd made sure they shopped locally and were as inconspicuous as possible. They kept the car in the garage, deciding that they would only use it when it was absolutely essential. They'd filled up with petrol as soon as they'd arrived – knowing that old CCTV footage from the garage forecourt would probably be erased. The house to the left was a holiday home and empty. They'd said hello to the neighbours to the right and had given them a similar story to the one they'd used in Ireland. This time, they were on an extended honeymoon; second marriages for both of them and their offspring hadn't come round yet so they were lying low until the children got used to the idea. Mary had even asked the woman next door for advice. That advice that had been given freely and at length. They'd dubbed her 'Nosey Anne' and she had asked Mary in for coffee. Mary had told Ben afterwards that a nosey neighbour was the best conduit for gossip so she was confident that their story would be disseminated and, if anyone came sniffing, their legend would be well known in the neighbourhood. She'd added that there was nothing so galling for those who want to gossip as a mystery and she'd made them sound incredibly boring while wanting solitude.

Ben had decided that, if the police and MI5 hadn't been chasing them, he could get used to this life. He would have to tell Mary this.

* * *

One evening, three weeks in, curtains drawn and half way through Midsomer Murders, there was a sharp knock on the back door. They were immediately alert. Ben raced upstairs and peered down into the garden. Through the gloom, he could make out a thin man in a tweed cap. He was too thin to be the neighbour – too short to be Michael. Ben silently opened the window to get a better look. The man looked up and mouthed to Ben, 'Let me in, you fool.'

Once inside, he shook himself and sat down at their kitchen table. 'It's fucking freezing out there. Got anything worthwhile to drink?'

Ben brought through the bottle of single malt that had been their one extravagance. Mary had done a good job of converting him to whisky. He watched as Chris gulped down a mouthful. 'God, have I had a journey. Bloody CCTV – been on the road for days.' He turned to Mary, 'Sorry 'bout the pong. Could do with a shower and clean clothes. Got anything to eat. I'm starving.'

While he was eating, he tried to talk but Ben stopped him. 'Look, it doesn't seem as though you've been followed. If you had, they'd have had the door down by now. Why don't you finish your food and have a bath. I'll find you some clothes and then you can tell us whatever it is you've come all this way to say. Yes?'

* * *

Chris stretched. 'God, that is so much better. Too much desk work, I'd forgotten what going grey meant. It's so good to be clean and warm and fed.' He smoothed down his tracksuit – Ben's tracksuit – and said, 'If you don't mind, think I'll go and buy some clothes tomorrow.' He turned to Ben. 'Got any cash? I got mine nicked in Downham Market.'

Ben smiled and nodded. They were seated again round the kitchen table. Chris was leaning back with the two front legs of his chair raised from the ground. It brought back a memory to Ben of schooldays when this has been the norm for teenaged boys bored with history, geography or whatever – seeing how far they could lean back without falling. Happiest days of your life. Not a chance! He was hoping these might lie ahead but, as yet, he knew that no chickens should be counted.

After a couple more sips of their whiskies, Chris set his chair straight and began his tale. 'Jane's on her way. With luck she'll be with us soon. Hope she's managed better than me. She'll bring us all up to speed. All I know is, I need a bloody good night's sleep. Those rough sleepers' shelters are all very well. Better than a hedge but, the racket! If ever I find a woman worth settling down with, she can't be a snorer. Oh, and the Prime Minister's been briefed and Knatchbull doesn't know we're on to him.'

He held up his empty glass. 'Ba gum, this whisky's reet gradely.' He leant back again. 'Learnt that from an old boy in the Downham Market shelter. D'you know, he's spent his whole life wandering the roads.' For a moment, Chris looked solemn. 'Bloody waste. Was in care in Leeds, got to eighteen and they just threw him out; cast him adrift. Gave him five pounds and his clothes in a cardboard suitcase. Can you credit that? Then he was in the army for a bit – got thrown out for fighting. Thought that's what they were supposed to do. Now he's homeless. Fucking unfair, that's what.'

Ben was impressed. Maybe a couple of weeks on the road had taught this young man more than all his past experience. He knew that Chris looked and acted like a City trader from the East End, but he suspected that this was a bluff to hide his privileged background; public school and Oxbridge was not always a good look, these days. He poured them all another drink and asked, 'So what else did you learn from going grey with the knights of the road?'

'Well, for a start, they aren't all knights. It was in the shelter that my cash was nicked.'

Mary looked hard at Chris. 'I can hear a "but" in there.'

Chris looked sheepish. 'Yeah. Been on the road for nearly three weeks. Met all sorts – some bastards – like the one who stole my dosh. But they've mostly got nothing and mostly look out for each other. D'you know, when my cash was nicked, they clubbed together to give me half their takings from the day – came to £3.53.'

Ben could see that Chris was moved by his tale. 'So what did you do?'

'Couldn't take it – took 60p for a cup of tea. Then they were happy and I was happy. I said I'd pay them back next time I was down that way. Honour satisfied.'

He sniffed. 'They shared such bloody awful stories. Like, every day they have to put up with people like me. The best ones ignore them – the worst beat 'em up. This guy told me about an undergrad at Cambridge. Rich guy. Came up to him and held out a twenty – right in front of his face. Then, as he reached for it, the bastard set it alight before he could take it. That twenty could have kept him in a shelter for a week. Bastard laughed. That's people like me.'

As they were talking, Mary had been making marmalade sandwiches. She put them on the middle of the table. 'Marmalade sandwiches. Best thing with whisky.'

Ben took a sandwich. He was used to this combination. Chris, however, was looking apprehensive. In answer to his unasked question, Mary added, 'Best combination ever. Why d'you think they make it in Dundee?'

Chris waved his sandwich while he continued. 'My mates in the shelters would love this. Warmth, food and a good bed. Maybe not the whisky. They mostly have trouble with booze.'

116

He took a bite of sandwich, then another. He gave Mary a thumbs up as he took a second sandwich. 'Those poor buggers.' He'd been knocking back the whisky and his words were beginning to slur. 'Good people. Need to give 'em hope. Realise what a plonker I've been. Going to have to do something for them. After this is over...'

Ben caught him as he slid sideways. 'I think, perhaps, it's time you went to that nice warm bed.'

Ben half carried Chris into the front bedroom. Mary followed with two paracetamol and a pint of water and stood over him while he drank all of it.

'You know – you're good people too. I'm going to be a good person...' He saluted them both as he fell back into bed fully clothed. Ben took off his shoes and tucked his feet in and Mary pulled the duvet over him. As Ben and Mary left the room, Chris was already snoring loudly.

Chapter 28

Over breakfast, Ben and Mary spent some time thinking what could they tell the neighbours. They were sure that 'Nosey Anne' would wonder about the young man who had gatecrashed their honeymoon. And it seemed there was to be a second gatecrasher in the near future. It was just about plausible that Chris could be Ben's son, although close inspection would suggest that Ben had started to reproduce at an early age. Jane was a bigger problem until they decided that she should be Chris's older wife. They would see what she thought of that. Mary was sure Nosey Anne would be disappointed at a family reunited – it didn't make such a good story – but Mary could embroider it.

Chris hadn't emerged, but Ben had checked on him. He was still fast asleep, curled up in the foetal position. Ben had left him to his dreams.

At a quarter to nine one of their phones pinged. A text message 'Nine o'clock, supermarket delivery.' And, on the dot of nine, a delivery van appeared, the driver unloaded several bags of shopping onto their front doorstep and rang the bell.

The woman was hardly recognisable as Jane. 'Bring these in, Guv?'

'Yes, of course.'

Once inside, she removed her beanie and shook out her hair. 'God, that's hot. Anyway, can't stay long. This is what will happen next. I'll come back tonight – late. Leave the bags till then. It's not shopping. Chris should be arriving soon. I hope to God he's OK. He's been out of contact.'

They were standing in the hallway. Ben opened the door to Chris's bedroom and pointed to the sleeper. 'Got here last night.'

'Good. I'll go. Keep acting normally and I'll see you tonight.'

And she and the supermarket van were gone.

* * *

Chris woke with a head 'like a herd of giraffes were rampaging through it'. Mary gave him more water and persuaded him that eating a good breakfast would help.

'Why giraffes?' Ben asked.

'Heads bumping on the inside of my skull, here.' Chris pointed to the top of his head. 'And bloody great hooves down by my neck, and the pain shooting up and down between the two. I could kill those bloody animals.'

Mary passed him two paracetamol to be downed with orange juice. Then handed him a full English. 'I've washed and dried your clothes. I've put them in your room. There's a few shops here if you want to buy more. Jane's coming tonight. She left some bags.'

* * *

They were half way through the box set of 'A Life on Mars' when Jane arrived under cover of darkness – dressed in fashionable black. Her large, black rucksack rather ruined the sleek image. Once inside she flopped down with a sigh. 'Too old for this caper. Had to walk bloody miles!' She reminded him of Chris when she immediately added, 'Any food? I'm starving.'

Chris grumbled about having to switch off the TV. 'Aw! I was really enjoying that. Great music and loads of punch-ups. Did the cops really get away with behaving like that in the olden days?'

Jane retorted, 'Chris, you sound like a teenager. And yes, they did.'

Over supper, Jane updated them on life in Cambridge. The family were all fine. Her brother was looking after them and had made sure they kept out of contact even with burners. Henry was 'having the best time he'd had in years'. Ben told them about the nosey neighbour and of Mary's suggestion that Chris's cover would be as Ben's son and Jane's as his slightly older wife. He had to laugh at the look of horror that passed between them. But they agreed that the legend of the second marriage of Ben and Mary and the family rift, was a good one.

After the remains of their very substantial supper had been cleared, Jane embarked on an outline of 'the plan'. Ben decided that she was trying to be conciliatory, and that it was not coming easy.

She was probably used to giving orders and expecting them to be obeyed. He listened intently, then let out a long breath.

'Let's get this clear. You want me to blackmail Knatchbull. You want me to meet him and get a confession from him. Then, somehow, you're going to arrest him before he has the chance to kill me.'

Jane had the grace to look slightly ashamed. 'Well, yes – if you put it like that. In essence, that's precisely what I've been sent to persuade you to do.' She rummaged in one of the supermarket bags and handed Ben a letter. It was on thick cream-coloured paper and Ben found himself back in Dr Clare's office looking at her walls – this beige, this taupe, this colour that was meant to soothe, to put you at ease, to make you feel safe. He had never felt less safe. He looked at the seal. The only place to go higher would have been the Queen and he thought they would not embroil her in this. 'The Prime Minister?'

Jane nodded. 'There was a Cobra meeting. They watched the video and they've moved in on the grandees. They're pretty sure they can keep them quiet with carrots and sticks. Bloody awful – but that's how it goes. But not Knatchbull. He's still in situ, he's still powerful so he's still dangerous and there's only partial evidence against him. We still don't know all the details of why the plot was abandoned. My lot need these in order to make it all watertight with no loose ends. We know Stanley Murdock was recalled to London very soon after he'd organised the murder of your wife. We don't know who ordered his return and on what evidence – people have died since then – and there's no paper trail. Knatchbull could say he was the one to foil the plot and we have no evidence to the contrary, just gut feeling. We need Knatchbull to talk so we can get right down to the bottom of this steaming pit of shit and cauterise this wound once and for all.' She smiled briefly. 'It was Knatchbull who ordered that everything to do with Murdock was to be buried. He didn't do his homework or he would have known that the bolshie undertaker burying Murdock was the widower of one of Murdock's victims. That seems to have been his only mistake.'

Ben raised his hand. 'Lots of people who cross people like you just disappear.' He thought of the two paedophiles who had killed Murdock's fellow blackmailer. He had seen one shot and killed in a sting, the other had disappeared from custody. 'Why not Knatchbull?'

Jane replied, 'Simple. He knows too much and we know too little. Like Murdock – he has a hold. We need to be sure that this plot is completely dead in the water. The Peace Process is still shaky. We must keep it secure. You going to open the letter?'

He broke the seal and brought out just one piece of paper. 'Signed by both the PM and his deputy.' He skimmed through it. The other three looked on expectantly. He flicked the letter. 'They usually come from charities.'

Mary said, 'What do?'

'Begging letters.' He handed it to Mary.

She read it through. 'Bloody Hell. No names, no direct reference to any of this. But God, are they rattled.' She passed it to the other two. 'Ever seen anything like this before?'

They read it and shook their heads. Jane said, 'I'm not surprised. The Peace Process is sacrosanct. No-one in the coalition is going to put it in danger. No sane government would put it in danger. They know it will take at least two generations of peace before they – we – can all breathe easily.'

Chris pointed a finger at Ben. 'Play your cards right and there'll be a knighthood at least. You could ask for a seat in the Lords. They'd be willing. Is that a carrot for you? It'll work for those old dodderers who were part of the plot.'

Ben curled his lip in distaste. 'Chris, you should know me better than that. Do you honestly think I would do this for advancement?'

Chris looked downcast – then brightened. 'Nah, not really. But you'll do it.' He pointed at Ben. 'You'll do it for the people of Northern Ireland who would die if the peace was shattered.'

Ben realised that there was no 'if you do it' in Chris's statement, so Chris did know him well, after all. Ben thought of all those men and women in Pretty Mary's – all those cousins of a Kevin who had never existed. He remembered drinking with them, laughing with them, enjoying their company. He thought of the heavies who had drummed the two of them out of town because they were asking too many questions and of Tommy, who had risked his life in the Troubles because he wanted peace. And then there was Michael Murdock's father – Stanley's brother – who had kept himself and Michael out of the war, only to be killed in crossfire.

Ben knew he would have to do whatever it took to prevent a return to that anarchy. Whatever it took.

Mary had been silent so far. She smiled across at Ben. 'I'll be with you.'

Ben smiled back then turned to Jane. 'OK. Tell me what you know. And then tell me what you want me to do.'

Chapter 29

Ben could see Jane's shoulders slowly descend as she visibly relaxed. He realised how much of her future was riding on this – Chris's too. Oh, and possibly the Peace Process.

Ben said, 'Explain to me why Knatchbull would rock the boat. I can't see what's in it for him.'

'We don't think he would. At least, we think he'd keep quiet – probably. But he's a loose end and a loose cannon. And we don't like loose ends and we certainly don't like loose cannons. Now that the Powers know how deeply he's been involved with Murdock and this plot, they know he can't be trusted. We kept Murdock under wraps for years, because we were told he knew too much. What we didn't know was that he had a protector in Knatchbull. The story was that we didn't know what he knew or what he'd do, and we didn't know what would come out if he disappeared. We appeased him and it was bloody difficult. With Knatchbull, if he was wedded to the plot and wanted it to go ahead, he could take over where Murdock left off – at any time. He could set something in motion now or at the time of his choice. Kill him and something could be set off remotely. We just don't know.'

'But surely he's lost contact with all those terrorists? It's been seventeen years.'

Jane shook her head. 'We've known that someone has been sending intel to the Protestant paras for years and they still are. Fifteen years ago, I got a tiny bit of info that led me to suspect Knatchbull. I took it to the high-ups but it was politely pooh-poohed. I was very junior and no-one believed me so I let it lie. Now he's in a prominent position, knows how to work the system and that makes him dangerous. Now we have partial proof, he's got to be flushed out.'

'And I'm to be the flusher.'

'Fraid so. We think that could work. We know that he knows something's afoot. He got you warned off and now you've disappeared. He was investigating Chris. Some rumours had started. As your handler, he was suspect too. I've just taken some leave owing. Said I needed a complete break.' She pointed to Chris. 'But someone set the ball rolling that we're in a relationship. We think that started with Knatchbull. He's trying to blacken all our names. He's worried, but what he doesn't know is that there is evidence against him. That's the clincher. He thinks he's in a strong position to crush us all. We have to make sure that doesn't happen.'

Mary said, 'I can see the rationale. Best case, he kills us all and it stops there. Worst case, he foments violence in Northern Ireland. Do we know if he has reason to do that?'

Jane shook her head. 'His security clearance shows no previous links with either the Protestant or the Catholic population there. He never visited before he joined MI5. His religion states he's C of E. But then, that's the default for everyone. Background, impeccable – Eton, Cambridge, Guards – they liked that sort of thing when he joined.'

Ben's ears had pricked up. 'Which college?'

Chris answered. 'Not Ethel's. But he did overlap with Murdock for one year. I looked at his history – probably what alerted him – but I wasn't able to concretize any meetings between them.'

Ben looked sideways at the younger man. 'What on earth is "concretize"? I suppose you mean verify, confirm, validate?' Ben laughed but, he realised, he was doing so primarily to relieve the tension. 'If you were really my son, sonny, you'd be speaking proper English like what I do.'

Chris smiled. 'Bollocks. That's a real word. Listen here, "Dad", the world moves on.'

Mary intervened, 'And so should we. Jane, tell us your plan.'

Jane glanced at Ben then directed her attention at Mary. 'If you both agree, this is what is envisaged. A copy of the meeting video is sent to Knatchbull but without sound. It is sent from central London – no fingerprints, no DNA – and accompanied by a note saying if he wants to hear the audio he's to text a number.' She searched in the shopping bag and brought out a phone. 'Phone and sim bought in central London two weeks ago.'

Ben picked up the phone. It was much higher spec than his. He turned it over. 'Anything special about the phone?'

'It records calls automatically. And when turned on, records all conversations. It transmits to a listening post in real-time. If it's placed in your top pocket, so...' She put the phone into a handy pocket in Ben's shirt, 'It transmits pictures too.'

He turned it over again, examining all its apertures in turn. 'Does it fire a laser or squirt poison?'

'Don't be ridiculous. It's a recording device. And it's only to be of secondary importance.'

Ben asked, 'How so?'

'We'll be arranging a meeting between you and Knatchbull where we want to get incontrovertible evidence of guilt. We'll do this from London. He'll text to a phone with an identical sim. He'll triangulate the receiver of the message but the phone and the replica sim will be smashed and in the Thames by then. The response will come through to you here. When you meet, he'll take your phone, so we'll send you in wired. The phone is just the first line. You OK with it so far?'

Ben nodded. 'Is it possible to keep the two phones going so that any response will come to both? That'll cut down traffic.'

'Good idea. I'll find out.'

'And how do I know who he is and how do I get his contact details?'

Jane turned her computer round so Ben and Mary could see the screen. He noticed she too had a pay-as-you-go dongle. Of course she would. She brought up a recorded sequence from the BBC Parliament channel. It was of Knatchbull giving evidence to the Home Affairs Committee. His name plate was visible in front of him, 'J Knatchbull, Home Office'.

'This was organised two weeks ago with the intention of giving you his name and a way of contacting him. It was also designed to rattle him. He was giving evidence about the De Silva Review. It's looking into the murder of Pat Finucane – loyalists killed him but with British collusion – a bit close to home. It was cobbled together in a hurry so a couple of members of the committee are missing.'

Mary looked aghast. 'You mean you got together a parliamentary select committee solely for the purpose of getting Knatchbull in front of TV cameras?'

Jane smiled. 'When you've got the PM and Cobra behind you, it's amazing what you can do. But don't worry, it wasn't just for you. His evidence will be sifted with a fine-toothed comb looking for discrepancies.'

Ben knew that, in meeting Knatchbull, he could be putting himself in extreme danger. The more disorientated Knatchbull became, the more likely he was to be erratic in his responses. Ben decided he would need all the back-up he could get. 'Phone – first line. Second line?'

For the first time Jane looked uncomfortable. She looked down at the table as she asked, 'Do you have your sack and crack shaved, you know, depilated?'

This was unexpected. Ben blushed and looked at the ceiling. Where was this going? This was not the sort of information he would usually share with anyone – let alone a woman he hardly knew. He swallowed, preparing to answer. At that point, Mary erupted in laughter. 'Ben, if you could see your face!' She turned to Jane. 'No, he doesn't.'

Jane looked relieved. 'That's good – they'll hide better. We have some new and very small transmitters. We're not even using them in the field yet. With Knatchbull's elevated status, we don't think he'll know about them. But we do think he'll expect you to be wired. So we're anticipating setting you up with some very clever bugs that he will find. They can't be too clever though, or he'll begin to suspect you. But these two,' she brought out a box with two tiny transmitters inside, 'These, we want you to place one on your scrotum under your penis and the other between your buttock cheeks. They are adhesive but you will have to shave a small area for each.'

Ben swallowed again. He dragged his thoughts away from the transmitters he was going to wear. 'Hang on. You want him to think I'm working alone – and my aim is to blackmail him?'

Jane nodded.

He continued. 'The phone will work. He'll think I might try recording on the phone. He'll destroy that. He might think I'd have some sort of crude device. He'll search me. If he finds anything in the least sophisticated, I'm dead meat or a bargaining chip. So it's got to be something I could buy on-line. He won't know who I am – right? But he might suspect.'

Jane nodded again.

'So I've either got to be myself or I've got to look different, be different and seem like a complete amateur. So, first we've got to decide who I am.'

Chris said, 'It would help us if you were someone else.' He pointed to Jane. 'It protects us – and the operation, of course.'

Ben thought of Chris's drunken speech of the previous night, how he was going reform and be 'a good person'. If this all went pear-shaped and he was lost, then Chris, at least, should have that opportunity to redeem himself. 'An amateur then. I'll need some ID, driving licence?'

'Noted,' said Jane.

Ben continued, 'So, how did I get this tape of the meeting?' He thought for a moment. 'Got it. Went into a charity shop in Cambridge and bought a DVD – some sloppy film – and it was inside. That would be a Murdock sort of thing to do – put it in an anonymous cover hidden in plain sight in his house. And after his death, the family give a pile of them to charity.'

Mary was already writing a list. 'So we must get Virginia and Alistair to back up that story. And you'll need some hair dye. We could make your silver into any colour. Must make it look really badly dyed.'

'Thanks, Mary.'

She grinned. 'I know. But it will grow out, eventually. And it's good. It helps him to underestimate you. That's what we want – him to be off his guard.'

Ben turned back to Jane and Chris. 'How do you expect me to get him to spill the beans?'

Jane replied, 'When you meet him, you'll tell him you haven't got the evidence with you but when you see the money, you'll get someone – one person alone – to bring it. That will give you time to get him talking. When we have enough, then we move in.'

'He'll only talk if he's expecting to kill me and my accomplice.'

Chris looked glum. 'Yep. But we won't let that happen.'

'Who do you expect to bring the evidence?'

Jane and Chris both turned to look at Mary.

Ben immediately shouted, 'Oh no! No. No. No.'

Mary patted his arm then replied, 'Ben, we made a pact, remember?' Then she spoke to Jane and Chris. 'What do you want me to do?'

'You'll wait till we give you the signal and then you'll go in with the evidence and a computer to play it on. He'll want to watch it straight away. He'll want to know if you have more copies. At this point, you need to say yes.'

Ben got up and paced the room. 'Otherwise he'll kill us both.'

Chris nodded. 'But then we'll move in.'

Ben took a deep breath. 'I don't want Mary to be involved. We can find someone else to do the drop.'

Mary also took a deep breath. 'Ben Burton, we have an agreement, remember? I have ghosts to lay too. And if you cut me out of this and you get killed, I'll never be able to speak to you again. But, if you cut me out of this and you survive, then I'll never speak to you again. Understand? I need to be there.'

Ben sat down heavily. He'd already lost one, and now, here was another woman he loved insisting on being put into danger. He hadn't been able to protect the first. How could he protect the second? Strong women. He liked strong women, he loved strong women, he admired strong women. He hoped his girls would become strong women but, by God, strong women could be a pain in the arse.

He tried one more time, his last ace in the pack, and one he'd been meaning to play in very different circumstances. He turned to Mary. 'Mary Amelina, I'm asking you to stay away because I love you. I was gathering the courage to ask you to marry me. That may not now be possible but I would rather you lived, with or without me.'

Mary smiled, then she laughed. Ben's heart sank into the pit of his stomach. Then she looked straight at him. 'Ben Burton, you are such an idiot. Hadn't you realised? I'm insisting on coming with you because I love you and I don't want to live without you. Not the most romantic proposal but, in answer to your implied question, yes please.'

There was a moment's silence then Chris started clapping. 'I do so love it when old people get together. My pretend dad getting married for real. That's the best!'

Jane was more prosaic. 'Congratulations, you two, but let's get this impending item out of the way first. We have the people sorted, we have your legends to…' She looked from Chris to Ben, 'verify, confirm, validate, concretize. We have to sort out timings and location for the meet.'

Ben reached across the table to squeeze Mary's hand. He mouthed, 'Thank you.' Then he dragged his gaze away from her.

Chris said, 'I've been thinking about this meet. It needs to be a place that's safe – away from the public. I thought of various locations and I kept coming back to the beginning.'

Ben scowled. He knew what was coming and he could already see the problems.

Chris continued, 'That god-forsaken hole where Murdock's body was found. Middle of nowhere; no witnesses, no danger of bystander fatalities. There's an old farmhouse and an outbuilding. Ben, you've been there. You must agree that it's a good place for a secret meet.'

'But what if Knatchbull knows where Murdock was found?'

'He won't. I never put the location in any reports. Didn't have an address so I just left it out. Got the body out and into your capable hands as soon as. The cops did all the spade work so I'm the only one who knows.'

Ben wasn't giving in until he knew that this was the best place for the meet. 'But – and this is a big but – it's in the middle of the bloody fens. No cover for miles.' Ben stretched his arms wide. 'Just loads of sky. And, if there are injuries, they'd bleed to death before an ambulance could get there. And thirdly, unlikely as it may seem, it might have been sold by now.'

Jane said, 'No problem. If this is as good as Chris seems to think, we can meet all those objections. We have a budget, substantial if we need it. Remember, this is sanctioned at the highest level.' She tapped the side of her nose. 'And they can't afford for this to fail.'

Ben rubbed his chin. 'Not convinced.'

Chris responded, 'Remember how much space there was in that farmyard. We can erect cover for our back-up team. And we can make it look like the cover has been there forever. He won't know, he's never been there. We can have helicopters on standby for possible injuries and we can requisition it if it's been sold.'

Ben still looked sceptical but he was thinking fast. 'So he has to be told the meeting place at the last minute so he can't reconnoitre. How long have we got to set this thing up?'

Jane replied, 'A week. Then they want the disk sent. I'm to go back on duty to see things through from our end. We've also got high-ups at GCHQ in the loop so between us all we should nail him.'

'Bloody Hell! A week?'

'The Powers are twitchy. They want to get him or clear him. Now that they know about the plot, they require answers – pronto.'

Ben needed one more bit of information in order to formulate his plan. He said, 'Is he left or right handed?'

'Left,' Jane replied.

'It figures. Sinister.'

'What?' said Jane.

Chris replied, 'The origin of sinister; Latin word for left.' He turned to Ben. 'There were some benefits to an expensive education. Not many, mind, but some. All finished?'

Jane nodded.

'Good,' he said. 'I can get back to Life on Mars now. I've got to get through the whole box set before we move out. Wish I'd been around then. They never played by the rules and the music is awesome.'

Mary had been sitting quietly, writing notes. She tapped her notepad. 'This plan resembles a sieve. I suppose the saving grace is that we now have a week to plug the holes.'

Chapter 30

Jane took off before dawn the next morning. Ben and Mary waved her off while Chris snored noisily from his bed. Ben envied his ability to sleep. Both he and Mary had tossed and turned the entire night, hence being up to see Jane disappear. While having a leisurely breakfast, they talked about the week's grace they had been granted. They were reasonably sure that their bolthole in Hunstanton was safe. Obviously, they must continue to be careful but they now knew that, barring accidents, nothing would kick off for at least a week. After much discussion about options – all of which were confined to just the following week – they decided that they would have a proper four-day honeymoon before getting down to the real business of planning their part of the coming exercise. Neither mentioned the possibility of failure, but Ben noticed Mary's sad smile when he caught sight of her face in repose. He supposed his face must mirror hers so he was trying to live for the moment – these oh-so-precious moments – and to let the future take care of itself. Suddenly, every minute was one to treasure. Even those mundane things like going for a walk together, shopping together for food, watching repeats on TV, each was going to be a pleasure to be stored away.

Later that morning, Mary had chatted over the fence to Nosey Anne telling her about Ben's son, who had come to stay, having left his wife. John, for that was the name that Mary had conjured for him, would be staying with them for the time being. Nosey Anne had gone into full flow about the younger generation and how inconsiderate they were so Mary had told her that John was in hiding from his wife. She'd confided that the wife was 'a very controlling woman and had been violent, so they felt they had to protect him'. Nosey Anne had agreed that any visitors to the house should be repelled and, of course, she would help them out if anyone arrived. She would tell anyone who rang her bell that her friends next door were on honeymoon and were not to be disturbed, and no, they'd had no visitors.

* * *

Their four days sped by, full of new experiences and busyness. They went to a local auction where Ben bought Mary a 'distressed' mirror. In Ben's view, it was just old and damaged but Mary informed him that 'distressed' was the coming thing. He decided he could put up with the 'distressed' mirror if he got the chance to share a house with Mary. If not, then distressed would be a truly apposite word.

They walked together through the dunes at the bird sanctuary and relished the silence. They were two travellers, alone in a sandy wilderness. They ate fish and chips out of paper and licked their fingers. They wandered the streets of King's Lynn and marvelled that this sleepy town had once been one of the biggest ports in England. The old buildings oozed the remnants of the wool money that had built them. They took a trip to see the seals and laughed at their languor. Those seals had not a care and, when Ben voiced the thought that he envied them, Mary squeezed his hand.

They visited all the villages along the Wash and they planned. When this was over, they decided they would to buy one of those carrstone cottages and spend weekends making it beautiful. Ben suggested that the distressed mirror should suit that environment perfectly and Mary laughed.

For the most part, they put to the back of their minds the thought that this happiness could be fleeting. It was only at the end of each day that they allowed their fears to surface. And then they made love with passionate intensity and consoled each other with gentleness and love.

* * *

Ben had got used to two sittings at breakfast, with Chris eating his at least two hours after theirs. On the fifth day, they finished their muesli and Ben reluctantly asked Mary to find her notes. He knew she'd hidden them and had not even told him where they were. He hadn't asked. She was protecting him in case of a raid. And if she'd wanted him to know, he was sure she would have told him.

'Let's start with the lure to draw him in. Remind me of the exact wording.'

She turned the page. 'It'll be posted in London the day after tomorrow. First class stamp, no DNA, no fingerprints. Hand-written in capital letters and they've purposely left it badly punctuated and with a spelling mistake. Hope it works. Not too late to change it.'

She put her notebook on the table so Ben could see it as she read aloud, '"*Found this in a charity shop. Its a video of you and some posh peeple planning some bad things. The real one comes with sound. I need money so if you want it back text this number this week or I go to the cops*" That and the bad hair dye, and your acting, of course, should make him relax his guard. That's the hope anyway.'

'I know. Act stupid, get him to talk then hope like hell our deliverers don't fuck up.'

'You talking about us?' Chris, looking young and tousle haired, was standing in the doorway.

'Mornin Chris,' said Ben. 'Yep. Last time, if I remember, they were trigger happy. Killed the suspect. Or was that the plan?'

Chris laughed but, to Ben, it sounded strained. 'No comment. But you wouldn't expect one. This is different. We want this dude alive – need him alive. We need to know what he knows. We need names. You can rest assured, we'll have the best out there. Those marksmen will be the crème. They'll have been in training specially since we've known about this. They'll be up there now planning and organising. They'll be working out the logistics of every eventuality. Don't worry. By the time of the meet, they'll have everything sussed.'

Mary smiled. 'And their ultimate aim is to take Knatchbull alive. So one of their logistic eventualities is that they might have to sacrifice one or both of us in order to secure their objective.'

Chris looked anguished. Mary patted his hand. 'Don't worry, Chris. We know the score. But we will need some last wishes fulfilled.'

'Of course. Anything. Well, anything within our powers, of course.'

Ben knew precisely what he wanted. 'I've got to see Mo and my girls. That's all I want.'

Mary said, 'And I need to see Henry Walpole. He's my oldest friend.'

'No problem. We can do that. We can get them here. And the cover can be that they're family trying to get me back with my bastard wife. Yeah – that works. That's good. I'll get dressed and get onto it.'

He raced from the room. Ben watched him go. 'He's worried. He's having as much trouble with the waiting as we are. He wants some action. But, at least, he has something to do now. You know, I used to dislike him. He was so brash and uncouth. I think he's having an epiphany. At last, he's learning what life is about and it's hard for him. He was an oik. He thought life was a game and now he realises it isn't.'

He started to pace the room. 'Should we tell them all of the danger? Or try to keep it from them?'

Mary got up. 'We need to be honest with them, but not brutally honest. Now, I'd better go and spin a yarn for Nosey Anne. How about, a family deputation is coming in force to try to get your son, John, to return to his wife. Better than Eastenders. She'll love it!'

Chapter 31

Jane had organised two cars, one to bring Mo, Sarah and Katy and the other, Henry Walpole, to Hunstanton. They were to start their journey early, under cover of darkness. Ben and Mary had organised their own surprise party to greet them. They'd decided between them that, if they were going to have a wake, they'd quite like to be there – hence the many bottles of fizz residing in the fridge. As Ben was in charge of buying, he'd eschewed champagne in favour of Cremant de Loire – his favourite. Mary had decided to organise a 'champagne breakfast' with Ben querying that it might be a copyright infringement as it wasn't real champagne. He'd laughed at her response, and pointed at Chris, who she'd dragooned into frying a mountain of sausages. He'd expressed surprise that she could use such language in front of an impressionable young lad. Chris had grinned widely. They had been touched that Chris had suggested that he should go out for the day to which both Ben and Mary had responded that he was now an integral part of their lives and, of course, he must stay. Secretly, Ben was wondering about Katy's reaction to the modified Chris. She'd certainly taken against the old Chris in a big way. He'd have to prime her to be kind to him.

* * *

Katy rushed in first. 'Hi Dad, you're looking sooo well.' She winked at him and whispered, 'Mary looking after you?'

Sarah and Mo followed at a more respectable pace. After hugs all round they moved into the kitchen. Ben noted that Chris had taken himself away while the family greetings took place. After the initial flurry, the welcomes and the kisses, Ben said, 'I'll go and get Chris to join us, and Katy, you be kind to him. He's been through a lot in the past few weeks.'

Then Henry Walpole's car arrived and there were more hugs and kisses all round. In the general chat that followed, Ben saw Mary in deep conversation with Henry. No doubt they were discussing tactics. He'd leave them to it. He also noted that Katy was chatting to Chris, and flirting outrageously. He had to smile as she fiddled with her hair and laughed at his utterances. A few short weeks ago, he'd have had to be in there calming Katy and rescuing Chris. As he watched, he was hit by the realisation that, not only had Chris changed, but so had he. He could see that Katy was big enough and strong enough to fight her own battles. In the circumstances, this realisation gave him immense comfort.

He was standing in a group with Mo and Sarah. He was brought back to the present by Mo saying, 'Ben, you're not listening.'

'Sorry. I was thinking that Katy and Chris were getting on well.'

Sarah answered, 'Well, I've only met him once before and I thought he was a jerk. What's changed?'

'He's spent the last few weeks in homeless shelters. It's taught him more than all the years of his expensive education. A bit of humility, for instance.'

'About bloody time but, I must say, they look good together.'

'Anyways, as I was saying before you two started matchmaking, it's all going fine at home. My mates down the nick say they're still being pushed around by the Met but they're resisting. They can't see that arresting you is a priority. And the security people are bored, but happy. Someone's paying them to look after us, so look after us they will. Eat a lot though! Good job you'd filled the freezer is all I can say. And Sarah's got something to tell you.'

Sarah looked embarrassed. 'Two things really. I've applied for promotion and I've got an interview.'

Ben grinned. 'That's brilliant. Well done.'

'But it will take me away. It's in Bristol.'

'Wonderful. I've never visited Bristol. I've heard it's a great place to live.'

Sarah hugged him again. 'Thanks, Dad.'

'And the other news?'

'If I get the job, Dani says she'll move there with me.'

Ben saw the far-away look and laughed. 'And she can put up with your moods? A saint, I'd say. I'm looking forward to doing the bad dad bit. Seriously though, I'm glad you've found someone to pick you up off that shelf.'

As Sarah belted him hard on the arm, Mary came to join them and Ben saw Henry Walpole excusing himself to Katy and dragging Chris off to talk to him. Mary pulled Ben away, and whispered, 'Henry wants to talk to us after we've waved the family goodbye. He thinks we ought to warn them that we're part of sting to get the person behind the arrest warrants. Make it sound like a police matter. But make them aware there may be some danger.'

'OK. Another speech. I think. I'll tell the good news first.' He tapped his glass and waited till they were all looking at him. 'I've got some really good news to share with you.' He looked across at Mary. 'I've asked Mary to marry me and she's said yes.'

There were more rounds of hugs with thumbs ups from both Katy and Sarah. Katy added, 'About bloody time!' and then whistled noisily.

'But before then, we've got to clear our names and sort out the person who's behind our arrest warrants. There's going to be a sting to flush him out and we're going to be part of it. We know he's got something to hide and sees us as a threat – so it's not totally without danger – but we can't carry on hiding for ever.'

Mo shouted out, 'Knew it'd be someone in the bloody Met. Never did trust them buggers.'

Ben mentally thanked Mo for taking it in that direction. He tapped the side of his nose. 'Well, you know I can't confirm or deny that! Anyway, Chris has been organising the sting, and we'll be back home with you all when it has come to a successful conclusion. And it's been really great to share our good news with you.' He raised his glass. 'Oh! And congratulations to Sarah and Dani. If she can put up with our Sarah, she has my deepest respect.' He raised his glass again. 'To Sarah and Dani.'

He looked across at his family as he hoped all this good news would be able to come to fruition and not be overtaken by the bad. He could see that Katy was crying so went across to her. 'What is it, love?'

She sniffed and he handed her a clean hankie. After noisily blowing her nose, she whispered, 'You weren't telling the whole truth, were you? Chris is clever but he's not that clever. I've worked out just who he is. And, if he's involved, it must be much bigger than your arrest warrants. And if it's that big, it must be that much more dangerous. How dangerous it it, Dad? And tell me the truth.'

He didn't try to prevaricate. 'Very – both for me and for Mary. She has her own reasons for doing this. Mine go back to your mum's death and why she was killed. It's tying up loose ends and catching the man who was complicit in her murder. And it could save hundreds – maybe thousands – of lives.'

Katy gulped and wiped her eyes. She looked straight at her dad and smiled a sad smile. 'Then you'd better get on with it.' She kissed him on the cheek and went to join her sister. Ben thought, as he watched her go, brave women, how lucky he was to be surrounded by them.

* * *

After the family had gone, in the same black minicab that had brought them, Ben mused to himself about their mode of transport. The cabs had looked ordinary but Ben, leaning in to say goodbye, had noticed the things he'd been accustomed to noticing in his Service days: the driver, super alert, the doors, rather heavier than would have been expected, the windows thick and shaded. They had been transported by professionals. He was glad about that.

He sat with Mary and Henry at the kitchen table. Chris hovered in the background until Mary invited him to come and sit with them.

Henry looked sombre. 'I have some news for you. Not good news considering the plan you're about to embark on. I've been garnering information from colleagues who know Knatchbull. They say he's getting erratic. He's always been an autocrat but he's getting worse, shouting, swearing. I think you young people would say he's losing it. He's asking for Northern Ireland files from way back, ones he wouldn't have had access to at the time. They've been told to stall him on everything. They have no idea why and they can't do that for long. He's also been asking about Josephine Finlay.'

Chris shook his head. 'That's impossible. Josephine Finlay's name is nowhere in the department. I made sure of that. I didn't even tell Jane. She said better she didn't know. The Friary bills were paid through an intermediary. So, how could he know about her? How come he knows she killed Murdock? I don't understand.'

Ben replied. 'I don't think he does know that. But it's our fault he knows her name. Our cover when we first went to Moira was using Josephine's credentials. An idiotic mistake, but we didn't know then that Knatchbull was involved. I don't even think that Diane knew who else was in the conspiracy with Murdock. But, don't you see, this means he must be in contact with people over there. He must still be getting intel from the men who forced us out of town. Chris. Get Josephine and Agnes somewhere safe. Now!'

Henry held up his hand. 'No need. They're safe. As soon as I heard, I got onto the security people in your house. They've squirrelled the two of them away somewhere. Agnes told Mo they were going on holiday so he wasn't to worry.'

Chris scrambled from the table and left the room.

Henry said, 'He'll be reporting the link between Knatchbull and current contacts in Northern Ireland. If they can run you out of town, it means that they are still operational. No wonder he's worried.'

Mary said, 'We're all worried. But worse than that, so is Knatchbull. And that makes him even more dangerous. We need to move fast. I'll tell Chris they'll have to set the plan in motion right away.'

Henry held up his hand. 'Hold on a minute, young Mary. You sure you want to do this? You can still decline their kind offer of putting you in mortal danger, you know.'

Ben looked at Mary and waited. She nodded silently as she wiped an errant tear from her cheek. 'It's not a want. It's a need. We must.'

Henry asked, 'What if they're not ready – your back-up?'

'No choice. They'll have to be ready!'

Chapter 32

After Chris's long and detailed explanation, Ben summarised. 'Chris, tell me if I've got this correct – and I mean entirely correct in every detail. Knatchbull gets the package and texts the number. It will come both to my phone and the clone phone in London. The first text from Knatchbull will give you his number. The response from the London phone will be to ask for £5000. When he has this he responds to the London phone. He'll already have had a trace put on it but all the texts are being transmitted from somewhere highly populated and each text will be from a different part of London. All right so far?' Chris nodded. 'Then, later, the location of the meet is relayed by text to Knatchbull from the London phone, with a time limit on his arrival. Otherwise the meet is off. We have to be there first. I get him talking. Mary is kept well away until she's called. If we get the info we need before she has to appear, she stays out of it. Then we have to rely on the back-up to capture Knatchbull and bring us out safely.'

Chris responded, 'Yep. That's about it.' He added, as if to himself, 'We can do this.'

Ben paced the length of the kitchen. He'd been pacing up and down all morning. 'Why hasn't he responded?'

Mary was scrubbing potatoes. She wiped her hands and pushed Ben gently into a chair. 'It's been posted. It's been tracked. It was delivered this morning. We've been told that it's reached his desk. He'll be weighing up his options. He'll be trying to find out about the phone. He'll be trying to contact the others on the video. We know they'll be silent but he doesn't. He'll be taking the letter and envelope to be analysed. He has to make up a cover story for his actions. He has a lot to think about before he texts you. He knows he has a week. He'll think in terms of five days – to be on the safe side. We'll just have to wait.'

Ben grunted. 'I hope he takes it at face value. Amateur and farcical will do.'

'So, to take your mind off it and cheer you up, let's get that hair dyed. The box has been sitting in the bathroom for days.' When he looked pained, she added in a whisper. 'I've never fucked a man with dyed hair, I'm so looking forward to it. Come on.'

* * *

Four hours later, Chris sniggered. 'God, you look awful. Old men who dye their hair black should be…'

The end of the sentence hung in the air. Ben knew that Chris had been about to say 'shot' but, in the circumstances, had swallowed his words. Ben lightened the tension by saying, 'Not so much of the old, thank you very much. I know I look preposterous. At least Mary had the grace not to laugh.'

'And I did buy a temporary dye not a permanent one, so it will wash out more quickly. And I've bought a dye remover bleach so we can get back to boring grey before your kids have a chance to laugh at you.' She walked all round him. 'It does seem to have come out a bit pink at the edges. But that just adds to it. Preposterous is the image we want to project. I told Nosey Anne that you were having a mid-life crisis. She understands. Says her Ted bought himself a bike and some lycra. She hasn't seen either since the whole family laughed at him.'

'I'm not wearing lycra!'

'No – that would be too ridiculous.' At Ben's downcast look, she added, 'But at least, with your running regime, you've got muscles. Poor Ted is scrawny.'

Chris joined in. 'I thought your tracksuit would do. It's vile. So last century.'

Mary giggled. Ben was captivated until she added, 'If only you had a shell suit to wear. Go on, tell me you've got a shell suit hidden in a cupboard.'

'How *could* you? I've never owned a shell suit. I've no doubt committed several sartorial crimes in my time – but not that one. We did used to go to Quo concerts dressed all in denim. Denim waistcoat, dancing with thumbs in pockets.'

Mary clapped her hands. 'Let's do it! They're doing a reunion tour this year.'

'Then we can do The Who and then Bowie.'

Chris groaned. 'Please, no dad dancing while I'm here. I couldn't stand it.'

Ben laughed. 'Just you wait till you're a dad. You have no idea how stupid you can be. Dad dancing is the least of it.'

Ben could almost see the cogs whirring in Chris's brain. Then the answer surprised him. 'Yeah, I'd like that, to be a dad doing stupid things. Yeah. That sounds cool.'

The discussion of fatherhood was terminated as one of Chris's phones beeped. As always he took the call in his bedroom. He emerged looking energised. 'Had intel that we should go and do a recce. See what they've done at the old ruin and work out some logistics. I've got to acquaint you with some of the hardware that came in Jane's shopping then first thing tomorrow we go to the farmhouse. All good?'

Mary answered, 'It'll be a relief to be doing something.'

'We meet up with a the commanding officer – name of Harris – not met him before but he'll be the best. They can't afford to lose Knatchbull.'

Mary looked at Ben and Ben looked at Mary. He raised his eyebrows, indicating for her to speak.

'But they can afford to lose us.'

Chapter 33

The place was indeed in the dead centre of nowhere. The house and shed-cum-barn at the back looked remarkably as Ben remembered them. One difference was that the big double doors to the barn, which had been hanging off before, had disappeared. How long had it been since he'd last been here? It could have been a lifetime. Ben realised with a shock that it was barely a year. Since then, he'd solved Murdock's murder and after that had been hushed up, he'd been, as he was to be again, the sacrificial lamb. That time it had been to catch the killer of his old tutor and a poor nun who had happened to get in the way. This time, the stakes were much higher.

A tall, rangy man in combat fatigues was marching towards them. He arrived and saluted. Ben saluted back – the first time he'd done that in seventeen years. The man then shook their hands, Mary then Ben then Chris. He had a firm grip but not too tight. For some reason that Ben couldn't fathom, that made him feel rather more confident that he might come out of this alive.

'Harris – but call me John.' John Harris waved his hand around the empty farmyard. 'Welcome to what has become our abode for the past week.'

Ben looked around. Nothing stirred. He surveyed the scene minutely. Still nothing stirred. 'Our?'

'Good. That's precisely what I wanted to hear. Come, let me show you round.'

They started with the shed where Stanley Murdock's body had been found. At first glance it looked just the same, except it was now minus its doors. The eel traps which had hung around the outside walls had been left precisely as Ben remembered. The interior looked just the same. There was still that clean circle on the floor around the place where the body had been found; still that small hole in the roof that let in a shaft of light, still the same roughness to the walls. Then he looked again. 'It's smaller than I remember.' And he smiled as he examined the back wall. He knocked on a side wall then on the back. They sounded the same. 'How have you managed that?'

'Magic. Got the engineers onto it. False wall which can hide three armed men. If you look closely, you can see three small holes – among all the others. Just the right size to take a pistol barrel. We're going to put the doors back because we want him to talk to you here, not in the house. The doors will be a bit stiff and heavy manually, but can be remotely operated and silent.'

'Who by?' said Mary.

'We're thinking of a hidden switch in here and remote operation as well. We think he'll want the doors closed but we may need to get in. We just have to keep in mind that he's a professional, so we have to keep one step ahead of the person who always wants to keep one step ahead.'

Ben said, 'Why not the house?'

'The house is more difficult to cover and make safe but we've made a few adjustments in there too. We'll secure the house doors so he'll have to break them down to get in. Not underestimating him so there will be back-up in there too. But the lines of sight are superior here, so here is where we want you to be. Before we go in the house, what about the yard?'

Ben looked round but could see nothing untoward. Then he began to think like a spy; to think as Knatchbull would think. He looked up at the roof of the house.

'Good chap,' said John. 'See that first chimney. We've put that up and it's hollow. Big enough for me and a marksman. What about the yard and field?'

Mary, Ben and Chris walked up and down the yard. Ben looked out across the flat land that surrounded the derelict farmhouse. There were no trees, no bushes, no gradient to the land, nothing to the far horizon. He wondered how anyone could live out here. There was a small gulley separating the farmyard from the field beyond. He walked up and peered into it. It was too shallow to provide cover. He looked up and reckoned that anything would need to be in direct sight of the barn doors. He could see nothing. 'I give up.'

'Good – let me show you.'

Harris stepped over the gulley into the field. He took out his phone and tapped a key. As of one, six marksmen, with weapons ready, arose from the flatness of the field. 'My god,' said Mary. 'It's as if they were wearing invisibility cloaks.'

Ben was peering into a hole left behind by one of the soldiers. 'It's like a coffin with a furry lid. Ingenious.'

'This is why we want you to keep him in the shed and not in the house.'

They went into the house and were shown every room. Ben had to agree that the barn and yard would provide a much better environment for capturing Knatchbull with minimal casualties.

As they moved back into the spring sunshine, Ben looked straight into Harris's eyes. 'Now tell me the bad news.'

He'd expected Harris to prevaricate, or at least to look uncomfortable. He didn't do either. 'Good man. Always has to be a downside. We're having difficulty with remote cameras. Broadband, electricity supply, both problematic. So we're sure we'll be able to hear you but maybe not see you. Longer timescale and we'd have had it cracked. Still working on it so it may be sorted but not guaranteed.' He looked all round him. 'We usually do Embassy sieges – that sort of thing. Can't choose the theatre there. This place was chosen because of its lack of connectivity but that does bring with it a few little niggles.'

As they walked back to the car, Harris fell in beside Ben. 'Chris tells me you'll be acting dumb to try to lull him into lowering his guard. Get him talking. Good plan. But, whatever you do, don't underestimate him. He's been around a long time.'

He shook them all solemnly by the hand. As Mary and Ben got into the car, he added, 'You won't see me when you come next. See you on the other side.'

Ben thought grimly, That could be taken two ways.

Chapter 34

Once it started, progress was fast. The expected lull after the first text had been followed by a rapid pinging back and forth until Knatchbull had been notified of the time and place of the meet. By the time the last text was sent, Ben was already within five minutes of the meet. He had to be there early, well before Knatchbull but he certainly didn't want to be hanging around. He'd already decided that it would become less terrifying if he thought of it as an exam. So exam it was. He knew what he had to do and was as prepared as he could be. He had to sit through the duration of the exam and hope he passed.

On arrival, he parked the battered Citroen, recently purchased in Aberdeen and re-registered to a man who only existed in spy world. The number plates were mud spattered so Knatchbull would have to clean them if he wanted to read them. As Ben was certain that Knatchbull would not want him to leave, other than feet first, this was a precaution that he thought unnecessary, but it showed a breadth of coverage that he found reassuring. He surveyed the bright blue sky, listened to the single skylark and smelled the slight dampness of the earth, all the time being uncomfortably aware that this might be his last chance to enjoy these pleasures.

A helicopter circled overhead then started to descend. This was the first time that Ben had qualms about the efficiency of his back-up. What on earth were they doing? Knatchbull must be on his way and they had no idea when he would arrive. A helicopter nearby would surely see him off. He watched it land in the middle of the field, well behind the soldiers in the 'coffins'. It was only as the solitary passenger emerged that Ben realised that this was Knatchbull. First change of plan needed.

Ben examined the approaching figure. Knatchbull was wearing a poacher's overcoat and was carrying a small plastic carrier bag – rectangular with no bulges so it probably only contained the money. His gun – for he must be carrying one – was well hidden. Ben reckoned it must be in his left hand pocket. Knatchbull was, Ben reckoned, in his mid-fifties but it was evident that he worked out. He had that easy stride and look of weightless strength that would make him a worthy opponent.

Ben shambled towards the approaching figure, hands in his pockets, shoulders hunched. He didn't know who else was in the helicopter and whether they were armed, so he had to get it to take off. Ben and Knatchbull met at the edge of the field. Ben spoke first, pointing at the chopper as its engine cut out. He'd been practising copying Mo's way of speaking. 'If I'd known you was that rich I'd've asked for more. Anyways, you'd best get that thing outa here. See, I live round here – know the farmer – lives that way.' He waved his hand in the general direction that the road took. 'He's a nosey old git. He'll have seen it come down and he'll be along to see what's happening. See if you've done damage. See if he can get compensation.' He looked sideways at Knatchbull. 'We don't want any nosey bastards interfering in our little bit of business, do we?'

Knatchbull looked around then at Ben. 'You alone? Your terms not mine.'

'Yeah, course. Like I said, s'our business.'

Knatchbull narrowed his eyes and surveyed the scene for some time. Only then did he turn and gesture for the helicopter to take off. The rotor blades started to turn, and Ben and Knatchbull turned their backs as it rose into the air. First problem solved, thought Ben. Now he had time to begin to assess Knatchbull. He'd got as far as the poacher's jacket and polished shoes before Knatchbull spoke.

As the noise died, he said, 'You live near here. How is it then, that your texts originated in London?'

Ben tapped the side of his nose. 'Clever, eh? See, I know you people tap phones and get up to all sorts of malarky, so I asked my sister in London to send them texts. I'm not stupid, you know.'

Knatchbull looked keenly at Ben. 'You people?'

'Yep. Looked you up. You're going to ask how I know what I know – yeah?' As he spoke, Ben was angling Knatchbull towards the barn with its wide open doors. 'We can talk in here. There's a few old bits of chairs so we can get nice and comfy.'

Ben could see that Knatchbull was examining the yard and surroundings as they walked towards the barn. Knatchbull suddenly turned and started to march towards the house. 'What's wrong with the house?'

'Locked and bolted. You'd have to break the door down. Leave evidence. Don't want to do that. Barn's open.'

Knatchbull retraced his steps and joined Ben inside the barn.

Ben watched as Knatchbull examined the doors and walls. 'What'cha doing?'

'Just checking.'

'Checking for what? We gets a lot of death-watch round here but I don't s'pose that's what you're looking for.' Ben went and stood close to Knatchbull, intentionally invading his personal space. He rubbed the back wall and watched as dirt and plaster covered Knatchbull's impeccable overcoat. 'What you lookin for? All you'll find here is dirt. Weren't clean when Fred were alive. Worse now he's dead.'

Knatchbull brushed the dust off his shoulders and moved away from the wall. He pulled himself to his full height. Ben reckoned Knatchbull had at least a couple of inches on him. Ben hunched himself even more to accentuate the difference in height and, by association, in status.

'Give me your phone.'

Ben took a step back. 'Nah. Got it new down the pub. State of the art. I ain't giving it away to no stranger.'

Knatchbull pointed to the edge of the yard, about fifty metres away. 'Put it in the gully and wrap it in this. He handed Ben a small cloth that was heavier than it appeared. 'I'll follow you to make sure you do as I say.'

When they had returned to the shelter of the barn, Knatchbull took the lead. 'I'll need to frisk you. Do you know what that means?'

'Yeah, no problem. You won't be the first.'

Ben allowed himself to be searched. The cheap recorder was easily found. Knatchbull ground it under his shoe.

'Bollocks – that cost me a tenner.' Ben looked across at the pile of money and grinned. 'Still, I can afford it now.'

'Down to business. I need some answers from you.'

'Kay.'

'How did you know who I was?'

'S'easy. Saw you on the telly. Was flicking through the channels in the middle of the night. See, I don't sleep too well since...' Ben paused and grimaced. He shook his head violently, then continued, 'Then, who should pop up but you. Recognised you right off. And you had this big sign with your name on. Wrote it down.' He tapped the side of his nose again. 'Told you I wasn't stupid, didn't I?'

'And then?'

'Asked the missus and she said you're one of the 'haves' and we're the 'have-nots' so why not try to even things out. She's reckoned you'd pay a bit cos you was probably doing something a bit dodgy with them old geysers.' He held up his two hands, palms up. 'Not my business. Done a few dodgy things in my time. Just wanted a few readies to get us out of schtook. You know, pay the bills, like. See, the gas bill is owing.' Ben was certain that Knatchbull did not see; that Knatchbull had never been in a position where he couldn't pay his bills.

'Remind me how this recording got into your hands.'

'Well, see, I was in this charity shop in Cambridge and I picked up this copy of Skyfall – James Bond – the wife loves him so I thought I'd get her a pressie. They was down to a pound for two. Real bargain. Didn't look inside until I got home and was right pissed off, I can tell you. Was going to take it back when the wife said p'raps we should keep it. This was last year so it sat on the shelf till I saw you on the telly.'

'How many copies did you make?'

'Well, just the one to send to you.' Ben scratched his head. 'Oh, and the one the wife said we should keep for insurance. That's in our flat. Should I have made more?'

'And who knows about this?'

'Just me and the missus. We thought what we was doing might be a bit criminal so we didn't tell no-one. We don't want no trouble. Just saw this as a windfall. That's all.'

'I need to see some ID.'

Ben showed the fake driving licence for James Smith, knowing that Knatchbull would be memorising the address to go and retrieve the other copy.

'And you have the recording with you?'

'Nah. I ain't silly. Need to see the colour of your money then the missus'll bring it.'

'She'll bring it here?'

Ben nodded and if he hadn't been looking closely, he'd have missed the slight glint that appeared in Knatchbull's eye. 'Very sensible.' Knatchbull held up the carrier bag. 'I've got your money. Do you want to count it?'

He lifted five bundles of twenty pound notes out of the bag and placed them on a spare chair. Ben fingered them in a reverential manner. 'Five grand, you say?'

Knatchbull nodded.

Ben picked up one bundle and checked that there were banknotes throughout the bundle. He put it down and said, 'Nah – I trust you.'

'Then we'll go and retrieve your phone and you can phone your good lady wife. Just tell her to bring it. Don't say anything else.'

'It'll take a while. See, we've only got the one car so she has to come on her bike.'

They walked together across the yard and Ben could swear that Knatchbull was sniffing the air. A battered jeep drove by and slowed as it passed the entrance. Ben pointed. 'Said the old sod would be out looking for your chopper. Good job he took off.'

He retrieved the phone and unwrapped it. He found 'Marge' in the list of contacts. The phone was answered on the first ring. Ben almost did as he was told. 'Just bring it. How long?'

Knatchbull grabbed the phone. He listened. 'Too long. Twenty minutes max. Understand.' And he ended the call.

Ben now needed to make a point of contact – to forge a connection – to get Knatchbull to talk. And he only had twenty minutes. As they walked back to the barn, he said, 'Since I seen that tape, been thinking 'bout Belfast. See, I was there. Eighteen, straight out of Catterick – then got sent to bloody Ulster. God, it was hell on those streets. In the Maze, they was all on bloody hunger strike.'

'Stationed where?'

'Shackleton – thought I'd be a Woofer cos me dad was a Brummie but they put me in the Cheshires. Bloody IRA ruined my life. I'd be dead now. It was only the missus what saved me.'

Ben paused. He sat down and dropped his head in his hands. He hoped that Knatchbull would ask him something – anything. He was not disappointed. 'What happened?'

'Injured in the Drop. Always remember that day. 6th of December 1982 – Droppin Well. Know it?'

Knatchbull nodded. 'INLA – killed eleven of ours.'

'Thirty bloody years ago. The day my life ended. INLA, Provos, all the same, bloody left-footers. Lost three good mates in that bomb. Me, I was invalided out. Fuckin army was no help. Then I had the flashbacks so I took to the drink to forget. I'd be dead now but the wife stood by me. An angel, that's what she is. And now they tell me I've got PTSD. Bit bloody late! If I could get my hands on those fuckers. Never forgive the bastards. Never.'

'Sounds as though you'd like vengeance?'

'Too bloody right, I would.'

'What if I tell you you can have vengeance?'

Jesus Christ, thought Ben. Is he trying to recruit me? This is good. Go with the flow.

'Vengeance? Bloody take it with both hands.'

Knatchbull leaned forward. His rickety chair creaked in complaint. Ben leaned forward to mimic Knatchbull's body language. His chair stayed silent. 'Look James – can I call you James?'

'Jimmy, friends call me Jimmy.'

'Jimmy, we have a lot in common. I too have suffered because of an IRA bomb. I had an uncle and two young cousins killed by the IRA. He was an important man; had great influence.' Ben saw a face that exuded hate. 'And they killed him when I needed him most.'

Ben smiled at him. He put his hand out, as if to pat Knatchbull's knee, and retracted it swiftly. 'Yeah, I know how it feels. It eats up your insides till you feel like lashing out. And no-one will let you.'

'Exactly. But maybe I can help.'

'How? I bin to see shrinks. Nobody can help.'

'You said it was just you and your wife who know about the recording?'

'Yeah – why?'

'Because I may have a proposition for you.'

Ben's mind took a leap. He *was* being recruited. He might even get out of this unscathed. But he had to keep Mary out of the barn. Just in case.

He looked sideways at the pile of money. 'I'd still get the cash?'

'Oh yes. No problem there. I get the recording and you get the money. No, this is extra. This will make you feel like you're in charge of your life again. Remember that feeling?'

Ben looked up and to the side, pretending to think. 'Yeah. I can remember what it was like before the bomb. No worries – except how to have a good time. Nah – you're having me on – no-one can bring that back.'

Knatchbull looked both ways, as if he was about to impart a secret.

Here it comes, thought Ben.

'How about you could settle some scores? Would that help you to feel better?'

Move it forward, thought Ben. Flush him out. That's what you're here for. 'Yeah.' He sat up straight in his chair. 'I'd be up for that. What you got in mind?'

'I think we need to wait until your good lady wife gets here. Seems like she's the one who makes the decisions in your partnership. She needs to be involved too.'

Shit, thought Ben. Need to keep Mary out of this. He said aloud, 'Nah. Ain't necessary. I'm me own boss. What you got for me?'

'No, Jimmy. I need to know that she's on-side too. In a sort of way, you've been through a vetting process. I can't tell you any more until she's been through one too.'

'Vetting process? What, like you do when you go in the army?'

'Precisely. Just like you do when you go in the army.'

Ben raised his eyebrows. 'And I passed?'

Knatchbull smiled and Ben noticed that the smile even reached his eyes. 'Yes Jimmy. You passed. Now let's just wait for your wife. What's her name, by the way?'

'Marge. She hates Marjorie so don't call her that. You could call her Mrs Smith if you was being formal. But you can call her Marge.'

Half a minute later, as if on cue, which she was, 'Marge' rattled into the yard on an ancient bicycle. She leaned it against Ben's car, picked up a large laptop from the front basket and looked around. Ben waved to her from the barn entrance. She waved back.

Knatchbull walked forward to meet her, leaving Ben to follow. Good, thought Ben. He's happy to turn his back on me.

Knatchbull's voice boomed across the yard. 'Ah, Mrs Smith. I think you've got something for me.'

Ben was amazed at Mary's transformation. He hadn't seen her in full battle dress before. Her suit was obviously old and too tight. With it she wore trainers and, incongruously, a wide-brimmed hat with feathers. She walked forward past Knatchbull and straight to Ben. 'You OK, lover?'

'Yeah, sure. This gentleman wants the recording. The money's in there. Then he's got a proposition for us.' He added in a whisper, loud enough for Knatchbull to hear, 'There might be a few bob in it.'

Mary turned to Knatchbull and gave him a broad smile. She thrust the laptop towards him. 'Brought this so you could view the goods, so to speak. Don't want to buy a pig in a poke, do you?'

Knatchbull ignored the laptop. He held out his right hand for the recording, keeping his left firmly in his coat pocket. Mary handed it to him and he put it in his right hand pocket. 'I'll have the computer too.'

Knatchbull took the computer, put it on the ground and stamped on it – hard – again and again until splinters emerged and it was flattened.

'Hoi!' said Ben. 'We ain't got another one.'

Mary held his arm as if to stop him moving forward. 'Never mind, Jimmy. We'll be able to buy a better one. Legit.'

'Oh yeah. Forgot that.'

'Shall we go back in the barn?' Knatchbull gestured towards the open doors and to Ben's eyes, he looked like any estate agent showing clients round a property. Except for his clothes – too expensive – and the glint in his eyes which Ben decided was a mixture of the predatory and the insane.

Once back inside the barn, Mary immediately picked up the money, looked through the bundles and motioned towards her bike.

153

Knatchbull shook his head. 'No. You need to stay here. I'll tell you when you can go. Stand by that wall. Close together, that's right.'

Knatchbull took the disc and a small DVD player out of his right hand pocket. His left hand stayed firmly where it was. He motioned to Mary to come and insert the disc. He motioned her back to the wall and pressed 'play'.

'You've watched all of this?'

'Me and Jimmy, we watched it together. Couldn't make much sense of it but we knew it was important. And valuable to the right person. And we needed the money.'

'Mmm. And what about the fourth realm – did you make any sense of that?'

Mary replied, 'Not really. Sounded like it was some sort of gang.'

Then Ben poked her arm. 'Tell him what we need the money for.'

'You sure, babe?'

Ben nodded.

Mary said, 'Jim needs more treatment. He gets flashbacks. He's bin taking it out on the people he's bin working with – Irish and Poles mostly. He needs more help.'

Ben joined in, 'But this gentleman says he can help. We might not have to spend the money on that.'

Mary turned to Knatchbull. 'You think you can help us?' Then she wagged her finger at him. 'You ain't kidding us?'

Knatchbull looked surprised. Ben wondered if anyone had ever wagged a finger at him. Perhaps, only his nanny. 'No. You see, I employ a lot of men like your Jimmy. I could have a job for him. A job he'd enjoy; a job he'd be good at.'

Mary waved a dismissive hand. 'A job! A job won't help him. He's had jobs. He's had hundreds. They don't last. He always gets in fights and then gets the sack.'

'This one is different. Tell me, how often does he get into fights?'

Mary raised her eyebrows and breathed out heavily. 'Ev'ry bloody week. That's why he needs more help.'

'I can get him fighting the people he really wants to fight.'

'Who's that then?'

'You tell me.'

154

Ben moved over to Mary and squeezed her arm. It was time to move in for the kill.

She said, 'I dunno. He don't tell me. You've known him five minutes and you think you know what makes him tick. Wish I did. So, Mr Clever, who would *you* get him fighting?

'IRA, INLA, Catholics – that's who he wants to fight.'

'Oh yeah. Him and whose army?'

'Him and my army.'

Then all Hell broke loose.

Chapter 35

The noise was deafening. Ben did as he'd been told. He pushed Mary to the ground and lay on top of her. The barn filled with smoke. He heard one shot. The sound ricocheted round the barn eventually leaving by the open doors. As the smoke cleared, he saw Knatchbull lying on the floor. Odd, thought Ben. They were supposed to take him alive.

Then he turned his head. Right beside him, he saw Chris lying in a pool of blood. The pool was increasing at an alarming rate – spurting from his leg. Ben ripped off his coat. He pressed it hard onto the wound. 'Don't die, you silly bugger. For God's sake, don't die.'

Mary joined him and shouted, 'Man down.' Then she set to work making a tourniquet with her scarf. Then, they both pressed as hard as they could on the wound.

Then the barn was full of soldiers. Three medics immediately took over from Ben and Mary. They wheeled in equipment. Ben thought this must be what a field hospital looked like. He glanced across at the prone and motionless Knatchbull. Three soldiers with rifles were standing over him.

Harris led Ben and Mary out of the barn. Both of them were covered in blood. Harris said, 'You injured, either of you?' They shook their heads. Harris continued, 'He's in the best hands. Those lads know what they're doing. Let's get you to our ambulance and get you cleaned up.'

The yard was now full of vehicles and army personnel. Someone was directing operations in the yard. Mary pointed across to the barn. 'D'you need to be with them?'

'No. They all know precisely what they're doing. I'd only be in the way.'

Ben had to ask, 'Was that the plan? That Chris would go in alone?'

Harris shook his head. 'No. We didn't like it but he insisted he had to protect you – said it was in his job description. He got his way. And he did his job. You're both safe. Now you'd probably like to phone home.'

After the briefest of phone calls, they retreated behind the ambulance as a helicopter landed in the same place that Knatchbull's had come down. His chopper had been covert – no signage – but this one had 'RAF Air Ambulance' printed in large letters down the side. A team with a stretcher trolley emerged and ran across to the barn. Within seconds, they came back with a patient swaddled on a trolley. Four medics were running beside the trolley carrying a variety of equipment to which the patient was hooked up. At the edge of the yard, they abandoned the trolley and carried the stretcher the last part of the race to the chopper. They bundled Chris and themselves in, and it took off.

Harris looked at his watch. 'Seven minutes since the injury. He's got a fighting chance.'

As they looked back at the barn, they saw another stretcher being carried out. Ben said, 'I thought he was to be brought out alive.'

'Oh, he's alive all right. Pumped full of anaesthetic from the watchers in the wall. How many shots did you hear?'

'Just the one.'

'That was his. Our men were silent. He's on his way to a location known only to a very few. He'll wake up…' He looked again at his watch. 'In about thirty minutes. Then the interrogations will begin.'

'And Chris?'

'Might be the RAF hospital at Lakenheath but probably Addenbrookes – maybe the QE at Lynn. They'll have contacted all three. They'll let us know – and I'll make sure you're kept informed. Now, when you've cleaned up, do you think you'll be up to an initial debriefing?'

After a hot shower in one of the several vans that had appeared in the yard, Ben and Mary had been given clean clothes, a sandwich and cup of tea. They had both declined the sugar, saying they were not suffering from shock. Ben had been relieved that it had been easy to remove the transmitters in the shower, the authorities having said that, in no circumstances would they want them back. He and Mary were now seated in another of the vans opposite Harris and four other middle-aged men. Ben didn't recognise any of them. They introduced themselves simply as representatives of MI5, GCHQ, Her Majesty's Government and Her

Majesty's Loyal Opposition. So these are the grey men in grey suits, thought Ben.

Harris said, 'Unfortunately, one casualty. We'll keep you all abreast of his progress. Knatchbull has been retrieved alive and taken for interrogation.'

The four grey men nodded sagely.

HM Government said to Ben and Mary, 'Thank you, both of you. You did an excellent job. We have the full recording and it has more evidence than we could possibly have hoped for.'

HM Loyal Opposition said, 'Absolutely!'

GCHQ said, 'The transmission worked splendidly. We have the entire encounter recorded. As of seven minutes ago, there is a team at his flat taking it apart. Another is at his office.'

MI5 said, 'We are all forever in your debt. Now the work begins to find his army and stand it down. We'll need to get on to that.'

Harris said, 'Yes. Our fault in part. A wake-up call for us. When we find them, they'll need proper support. This time, they'll get it. It's obvious the services have failed them. We must rectify that.' He looked at the other four men and they all nodded. Ben was reminded of those rows of nodding dogs in the back windows of cars.

Ben and Mary sat quietly. Ben wondered if they would be asked anything. Their job was done and he was more than ready to go home.

He said, 'Do you want anything from us?'

MI5 said, 'Ah yes. Sorry. Just any impressions from your meeting. We only had audio. Anything you saw that might help?'

Mary said, 'He's quite deranged, of course.'

Ben was annoyed that the GCHQ man was fiddling with his phone while Mary spoke. The man looked up. 'Another cock-up.'

Ben thought for one awful moment that Knatchbull had escaped, but GCHQ continued, tapping his phone as he spoke, 'He was related to Louis Mountbatten. That was the uncle he spoke of – distant cousin really. That was never picked up.'

MI5 added, 'Or if it was, it would have been seen as a plus. Friends in high places.'

GCHQ and MI5 exchanged glances and nodded almost imperceptibly. Ben wondered what that was about.

HM government said, 'Deranged, you say? How do you know?'

Ben said, 'Just look into his eyes, then you'll know. Can we go now?'

MI5 said, 'Of course. I'll show you to your transport.' He took them to a chauffeur-driven car.

As they got in, Mary said, 'If it's real money, can it go to a charity?'

'Fraid not. It's evidence. It'll be dusted. Where will you be? Cambridge or Hunstanton? We'll need to see you in the next day or two to take your prints, DNA, plus any further insights you might have.'

Ben looked at Mary. She said, 'We'll go back to Hunny for tonight. Then probably on to Cambridge tomorrow. We have people to hug. What about Chris? When will we hear?'

For the first time MI5 smiled. 'We'll keep you posted, I promise. And, if you don't hear anything for a day or two – that will be good news. Bad news will come more quickly.'

Chapter 36

Ben asked the driver to drop them off some way from Josephine's bungalow. He needed a walk in the fresh air in order to regain some balance and digest what had happened. On the blowy clifftop, he and Mary walked together, hand in hand, in silence. After some time, he spoke. 'I feel numb; as though I'm in suspended animation. There's nothing we can do for him but wait. I hate waiting.' He squeezed Mary's hand and she returned the pressure.

Then he phoned Mo to tell him more news about their escape and Chris's heroic act. Mo would pass on the news to all the family and the friends who needed to know. He told Mo they'd be back in the morning but wouldn't be able to answer any questions. Mo asked if he needed to see Dr Clare. He could make an appointment for him. Ben was relieved to realise that no appointment would be necessary. Not yet, anyway.

In a show of optimism, before the meet, they'd booked dinner at the only Michelin starred restaurant in Hunstanton. They'd decided that, if they both survived, this was to be a celebration of the beginning of the rest of their lives. Ben phoned to cancel. The rest of their lives would be on hold for the time being. Instead they bought takeaway fish and chips. It was Mary who declared them tasteless. They stood at the door of Chris's bedroom surveying the mess and the silence. After that, they went to bed and hugged each other tightly both weeping into their respective pillows.

The next day dawned grey and lifeless. Fog had settled just off the coast and it reflected their mood as they packed the few things worth taking home. They filled a small bag with Chris's possessions. There was a scrap of paper on his bedside cupboard with the names of all the people from the Downham shelter, together with his first thoughts on how he might help them. Seeing this, Ben sat down and wept anew.

They drove back, mostly in silence, the only punctuation being the occasional traffic alert. When they got back, the family were all waiting. Those necessary hugs were exchanged. Sarah introduced Greg, their watchman. Ben surveyed him and decided he looked like a fine young man.

After the welcome, Mo busied himself making tea and Katy gave him the news that a woman called Jane had phoned.

'And?'

'She told me that Chris is in intensive care at Addenbrookes. She could only tell us that they've put him into an induced coma and his mum is with him.'

'Oh shit,' said Ben. 'His mum? I never even thought about his family.' He sat down and put his head in his hands.

'Let's be practical,' said Mary. She turned to Greg. 'We've got a quick way of contacting Jane?' He nodded so she continued, 'Let's see if there's any way we can help. For a start – has his mother got anywhere to stay? There's plenty of room here. She'll want to be at his bedside most of the time but she's got to sleep.'

'I'm on it,' said Greg and he wandered off with his phone in his hand. Two minutes later, he was back. 'All arranged. Jane's going to pick her up this evening and bring her here. And Ben, Jane says she needs to talk to you urgently about the man in custody. Can you phone her back. Here's the number.' He showed Ben the number on his phone, adding, 'Best you do it on one of your burners. Safer till it's all dismantled; still need to be careful.'

Ben went to his study, motioning Mary to join him. After a brief phone call in which Ben expressed many expletives, he pressed the end-call button and turned to Mary. He was shaking. 'Can you believe that man. What a bloody nerve. We catch him making preparations to kill God knows how many in Northern Ireland, he shoots Chris and we don't know whether he's going to live or die. Then he has the effrontery, the, the, the damned insolence to try to call the shots.'

Mary said quietly, 'What does he want?'

'He says he'll only talk to me. Says he admires me because I got the better of him. He says – no, he demands – that, unless his terms are met, we'll never know the truth. Who the hell is he to make demands?'

'He's an entitled white man who, I suspect, has always been privileged. He will have made demands all his life and they will always have been fulfilled. What do you expect?'

'I don't know. Piss you off though, don't they, his type. I'd expected to be able to leave this all behind me. You know, crescendo then fading away. We've had the big build up and now there's more to come. I don't know if I can bear to see him. Maybe I'd feel better if I went and beat him to a pulp.'

'I expect you'll see him, and you won't beat him up. D'you know why?'

'Tell me, because I don't know why.'

'I think I know you by now. Here's why you'll see him: One – sense of duty – the job isn't finished. Two – saving people – you have this need to save people. You'll think of all those people in Northern Ireland, and those soldiers, wounded in mind and body, who really don't need to go back to war. You'll think that's the last thing they need. And this is the best one – you'll really enjoy doing it. No! Maybe enjoy is the wrong word. You'll find it satisfying. Don't tell me you haven't felt more alive in the past few months than you have for years.'

'Could it be that meeting you made the difference?'

'Oh, I would love to think that. So good for my ego. No. You started on this road long before I came on the scene. If you were in a really benevolent mood, you could thank Stanley Murdock for that.'

'Kind and generous, though I am, I can't bring myself to thank Murdock. But it could be that he was still part of the plot. I'd love to know.'

'Only one way to find out. Now, let's do something positive and make sure Chris's mum's room is ready and welcoming.'

Chapter 37

Two days went by – dragged by for Ben. They'd settled back into some kind of normal, and then there was Chris. Ben had told Jane that he would meet with Knatchbull but not for a few days. First, he would have to come to terms with Chris's condition. Chris was stable but the doctors were worried. They'd reduced the drugs and he should have started to resurface from the coma but there had been no change. His mum had been going back and forth to Addenbrookes, coming in, having a meal and then going to her room. She was very quiet and Katy had taken her under her wing. It looked incongruous but it seemed to work. As they weren't supposed to know her surname, Katy had named her 'Mrs Chrismum' and they had all followed suit. Mrs Chrismum said she rather liked her new name. It reminded her of Christmases past.

Mary had moved in, temporarily, she said. Sarah was still there. Dani had moved in and they'd been in separate rooms until Ben had laughed and told them life was too short to resist temptation. Suddenly, Dani's room was empty. And, just as suddenly, Ben realised how far he'd come in his journey towards 'letting go and moving on'.

Agnes and Josephine were back home in Cherry Hinton and Mo had gone to stay with them – to protect them, he'd said. Michael was looking after the business and living in Mo's house with Pam. Ben had compared their daily life to being in suspended animation, waiting again for something to happen. He knew he would rather be doing something, anything to relieve the situation, but he didn't know what.

It was Katy who came up with a solution. At least it would mean they were active participants. She'd discussed it with Mrs Chrismum when she'd driven her back to the hospital. As soon as she returned, Katy gathered the family together, Ben, Mary, Sarah and Dani. 'I've been reading up on coma. There are things you can do that the medics can't. People who know the person can help. First thing they say is you should play them music they like.'

'Life on Mars,' Mary said. 'He loved the music from the series.'

Katy squeezed Mary's hand. 'You two got to know him quite well, didn't you?' She didn't wait for a reply 'Good. I can get the music sorted. And Google says he's got to have a reason to come back to us. Something to live for. Any ideas?'

Silence. Then Ben said, 'He wanted to be a good person.'

'Downham!' Mary pointed to Ben. 'Remember he said he wanted to help the people in the homeless shelter in Downham?'

Ben leapt up. 'I've got his list.'

He ran up the stairs two at a time and returned with Chris's list. It had the names of all the homeless men who had wanted to bail him out when his money had been stolen. 'They could visit, talk to him. But I wonder will the hospital let them in? They'll be a bit ramshackle.'

Mary smiled. 'Look, we have the Prime Minister owing us, we have MI5 owing us. And they sure as hell owe Chris. I'm certain they can get the Health Minister to pull strings if we need it. But let's hope the doctors will think it's a good idea. Ben, Katy, lets go and invade the hospital and beat them into submission. Greg, can you phone Jane and get her to sort it from her end?'

In the ten minutes it had taken to drive to the hospital, the phones must have been red hot. They parked and paid and arrived at the main entrance. A phalanx of besuited men – and one woman in a white coat – were waiting to greet them.

A very smartly dressed man stepped forward. 'Welcome to Addenbrookes. Let's get to it and try to get your young man back on his feet.' He ushered them into a lift with the five other besuited men and the woman in the white coat.

They arrived at a large office and were introduced to all the Misters and Doctors and Ben immediately forgot all their names. They sat in a circle and the woman took charge. 'You'll forget my name...' Clever woman, thought Ben. 'But I'm the consultant looking after Chris. In a nutshell, he lost a great deal of blood at the scene so his blood pressure went very low.' She smiled at them. It was a warm smile that gave Ben confidence. 'We know that you saved his life by your quick thinking. Without that tourniquet, and the pressure you applied, I'm sure he'd no longer be with us. As is normal in these cases, we put him into an induced coma. It gives the body and brain time to recover. He did exceptionally well physically – he's a very fit young man – so we had every expectation that, when we weaned him off the drugs, he would regain consciousness. That hasn't happened. We've done a brain scan and can see no physical reason for his prolonged comatose state. But the brain is a complex organ; it doesn't always conform to our expectations. He's still scoring low on the Glasgow Coma Scale and we just don't know why or for how long this will last. So we wait and hope. Now, I understand you have some ideas which might help.'

Ben spoke for them. 'Two things. First, he'd recently become a fan of "Life on Mars", the TV series...'

White-coat interrupted. 'Oh! That's...' She paused. 'A coincidence – and I don't believe in coincidences! So, for God's sake, don't play him the end. Carry on.'

'We just thought of playing him the music from the sound track. He loved the music.'

'Good. And the second?'

'He'd made friends with some homeless people in Downham Market. He was intent on helping them, so we wondered if it would help to bring some of them here to talk to him.'

'Yes, good idea. But would they be willing to come? In my experience, people who live that kind of alternative lifestyle are sometimes reticent when it means going outside the parameters they know well. They might need to be persuaded.'

Mary spoke. 'We have the names of those he was particularly close to. We'll need to talk to the Warden first, then we'll plead with them. And we'll need a photo of Chris as he is now.'

'I'm sure his mother will allow that. In fact, she'll have to take the photo. Infection control. But you can come and look at him through the glass screen and ask her. To warn you, we've taken a lot of the tubes away but he's still hooked up to several monitors. Shall we go?'

* * *

Katy's face was ashen. 'That was bloody awful – and don't tell me not to swear.'

Ben hadn't even noticed. He too was troubled. 'Yeah, bloody awful. I wasn't prepared for that. I thought he would look

165

peaceful, as if he was asleep. But the way he was thrashing about and trying to pull out his tubes. Normal – they said. Look, we've got to get him back from wherever it is his brain has taken him.'

As soon as they were home, Ben phoned the Friary and talked to Dr Clare. She told him that Chris was booked to move into the Friary after discharge from Addenbrookes. And she agreed that their two ideas were worth trying. After talking to her, they decided to go to Downham Market on the off-chance they would be able to talk to the warden. If nothing else, it gave them something to do.

* * *

They were in luck. They told their tale, they showed a photo, and yes, the warden remembered Chris. He said he was younger than the usual clientele and seemed like 'a nice guy'. They could tell he was shocked when they showed him the photo from the hospital. He couldn't look at it for long. Ben warmed to him immediately. They told him half-truths and left the warden to fill the gaps in his own way. They said Chris had been beaten up and was in a coma and they'd been told that he might come round if people he knew talked to him. That's why they wanted to talk to anyone who might know him. Ben handed over the list.

The warden pointed to the photo. 'Perennial problem – attacked from all sides, poor buggers. Yeah. They're all still around, either here or at Lynn. They're only allowed to stay three nights in a row then they have to move on. Not my rules, you understand. Some of them alternate between two or three shelters. It works. They'll be congregating outside from about five. Shall I copy this list and talk to them.'

Mary nodded, 'Yes please. You might show them the picture. You know them so you'll know if it will help. We're particularly interested in a man from Leeds. He was in care then in the army. Speaks with a Yorkshire accent. It seems Chris was close to him.'

'That'll be Long John. A lot of them call themselves John – no surname – so we need to be able to distinguish between them. Homeless people tend to go by other names. It's a form of protection. A lot of them are hiding from someone or something.

166

He'll be around tonight, I think. Been away for three nights so it's time.'

Ben gave him his card. He looked at it and then at Ben. 'Undertaker, eh.' He did a strangled giggle. 'Hope that's not an omen! Sorry – that was crass. You must get all sorts of stupid remarks. I'll talk to them. Persuade them it's a good thing to do. How are you planning on getting them to Cambridge?'

Ben asked, 'Do you think they'd like a limo or two? Make it a bit special?'

'Could do. Yeah – they might like that – something special. I'll tell 'em that. They're a good lot so I'm hopeful. I'll get back to you this evening.'

And they had to be content with that.

Chapter 38

It reminded him of his visits to Michael in prison – not so long ago – but, in other ways, a lifetime. Or several lifetimes. When he had first visited Michael, Stanley Murdock had already been dead but his death had been followed by that of Professor Dobson, Sister Theresa and Doctor Neville-Taylor and possibly Professor Pedersen. And, of these, the only one he mourned was that poor nun who had got on the wrong side of a homicidal paedophile.

He stood in the car park and looked around. Same high barriers to stop sudden exits. Same greyness and depressive silence. But this prison was different. This one almost certainly held only one prisoner. Its presence was omitted from maps. It was sited in the middle of a forest with barriers across the entry road and a complete lack of signposts. He'd had to phone a code from the barrier and then follow a winding forest road for a mile and a half. Then suddenly, there it was – austere and drab – shielded and protected.

He was met by two soldiers in camouflage gear, holding large automatic weapons. He had been warned that, although he was expected, he should not make any sudden moves. He didn't. Holding his hands well away from his sides, he introduced himself to the two soldiers guarding the entrance. One asked for ID, so he slowly extracted his passport and driving licence from his jacket pocket. He showed them the small recorder he would be using. He didn't show them the microphone he had taped to his scrotum. That would be far too indelicate. The second soldier kept him in his sights while the first examined his documents. He handed them back and tossed his head. 'This way,' and the second soldier lowered his gun.

After a pat down search, he was led by another armed soldier into an empty room with a partition down the middle. He'd seen something similar in American gangster movies. It seemed they weren't taking any chances, but he knew that he needed to build rapport with this man and that this physical divide would make that difficult if not impossible. This was one dangerous man but Hannibal Lecter he wasn't. He pointed to the screen. 'Is this necessary?'

'You're a civilian. We can't afford for you to come to harm or to be taken hostage. He says he'll only talk one-to-one so you'll be alone. The commander thought it best.'

'I'd like to talk to the commander please.'

The soldier pointed to a phone on the wall. 'That's for emergencies. Pick it up and press one and they'll put you through.'

The call to the commander was brief. The commander insisted that the barrier was necessary. Ben insisted that it was not. Ben also intimated that he would walk away if the room allocated had a screen between himself and Knatchbull. The outcome – another room would be found.

Ben waited in the more relaxed atmosphere of the dining hall. He sat on a plastic chair, leaned on a plastic table, surveyed the room. Grey again, always grey – and he waited. Then he waited some more. He'd known that Knatchbull would keep him waiting. It was one of the few means that man now had for expressing power. Knatchbull's other advantage, and this one was the one Ben had to crack, was the extent of the knowledge that he, and probably he alone, had of 'his army'.

Ben had made strides in knowing his adversary. That was his only advantage. Knowing Knatchbull while Knatchbull didn't know him; that might give him just the little bit of edge he needed. He had been totally immersed in all things Knatchbull for the past three days. He'd had access to Knatchbull's MI5 file. He'd talked to people who had worked for him, alongside him and above him. Obviously, they'd known something big was up but he was sure most of them had no idea of the details. From what he'd been told, he'd surmised that there was no love lost anywhere. Knatchbull was respected for his intellect but was not liked. It seemed that no-one was close to him.

He'd visited Knatchbull's flat in Knightsbridge. It was his main and, as far as anyone knew, his only residence. MI5 and GCHQ had swept it and had found nothing. It was cold and sterile. Everything was in its proper place. It reminded Ben of Josephine's flat – and she'd been mentally ill. Or Dobson's house – and he had been a lonely unhappy man. When he'd talked to the neighbours, under the guise of a colleague who was worried about him, they'd all declared ignorance. Except one. He smiled at the memory. Every place had its Nosey Anne and he'd found this one. The neighbour across the hall from Knatchbull vouchsafed that, in ten years, he'd only seen one visitor, and that one had stopped coming about a year before. Ben had looked through his phone and luckily, still had a picture of the dead Stanley Murdock looking serene. He showed it to the neighbour and yes, that had been the man who had been Knatchbull's regular and only visitor. He'd passed on that bit of information to the people who needed it and knew that a statement would be taken.

Thinking through, Ben had decided that he would get more if Knatchbull felt he was calling the shots. He also knew he had to gain rapport. Mountbatten's murder might be the starting point. This was going to be bloody difficult.

It had been barely a week since the show-down in the barn. Ben wondered what that week had done to the prisoner. The door opened and he found out. Knatchbull looked precisely the same as he had the last time they'd met. Whatever had happened to him in that week, either it had had no effect or Knatchbull was going to hide it from his visitor. He walked in, tall and straight in his immaculate suit, turned to his guards and, with a dismissive gesture said, 'You can go now.' They retreated and closed the door.

Knatchbull came and sat down opposite Ben. He leaned back in his chair and linked his arms behind his head. He took several slow breaths and looked around. Ben remained silent. Eventually Knatchbull spoke. His voice was low and slow. 'So here we both are. Know why I called for you?' He didn't wait for an answer. 'Wanted to know who you are.' He pointed to Ben's head. 'The hair suits you. Gives you gravitas. Clever, that dreadful dye. So who *are* you? What do I call you? Not Jimmy, I'm sure.'

'Ben. You can call me Ben. And what do I call you?'

'You'll have done your homework, I'm sure, so you'll know what all my titles are. But you can call me Jerry. Do I get your surname?'

'No. So, Jerry, how are we going to play this? You know what I want from you. So what do you want from me?'

'A man after my own heart. Cards on table. But I know you've still got some close to your chest. I want to know what they are.'

'Ask me.' Ben took the recorder out of his pocket. 'Can I record this?'

Jerry replied, as expected, 'You know the answer to that.' Then he took the recorder, placed it on the floor and stamped on it. He looked Ben up and down. 'You look like a soldier.' He pointed to the scar on Ben's head. 'Wounded in action, by the look of it. What medals do you have?'

Ben was surprised at the question but decided to respond honestly. 'Distinguished service medal and Victoria Cross.'

'VC – oh, so you *are* brave. Had to be, to do what you did.'

'Or foolhardy.'

Jerry laughed. 'Indeed. And what foolhardy act deserved a VC?'

'They tell me I rescued two soldiers from certain death and warned several others so they stayed back. I don't remember it. Now your turn. What are you planning in Northern Ireland?'

Jerry looked pained. 'Oh, Ben. Ben. We're only just getting acquainted. It's far too early to get me to talk about Ulster. Ask me something else.'

'I'm sorry about your uncle. I lost someone to a bomb. I know how much it hurts.'

Now it was Jerry's turn to look surprised. Ben could see pain cross his face and disappear in a trice. 'Did you indeed? Someone close, obviously. That's what's driving you, isn't it? What do you want from this? Revenge?'

This time Ben wasn't being entirely honest. 'Revenge would help. But I also want peace inside my head. To stop feeling guilty.'

'Ah! Survivor guilt. Yes, a powerful motivator. I understand that. See, when that boat was bombed, I was supposed to be on it with Louis and Nick and Tim. I'd had an argument with Nick – some ridiculous teenage thing. So, in a fit of pique, I decided not to go. I watched them from the shore thinking I'd pay Nick back but I never got the chance. I saw the boat go up. I watched them die.'

Ben had never for a moment thought that he would feel anything but antipathy for this man. After all, he had been prepared to commit genocide. But he had a niggling feeling of empathy for a man who had seen his relatives die.

Jerry leaned forward towards Ben, 'Who did you watch die?'

171

'My wife.'

'Ah, that's tough. I never managed to get one of those. Never seemed to be the right time.' Jerry sighed then sat up straight. 'Too late now.' Then he said, 'Where did she die?' And before Ben could answer, he added, 'It was Ulster, wasn't it? Of course, it must be! So, if you're after me, it must have been the Prods that killed her. Yes?'

Brilliant, thought Ben. It took them away from the real killer – Stanley Murdock, erstwhile visitor and co-conspirator of this man sitting opposite – this Jeremiah Knatchbull.

He feigned surprise. 'A good assumption. How did you know?'

'You've got that look about you. I could see it when we met in that barn. The hurt, the loss. I thought you were ripe for the picking but I underestimated you. I took a gamble and I lost.' Ben could see a gleam appear in Knatchbull's eyes. He prodded his finger in Ben's direction. 'Our glorious revolution – the one to sort out Ulster once and for all – to make sure it stayed British for ever. Lost now. We were just waiting for the spark to light the tinder-box. Something to shake the so-called Peace Process. Something to shake up the Ulstermen. Then we were going to strike.' He sat back in his chair and the light in his eyes went out. 'It's over now. Good for you. Not many people get the better of me. Clever.'

Ben was nonplussed. This man sitting opposite him had been prepared to organise mass murder. Yet he was conversing in a normal manner. He was showing some anger, yes, but overall he seemed so sane, so ordinary. 'I'm interested. Tell me about your army. You won't get the chance to lead them into battle so they need to be demobbed and supported. They'll need help. I can organise someone to take responsibility for them. The regular army should have done this but they didn't.'

For the first time, Jerry looked less than confident. He looked down at his hands. 'Can't do that. Wish I could but I can't.'

In response, Ben began to feel anger rising in him. He kept his voice calm. 'What d'you mean, "you can't". You recruited them. Presumably, you trained them. You have a responsibility towards them. They're your men.'

'They're not my men. Someone else did the recruiting – someone else did the training. I was in the inner circle but I had to report to the leader. My job was to provide the money for the weapons. I did my job. The money was there. When our leader died, I took command. He held all the intel. He told me that if he died before the mission was accomplished, I had to take command.' His voice changed from conspiratorial to adversarial. 'The information I needed was sent to me but you'll never find it.'

'What information? Where did it come from? Who did it come from?' But Ben already knew the who.

Knatchbull didn't answer but posed a question of his own. 'That disk – you didn't find it in a junk shop, did you?'

Ben had been prepared for this and had prepared the lie. He stayed as close as possible to the truth. 'No, I didn't. It was handed in by a member of the public. He found it and didn't know what to do with it.'

'You haven't asked who made the recording. He's never in the picture.'

'OK. Who made the recording?'

Jerry sat up and looked defiant. 'You didn't ask because you knew I wouldn't tell you. Right?'

Ben nodded.

Jerry continued, 'You knew I wouldn't tell you because you wouldn't have told me if our roles had been reversed. You knew because you understand that it's the only bargaining chip I've got left. It might just keep me alive. So that's my insurance – I won't tell you who made the disk, who sent me the army list or where I've hidden it.'

Ben sat back and relaxed his shoulders. He hadn't expected anything else. Knatchbull was right. He wouldn't have told. 'Fair enough. What about the only person whose face isn't visible – the army type?'

'He's our enforcer. You won't get his name from me either.'

Ben noted the present tense. So the army officer was still operative. He took a different tack. 'The army list, not the who but the where. Give me something. It will help you if you can be a little bit helpful. Where did the army list come from?'

Jerry looked jubilant. 'Oh yes! I can tell you that. But it won't help you because it was stored in the Cayman Islands, posted from the Cayman Islands. So you'll never be able to trace it back.'

That confirmed it for Ben. A remembered conversation with Josephine brought back the germ of a possible solution. He needed to check with Josephine and, if he was right, another search would have to be organised, and soon.

'Anything else to tell me?'

'No. I think we're done for the moment.'

'That's it then,' said Ben. 'Call me if you want to tell me more.' And he got up to go.

'Is that it? Aren't you going to ask me more?'

'No. You said we're done. Call me if you have anything else to tell me.'

But Jerry Knatchbull wasn't quite finished. 'I want you to promise me something.'

'Tell me what it is.'

'If I ever get to a prison, you'll come and visit me.'

To his enormous surprise, Ben found himself saying yes.

Chapter 39

The immediate debrief with Jane and another officer from MI5 was painless. The same could not be said for the removal and disposal of his intimate transmitter. The MI5 officer was obviously disappointed. 'Didn't get anything new. We were hoping he'd open up to you. But, at least, he wants to see you again.'

Ben was almost tempted to try a Belgian accent but couldn't quite restrain himself from doing a Poirot impersonation. 'On the contrary, mon ami, he told us a great deal. Those little details tell us so much.' Then he tapped the side of his head. The young officer looked bemused so Ben omitted reference to his 'little grey cells' and reverted to normal, 'I've got to check on a few details. Then, I think, we should be able to wind this up and reel in any other conspirators. And we'll have to keep Harris and the army to their side of the bargain. Those foot-soldiers will need help.'

Jane looked confused but concurred. 'Absolutely, we'll make sure that happens.'

Ben changed the subject abruptly to the person who was uppermost on his mind at present. 'That can all keep. Knatchbull's not going anywhere. Have you been to the hospital?'

Jane shook her head. 'They won't let me in. He's my responsibility and I feel so powerless.'

She looked truly desolate and Ben's heart went out to her. He squeezed her hand. 'Has Greg told you of Katy's plan?'

'No. He just said you need finance. So I said yes.'

'Katy has a plan and we've started to put it into operation. She's organising the music that Chris was listening to in Hunstanton to be played to him and we're hoping to get some of his friends from the homeless hostel in Downham Market come to visit. That's the more difficult. I've been told that they might not be too keen to leave their immediate surroundings.'

Jane looked thoughtful. 'Another group of vulnerable people caught up in this affair. Keep me posted and we'll make sure you get everything you need.'

'I can tell you one thing I want for the longer term. A permanent hostel where they can put down roots if they want to.

But, for now, a fleet of limos might be the thing. I'll keep you posted.'

'Thanks, Ben. You're a star!' And she walked away.

* * *

It had proved easier than Ben had thought to bring five homeless men from Norfolk to Cambridge. The warden had been a boon in helping to organise the five to be ready and eager for their trip to Cambridge in a stretched limo. He said he'd make sure they were all scrubbed and wearing clean clothes and had agreed to accompany them to 'make sure they behaved themselves'.

Ben arrived at the hostel at the appointed time. He'd acquired a chauffeur's uniform to make sure that they travelled in style. A motley crew were standing waiting on the steps. They were all wearing suits, ill-fitting and old-fashioned. Ben had to hide a smile as he remembered his first suit with flares and wide lapels. He eyed the group in front of him and wondered when was the last time any of them had worn a suit.

He got out of the car, approached the assembled company, removed his peaked cap and gave a deep bow. 'Thank you, gentlemen for agreeing to come to the hospital to visit Chris. Shall we get going and I'll explain on the way what we hope will happen.'

He could see that they were looking confused. The warden intervened. 'He called himself Col when he was here. Short for Columbus, I suppose.'

The tallest man in the group spoke up. He had a strong Yorkshire accent. 'He were a good lad. Runnin from summat just like the rest of us. We'll do what we can. Least we can do.'

'Thank you, John,' said Ben as he bowed and held the car door open for them. John beamed a gap-toothed smile. 'We've not been introduced so he must have spoke about us. Aye, a good lad.'

When they arrived at the hospital, it was as though royalty were visiting. They were ushered in and taken to what was obviously the hospitality suite. Ben could see the visitors eyeing the coffee and pastries. At Ben's invitation to 'help themselves', the entire pile of the pastries disappeared into mouths and pockets.

Ben was beginning to value having friends in high places. It opened doors. He was convinced that, if he could find the last piece of the jigsaw, he would be in a strong position to ask for some very big favours. He now had a good idea where he would find Stanley's stash and finish this obscene thing once and for all. Then he would have to think what he would want the authorities to change.

When they arrived at Chris's room, they were told that they could go in two at a time. John took charge. He pointed to Ben. 'Thee and me, lad. We'll go first.' He turned to the other four. 'Remember what we said. Hard man, soft man and your best singing.' He turned to Ben. 'We've bin practising.'

John looked startled when he saw Chris. Mrs Chrismum was sitting holding Chris's hand. John spoke first to her. 'Sorry 'bout yer lad. We were close to him when he needed help. Looks like he needs us again. Let's see if we can waken him.' He eased himself into the chair at the other side of the bed. It was then that Ben realised what a life on the road had taken out of him. He sat down like an old man, but his voice was clear and urgent. 'Col, you silly bugger. It's Long John here. What've you done? You told me you always walked towards the action. Fucking stupid.' He turned to Mrs Chrismum, 'Beggin your pardon, missus. That's how we talked together.'

She nodded and smiled. She let go of Chris's hand. 'Carry on, please.' She stood up. 'I think I'll leave you and get a cup of coffee. Then you can swear at him all you want. I know I've wanted to. I hope you can get through to him.'

Ben watched her go and saw her talking to the four men who were now sitting in silent contemplation outside. He saw one of them surreptitiously reach into his pocket and take out a bite of pastry. This made him angry – not with the eater – but with the hunger that was so obviously a regular part of their lives. He sat beside the bed and turned down the music. 'Live and let die'. Not entirely appropriate, he thought, but part of the soundtrack to the series they'd watched together in Hunny. Ben suddenly felt fearful. He'd been pushing to the back of his mind the possible outcomes for Chris. Now they came creeping forward into his consciousness. He swallowed hard as he pushed them back into that box at the back of his brain. Then he locked down the lid. He watched John heave himself up and change places. He realised it was so he could take the hand that Chris's mum had let go, the hand without the cannula. He watched as John squeezed Chris's hand and he listened to John's spiel.

John was leaning over close to Chris's ear. 'C'mon Col. We agreed we're fighters. I told you what I bin through. I haven't given up on life and mine's been a damn sight harder un yours. So you better wake up. You fuckin better wake up. You said you ain't seen hardship before. You promised us you'd come back to help us. Anyway, you still owe us. I got Jack and Jim and Petey and Johntoo outside. Listen on. You said you'd pay us back for the tea money. Well, you can't fuckin do it while you sleep the days away here. You got debts to pay, lad!'

He turned to Ben. 'Your turn.'

Ben suddenly knew what to say. 'Chris, it's Ben. Debts. Me, I've got the biggest debt of all. I owe you big time. We owe you enormous time. You saved me and you saved Mary. And we can't thank you till you can celebrate with us. Listen Chris, remember I told you we're going to get married. Well, we're waiting till you can be there. And you told us we were already ancient. So, we can't wait too long. We're two old people in a hurry but we're waiting for you. And we miss you. Come back to us.' He had to stop because the tears were getting the better of him.

John took up the tale. 'See, Col, we all need you. I'm going to fetch your old friends from Downham. Don't you disappoint them, you hear?' He said to Ben. 'Hold his hand while I go and talk to the others.'

Ben took his place and held Chris's hand. Suddenly he felt angry with Chris, angry with the world but mostly, angry with Knatchbull. 'Listen, you stupid bugger. This "Life on Mars" thing has got to stop. We need you here so get your arse in gear and come back to us.'

John came back in with the four other men. They stood in a ragged line at the bottom of the bed. 'They said we could sing to him. Male voice choir. We used to at the hostel, sitting round in the evenings.' He raised both hands as a conductor and said, 'One, two, three,' and they launched into a rousing chorus of Ilkley Moor Bar Tat.

For the first time, Ben listened to the words and he realised how appropriate they were. Not only was it a Yorkshire anthem for

John but it was also a cautionary tale for Chris. He hoped it would work. It was when they got to the last verse, 'That's wheear we get us ooan back, ooan back', that the doctor burst in. He looked at the beeping machines and grinned. Ben could see no difference but then he felt the faintest of pressure on his hand. He said to John, 'Bring his mum in. He squeezed my hand.'

The doctor said, 'Whatever you did, do it again.' And Ilkley Moor was reprised with gusto.

Chapter 40

After driving back to Downham Market via a chip shop where all five men had partaken gustily of large portions of fish, chips, mushy peas and curry sauce, he'd taken the limo back to the hire firm. He wasn't sure what the hire company would make of the fish and curry smell, but he was sure they'd coped with far worse. This was a university town after all. He'd promised to take the men back to the hospital the next week, or sooner if they were needed. He'd given the warden enough money to keep each of them in the hostel, or a nearby one, for the week. Now he had to see Josephine.

It was a fine spring day so he decided to walk to Cherry Hinton. It certainly was living up to its name. The blossom was waving gently in the breeze and, as he walked through Cherry Hinton Hall Park and on through the allotments, he could hear the buzzing of countless insects. His heart felt lighter than it had for as long as he could remember. The prognosis for Chris was positive. He still wasn't fully conscious but was showing signs that he could hear and respond. His mother had told them that he could click his fingers when asked to, and the doctors saw this as a very good sign.

Of the two leading conspirators, one was dead and the other was in prison with a twenty-four hour watch, so imminent danger from them had receded. Now he was hopeful that Josephine could fill in the missing piece of the jigsaw. It would give him great pleasure to be the one to produce the remaining evidence of wrongdoers, and if it included plotters both sides of the Irish Sea, that would be a bonus. Harris, and the army, needed the list of the unfortunates who had been ensnared as foot-soldiers in this plot. From his brief contact with Knatchbull in the barn, Ben had become aware of how easy it would be to garner people's feelings of abandonment and turn them into destructive action.

He quickened his step. He was looking forward to seeing Mo, who had more or less moved in with Agnes. This suited Michael, as Mo's departure had allowed Pam to move in with him. Sarah and Dani were quickly becoming like a married couple. They had shown no inclination to move back to Sarah's flat. The lovey doveyness had become too much for Ben so he'd had a valid excuse to move in with Mary. Katy was the odd one out but, ye Gods, she was planning to visit Chris every day. Where would that go, he wondered? If Chris had any sense, he'd retreat back into his coma. But Chris had leapt out to save him, so a sense of self-preservation must surely be lacking. Certainly, Katy was a force to be reckoned with so he felt Chris didn't stand a chance. They still didn't know the long-term effects of Chris's shut-down but the latest brain scan had revealed no discernible injury so the signs were positive. But, Ben knew, from his own experience of head injury, it could still be a long haul.

He arrived at the small Victorian terrace and noted the new paintwork on Agnes's house. The tiny front garden was effervescent with spring flowers. The perfume of the hyacinths accosted his nostrils and reminded him of the lily smell he so hated. But then he stood stock still and considered his good fortune. He had avoided the most common effect of head injury, loss of the sense of smell. The moment passed, but he still couldn't stand there breathing in this stink, so he rang the bell long and hard.

This was the second time Ben had seen Mo since what Agnes had insisted on calling 'his ordeal'. Mo's hugs this time were just as strong and just as long. Eventually he'd had to extricate himself. Then a hug from Agnes and the promise of a cup of tea. Lastly, a hug and a kiss on the cheek from Josephine. This one had surprised him. The woman who had been touch-phobic was hugging people. Dr Clare was certainly doing a great job.

After the pleasantries and the inevitable cup of dark brown tea, he went straight to the point of his visit. 'Josephine, I'm hoping you can help me, but I don't want to cause you any grief. There are things I need to know, things you told me soon after we met, about Stanley Murdock.'

Josephine grinned. 'I was in a bad way then, wasn't I? I'd just killed the man who'd raped my mother and was planning to rape me. And then I fixated on you. I have a lot to thank you for, including not giving up on me.'

Ben found himself blushing. 'I'm just so pleased to see you recovering.'

'You've no idea how my life has changed and I've got you and my mum and Alison to thank for that.'

Agnes joined in. 'That Dr Clare is a miracle worker, an angel sent straight down from heaven. Did you know I'm seeing her too? She tells me it's included in the package.' She grabbed Ben's arm and squeezed hard. 'But Ben, you can tell me. Who is paying for this package? It's worrying me. Dr Clare says not to ask, just be grateful the bills are being paid.' She pointed a thumb at Mo. 'Maurice says the same. But I can't just accept charity, leastways without being able to say thank you.'

Ben certainly couldn't tell her that MI5 were picking up the tab. He decided to tell a near-truth. 'You know you had to go into hiding recently, to keep you safe?'

Agnes nodded.

'Well, that was because an associate of Murdock's was on the run, but now he's been caught. When Josephine killed Murdock, she brought down a very serious criminal. And now his accomplice has been caught. And a grateful nation, by way of a sort of police compensation scheme, is paying her bills. And don't feel beholden. See, they're doing it to spare their blushes. Josephine started the dominoes falling and very soon, they'll all be down. And that's where I need Josephine's help again.' He added quickly, 'And there's no danger. I only need information.'

Josephine nodded. 'Of course I'll help. But first I need a straight answer from you. There are four men who could have been my father. I need to know if it was Murdock? I'm willing to take a DNA test and I'm sure Virginia and Alistair will help.'

Well, thought Ben, this is a pretty mess. He knew that Josephine was Murdock's biological daughter. Chris had told him. He'd also told him that Virginia and Alistair were not, and he hadn't told them that yet. He'd had to leave that till after the showdown. Now Chris was on the mend, a trip to Brighton to visit Virginia and Alistair was moving swiftly to the top of his agenda.

He looked at Josephine, then at Agnes. They both looked eager but serene. Agnes answered his unasked question. 'Of course we can cope. It will set our minds at rest to know the truth.'

'Then I can set your minds at rest. Yes, Stanley Murdock was your father. The police did something they shouldn't have. They did a DNA test on your hairbrush when they cleared out your offices. They shouldn't have done it without your knowledge but they did.'

'Good,' said Josephine. 'I thought he was.' She turned to Agnes and smiled. 'I'd better make sure I turn out like my mum then, hadn't I?'

After all their difficult years and their estrangement, Ben could see that a close bond had developed between these two women. He had to take a few deep breaths before he could speak again. 'So, my question?'

'Yes.'

'When we first met, you said something about seeing a letter – or something – from a bank account in some far off place. You said that Murdock took it from you and told you to forget it. Do you remember?'

Josephine frowned in concentration. 'Yes. He was very open with me about his finances. Useful, as I was the one drawing up his will! His affairs were all very complicated. I worked with his accountant both before and after his death and we got all of it sorted and accounted for. But there was something we never included because he'd insisted that it was inconsequential, and not to be part of the inheritance. Who were we to say other? He was our client and he was adamant. Now, what on earth was it?'

She paused, and it seemed that everyone in the room held their breath. They breathed out as she exclaimed, 'Oh yes.' And Ben breathed out further when she added, 'Cayman Islands. That was it. There was a statement from an account in the Cayman Islands with only one recipient. It was weird. It was a regular payment to Cambridge City Council – forty, maybe fifty pounds a month. And there was a sizeable amount in the account. Enough to keep it going for years. He whisked it away from me as though it was hot. But, why would he want to keep that secret?'

But Ben knew why and now he had the confirmation he needed.

After he'd finished his tea, Josephine insisted on showing him out. She obviously had something she wanted to say to him alone. And what she said brought him up short because it hadn't even occurred to him. 'Thank you again for all you've done, and you have no need to worry about Mo. He's made my mum so happy. He's sort of a dad figure, the sort I'd want, given the choice. I was worried, so I asked Alison if there was any chance that I could harm him and she said no.'

'Oh, good,' was all he could think of saying.

* * *

Ben's next trip had been a joy. As he'd had such very personal information to impart, he'd decided to go alone. Virginia and Alistair had been delighted to see him and had been even more delighted to find out that the hated Stanley Murdock was not their biological father and the much-loved Tommy was. They had whooped with joy and danced round the kitchen. Then they had all laughed together.

They had readily agreed when Ben had told them that this must be a private matter as no-one in authority wanted old wounds to be opened. He told them the tale that their police DNA tests had only recently come to light and hinted at police incompetence over the storage of the DNA, and that the test results had now been destroyed. They readily agreed to let that lie.

He then told them half a story about his meeting with Tommy. After that, he had got the distinct impression that he was surplus to requirements and that, as soon as he had departed, they would be on the phone to Northern Ireland. He'd left two very excited adults, behaving like children on Christmas Eve, and it had brought joy to his heart.

On his journey back from Brighton, he parked near the place where he and Mary had been forced off the road. He smiled to see that there was still a dent in the hedge that had saved them both from serious injury. Then it came to him in a rush; the enormity of what they had achieved. He took a deep breath, got back in his car and drove on home, for there was still a job to finish.

Chapter 41

He'd gathered together those he thought of as 'his big brains' – Katy, Mary and Henry Walpole. He was feeling frustrated because he'd thought he'd understood how the last part of this tangled mess fitted, but no. He was at an impasse, again, and he needed their help. They looked expectantly at him.

'I need your brains. And Katy, I really shouldn't be sharing this with you.' He waved his hand towards Henry and Mary. 'They've signed the Official Secrets Act and some of my revelations could well be official secrets. But I think you might be the one to solve this puzzle. Is that OK with you? Will you be able to keep this secret? If you're worried about it, I'll understand if you want to back out.'

Katy laughed. 'Dad, I love you so much. You're still trying to protect me. But heh, I don't need that much protection. A teeny bit maybe? See, I winkled a whole lot of information out of Chris at that get-together you had in Hunny. He'd had a few and he really needed someone to talk to. He should never have mentioned the name Knatchbull. Am I right?'

'Bloody Hell!' said Mary and Ben in unison.

'Clever, clever girl,' said Henry.

'He thought he might get killed, so he was vulnerable. He couldn't talk to you two because he didn't want to add to your worries. So I listened. And I find I'm a really good listener, specially when I'm hearing something so bloody explosive.'

Ben's eyes widened. 'You knew how dangerous it was going to be and you still didn't try to stop us?'

She looked witheringly at him. 'Dad, you know this already. You have to let go. You have to allow people to take their own risks. Then you pick them up afterwards if they fall. Remember outside the garden centre in Shelford. You picked me up and you looked after me.' She smiled. 'I just did the same. See, I've had a good teacher.'

Henry Walpole clapped his hands in a round of applause. 'Ben, this young lady of yours is remarkable. I love her. She's wise way beyond her years, and she's a credit to you.' He turned to Katy.

'Miss Burton, I'm a very old man and I'm gay. I've got pots of money that I don't know what to do with. I can't go down on one knee because I'd never be able to get up again. Will you marry me?'

'Whoa now!' Mary said, after the laughter had died down. 'Hold your horses, Henry. You've just lost me to another. Have you thought you could be acting on the rebound?'

'Oh, perfectly possible. Anyway, thinking about it, I'm very sorry, Miss Burton, but I've realised that you are far too young for me. So, I'll retract my offer of matrimony but I would be honoured if you would agree to be my friend.'

Katy grinned. 'And I'd be honoured to be counted among your friends.'

'Good, that's settled.'

'Enough bonding,' said Ben. 'Can we get down to business?'

They all pulled in their chairs and sat up straight and looked expectantly at Ben. He continued, 'Josephine has confirmed that Murdock had – well, still has, I suppose, an account in the Cayman Islands. Its only function is to pay out every month to Cambridge City Council.'

Katy jumped up, nearly knocking over her chair. 'The lock-up!'

The other two looked bemused. Mary knew about the lock-up but Henry didn't. Ben explained to him. 'Murdock has a lock-up garage he rents from the City Council and it's where he hid his blackmail evidence. We searched the garage thoroughly and we found the bag of incriminating stuff hidden in the roof struts. Now, the fact that he'd set up such an elaborate and secret means of paying for the garage, well, that suggests to me that it was of prime importance to all his nefarious endeavours. So I went back. I've been back three times and I've been through that garage with a fine-toothed comb. And I've come up with precisely nothing.

'I've been round all the walls, bearing in mind that the army put up a false wall where we met Knatchbull and it didn't sound any different from the old solid walls. I drilled holes through all the walls and they're all single brick and all legit. I've probably broken all the terms of the lease, but I have reinstated where I'd drilled. I've been up in the roof investigating the roof struts where we found the bag of blackmail evidence – nothing. I've gone over the floor –

swept it and even washed it over. I had to sweep the water out because the inside drain hole was clogged so the water didn't drain away.'

Katy was doodling as she listened. 'We have to think like Murdock. He was clever and devious and evil. Let's not do the evil bit, but clever and devious will help us. This thing we're looking for, what do we know about it?'

'Evidence. We know from Knatchbull that Murdock was the keeper of the logistics, the man who recruited the personnel, the chief organiser, so he must have kept some sort of record. Could all be on disks or even on SD cards. Could be tiny.'

Katy was still doodling. 'The blocked drain hole. It was inside the garage?'

Ben nodded.

She stopped doodling. 'Did you try to look in there?'

'Totally seized. And there was no lip so I couldn't see a way to get any leverage on it.'

Katy sounded urgent, 'Did you try?'

And she breathed out forcefully when her father answered, 'No. I couldn't see a way of attacking it.'

'Phew, well done, Dad. Your drilling? Was there electricity or did you have to use those manly muscles?'

'No, it was bloody hard work. My manly muscles need a bit of honing. I had battery drills but that's one reason I had to go back – batteries needed a recharge – the drills and mine.'

Then she asked, 'Did Murdock do Maths at Ethel's?'

Henry nodded. 'Started with maths with physics, then transferred to music, I believe.'

'Oh brilliant!' said Katy. 'Levers and pulleys.'

Mary looked perplexed. 'Care to elaborate?'

'Oh, sorry, yes. Of course. You two didn't see Murdock's safe. It was amazing. It was in his study in his house in Grantchester, and it was completely hidden. We were there to witness the opening of the safe after his death. Anyway, that one was electrically operated. You pulled a tiny hidden lever and a section of wall swung open to reveal the safe. He'd shown it to Josephine when she was doing his will and even his kids didn't know it was there. I had a quick look at it before we left. It was sooo clever. I'm pretty certain he could do something similar in the garage.'

Katy held up her doodle. 'This is how I think it works. See the drain? Well, the drain isn't a drain. It's a cover for a hidey hole. It opens remotely. We just have to work out how to open it. If we can't find any mechanical arrangement, I think you'll have to bring in reinforcements. And knowing Murdock's evil mind, we need to be aware that it's probably booby-trapped.'

Ben looked amazed. Whenever he'd doubted Katy's analysis in the past, he'd been proved wrong. This seemed far-fetched but, at least, it gave them an opening, closed though it was at present. 'You could be right. But what got you started down that route?'

'Drains. Who puts a drain inside a garage? The logical place for the drain is outside – unless it's a garage for repairing cars or, I suppose, if you expect the roof to leak loads.'

Henry asked, 'What sort of garage is it?'

Ben answered, 'It's one of a run of say...' He counted in his head. 'Ten garages in a row with another ten opposite. Council owned, east side of Cambridge on the way to Cherry Hinton. They all look run-down. I think he chose it cos it's quiet there and not overlooked.'

Henry wiped his eyes and beamed at Katy. 'Ben told me about you and the puzzle box. I'm sure you know that you have some very special talents and a devious mind. I'm looking forward to a delightful friendship. Tell me, do you drink gin?'

'No – I'm generally a beer girl – but I may have occasion to drink gin with you. I'm starting at Ethel's in October.'

Henry beamed. When he spoke, to Ben's ears he sounded so much younger. There was a vibrancy that had been dimmed of late. 'Oh, how splendid. Pratchett – read him? Leonard of Quirm – Murdock – but Leonard was an innocent.'

'I love Pratchett,' said Katy. 'We could have a two person book club.'

'You'll make friends. You could bring them along. I'll have cleared my rooms by then.'
He turned to Mary. 'You will still help me, won't you?'

'Of course I will, you old duffer. You're my favourite non-husband. You must know that.'

'It will be such fun to have young people around again. Mary and Ben, you won't be allowed in our reading group. Too old.'

Ben answered, 'We'll drink gin with you at other times. Now, let's get on. Katy, how certain are you?'

'Not at all certain, but it would be just like him to do something like this. If he's set up a secret account to pay for it, then I think that he'd use that lock-up for more than just local blackmail evidence. I'd say, seventy per cent sure – final answer.'

'OK, what's next to be done?'

'Go to the lock-up, of course.'

Chapter 42

However, the trip to the lock-up had to be postponed. Ben had a call from Mrs Chrismum. Chris was stirring and he'd said his first two words. Long John, he wanted to see Long John. So Ben and Mary hurried off to Norfolk to try to find him and Katy went to the hospital.

It took an hour to reach Downham Market and another hour to seek out Long John. They talked to the warden and to a couple of John's associates, then searched his usual haunts. Eventually, they found him sitting on a bench, watching the river amble its way through Kings Lynn and out into The Wash. He turned at their call. 'How's t'lad?'

'He's waking up. He's asked to see you.'

And then Long John broke into racking sobs interspersed with ferocious fits of coughing. Ben gave him a clean white handkerchief and John proceeded to puff on his inhaler and blow his nose. Mary sat down next to him and put an arm round his shoulders. Once he'd recovered from his coughing fit, he said, 'When I saw him, I thought he were going to die. Seen too many deaths. Old codgers like me – but he's too young.' He stood up. 'Wants to see me, eh? Well, what're we waiting on? Got tha limo?'

This time there was no limo, no fanfare, no greeting party, no pastries. Instead, there was hope. When they arrived at the Intensive Care Unit, they were taken down a different hallway. The nurse explained that Chris had been moved as he no longer needed the degree of support that he had previously. John had a twinkle in his eye as he said, 'Been downgraded, has he? Well, that's gradely.' Ben had to translate for this southern nurse that gradely was a good thing.

When they got to his room, Chris looked just as the last time they'd seen him, except most of the machinery was missing. His mother and Katy were sitting either side of his bed each holding one of his hands and taking turns to talk to him. The 'Life on Mars' soundtrack was playing softly in the background.

Katy hugged them all, including Long John, who looked a mite surprised. She brought them up to date and explained that it

190

wasn't like in the movies where the person in the coma suddenly wakes up and starts talking in complete sentences. They'd been told that he was probably sleeping ninety per cent of the time but his vital signs had definitely changed. John said he'd stay until Col woke again or they chucked him out. He took Katy's place and took Chris's hand. Then he chided Chris big time.

'Tha's a gret southern softie. Nobbut a babby. They tell me you was shot. Shot? C'mon, yer daft ha'peth, it were yer leg not yer head. Now lad, it'd be champion if yer could give your mam a present and wake up proper like. She'll be chuffed t'bits. What d'yer say?'

There was a small grunt from the bed. It might have been a word or it might not but it encouraged John to add, 'If tha's all yer can do, I'll have te tell yer mam I'm reet disappointed. C'mon lad, tha can do it.'

The nurse ushered the extra bodies from the room with, 'only two visitors allowed'. They left Mrs Chrismum and Long John with the promise that both would be collected at 'chucking out time' and both would have a bed at Ben's house. John said that would be grand and Mrs Chrismum nodded. As they left, they heard Long John starting to recount his life story.

* * *

Ben and Katy decided to look over the lock-up, just the two of them, leaving Henry Walpole fretting in college, with Mary helping him with the continued blitz of his rooms. They'd decided to keep Dr O'Connor in reserve in case they got nowhere and needed additional knowledge of the physics of the thing. Ben knew that, as a former blackmailee of Dobson and possibly of Murdock, O'Connor would be delighted to help. As they drove to the lock-up Ben whistled loudly – and continued despite Katy's cries of disgust. He marvelled at the number of friends and allies they had made in the quest to discover Diane's killer and latterly, Murdock's secrets. Yes, life was good.

When they arrived at the lock-ups, Katy looked around. She whispered, 'You wouldn't expect this quite so close to the Cambridge dreaming spires. It's perfect for a hidey hole.'

Ben said, 'Why are you whispering?'

She pointed up to the overhanging trees. 'I don't want to disturb the birds, silly.'

Ben led the way to the right garage. Katy stopped him from opening the door. She surveyed the run of garages. Murdock's was in the middle of the run. She studied the door and the front of the adjoining walls. 'I wouldn't expect anything funny on the outside. Too public. And see, there's a sloping drain right outside with gutters and downpipes. No need for an inside drain. Can you open up, Dad.'

Ben unlocked and raised the up-and-over door. Katy knelt down by the inside drain cover. 'There's no slope towards it. That's promising.' Then she looked up and surveyed the walls and door. 'See, it's near this wall and away from the door. A good place for a hidden compartment. Now we just have to work out how to get into it.'

She started to examine the wall, brick by brick. Ben could see her eyes light up as she pointed to a brick high on the wall above the drain. Attached to it was a small rusty coat hook hardly visible up near the rafters and far higher than you would want in order to hang a coat.

'What d'you think, Dad?'

He stood up and looked at the hook. It was within Ben's reach but too high for Katy. 'I'll get the steps from the car,' said Ben.

Katy climbed the ladder, took her phone out of her pocket and turned on the torch. She examined the hook from all angles. 'Looks like something I've seen online. Shall I go for it, Dad?'

'D'you think it will blow us up?'

'No, but I might lock it so the garage will need to be demolished.'

'Is that all? Go for it.'

Katy gingerly turned the hook. There was a muffled click and the drain cover opened a small way on a hinge. Katy said, 'I'll hold this steady just in case. You open it up and get everything out.'

'Yes Ma'am.'

Chapter 43

As Ben walked around Front Court, he breathed in the fresh Spring air and marvelled again, at the change in his fortunes over the past year. For the first time in eighteen years, he could say he was truly at peace. Well, almost. He was as sure as he could be that the turbulence of the past was behind him. Diane's ghost had, at last, been laid to rest. He knew who had killed her and was well on the way to understanding why. His flashbacks had disappeared, his hyper-vigilance had receded and his relationship with his girls had become one of equal adults. Chris was on the mend, though it would be a long haul. And he had found Mary. If he'd believed in miracles, then that would have been one. And now, there were loose ends to be tied up and he was unsure which knots to choose, hence the arrangement for a meeting with Katy, Mary and Henry.

As usual, he was early, so he decided to take a stroll round the pond and commune with the ducks. He patted his hold-all and checked again to ensure that his precious parcel was still there. He grinned to himself, remembering Josephine's OCD and realising he was being obsessive about this package, but with a totally logical reason. He and Katy had had a discussion about whether they should look at the contents yesterday, when they had discovered the cache. They had even discussed whether they should look at all, or just hand the whole lot over to MI5 unopened. He had placed it in his hiding place in the chimney overnight and had laughed at himself as he had checked it at two-hourly intervals. He'd realised how ridiculous he was being as no-one except his three confidantes even knew of the existence of the package or its whereabouts. Even Knatchbull hadn't known what Murdock had stashed away or where he'd hidden it. If he had, Ben was sure he would have removed it after Murdock's death. It had been Knatchbull who had ordered that Murdock's wishes were to be followed so that everything from the safe was to be buried with him unopened. So Knatchbull must have believed that he was in the clear; that he was the only one who knew the entirety of the plot. Knatchbull's mistake had been in not checking the identity of the undertaker who was burying his co-conspirator. Such a small error.

Ben passed three fresh-faced undergraduates chatting animatedly and wondered if his 'watcher' had taken his advice and steered clear of espionage in all its guises. He hoped so. His own brush with 'the Services' would soon be over. He was looking forward to a settled time, buying a cottage with Mary, putting up her dreadful mirror, spending some of his inheritance from Dobson. And going to some weddings.

When he arrived, the others had already gathered in Henry's rooms. Ben brought out the package. It was a heavy duty waterproof box about the size of a house brick. 'This is it. Now, I need advice. Do we look inside or do we give it, as is, to Jane and leave MI5 to sort it out?'

Henry looked at the box. 'I'm sure you have – but I have to ask you anyway. Have you checked it for booby traps?'

Katy picked up the box and pointed to it. 'See, it's transparent, heavy duty plastic. Sooo bad for the environment but useful when looking for small bombs. I found the same box on-line, compared them and I'm pretty sure it's OK.'

Henry beamed at her. 'I wish we'd had the internet when I was young. How I envy you young things. But, we have a dilemma, do we not? Or rather, Ben has. Open it and you may find answers that will help you, or those answers may cause you further grief. And they are answers that the Services will certainly not want you to have. Pass it on unopened and you'll have to live with not knowing.'

Katy said, 'I found it so does that mean it's mine?'

'I think you'll find it belongs to Murdock's children,' said Ben. And that reminded him of his joyful trip to Virginia and Alistair to tell them that Tommy was their father. It would open a worm-can if it became common knowledge that they were not Murdock's offspring. That was a secret he would continue to keep.

Mary was thoughtful. 'But his children can't be allowed to know.'

Ben jumped. 'Know what?'

Mary gave him a weird look. 'About this box.'

Katy looked at the box. 'True – blissful ignorance is a great thing – and we don't have it. I, for one, couldn't bear to live my entire life without knowing what we'd found.' She looked around the rest of the group. 'And I've got a lot longer to live than you lot. I'm hoping to live to a hundred so I've got a lot of living to do.'

Henry Walpole laughed. 'Even I've got a few years till I reach that exalted age. I, too, would like to know, but I think the choice ultimately lies with Ben. I am one step removed from the effects of Murdock's work. Katy less so. We now know that Murdock had a hand in killing your mother. Then, Ben put himself in danger, although Mary too has done that.' He looked at Mary. 'Your view, my dear?'

She turned to Ben. 'Sorry. It's your choice, and I really can't help you decide. In reality, it should go unopened to MI5. Murdock was a spy, he was plotting mayhem in Northern Ireland. As ordinary citizens, we shouldn't interfere.'

Katy interrupted. 'My dad – and you too, Mary – you're not ordinary citizens though, are you? You both know far more than is good for you already. And they owe you. The question is, Dad, could you live without knowing what Murdock had hidden?'

'No Katy, I don't believe I could. Shall we get on with it?'

Ben took the box and, before opening it, said, 'I think we should wear gloves and visors. Just in case – I don't trust that bugger not to have booby trapped the contents – plus, we want to leave as little trace as possible for the authorities. Until we know what we've got, we don't know if we'll want to plead ignorance of the contents.' He proceeded to distribute thin latex gloves and industrial visors to the four of them and told them to stand back. Then he carefully released the catch on the lid. It opened with a quiet click and the four of them breathed out in synchrony.

The first item, laid on top of a bundle of papers, was a surprise. A crisp white envelope held, in swirling copperplate handwriting, the dictum, 'To whom it may concern'. Ben turned it over. The envelope was unsealed. He carefully drew out a single sheet of thick white paper, unfolded it and started to read it aloud:

'Congratulations – I am in awe of you, for you have out-manoeuvred me. And your prize – my archives. For what use are they to me? If you have found this, I will already be dead or am about to be killed by the unseen forces of the state.

You are not a mere council employee who has inadvertently come upon this box while destroying the garage underneath which it has resided. If you had been, you would be dead because the professional I employed to dispatch the beautiful Margaret, has provided my archive with a fail-safe way of ensuring its security.'

Ben stopped reading. Katy grabbed her father's arm. 'We did close the drain and lock the garage, didn't we?'

Ben nodded. 'Yes, we did. They'll have to get the bomb squad in, but this tells us it's safe as long as no-one interferes. And we know that the beautiful Margaret is a yacht belonging to one of his co-rapists.'

Mary pointed to the open box. 'Not is. Was. Look at the photo.'

Katy carefully lifted out a photograph of the shattered hull of a boat, beached on a white sandy shore. The name 'Margaret' was just discernible in flaked and filthy paint. An enormous hole could be seen in the stern just below the water line. She turned the photo over and read the inscription on the back. It was written in the same florid handwriting as the letter. She read it out.

'Revenge for the Swiss francs. Pity about the heart attack. He's no use to me dead.'

Ben explained, 'You saw his note – eggs is eggs – bombs are bombs.' A look of acute disgust crossed his face. 'I wonder how many people he has caused to die?'

Henry thumped him on the back. 'No point in thinking about it, dear boy. Can't change it. What else does he say?'

Ben read on:

'If you are reading this, then our plan to rid the North of taigs has failed. We got some of them but the Fenian lovers in England will have won this time. But be warned, we just need a ripple in the fabric of peace and the forces will stir again. We've lost the battle but the war will continue. There will be an uprising and it will ensure that there is never, ever, a chance of the North being overrun by the left-footers from the South. As long as there are Ulstermen, there will never be a united Ireland.'

Henry exhaled loudly, 'Gracious me. I hadn't thought so, but it seems that Murdock was a rather dangerous fanatic.'

Ben looked unutterably sad. 'So that was why he tortured his poor wife.'

At their looks of incomprehension, he added, 'When they came back to Cambridge, she defied him by becoming a Catholic. It was the only time she stood her ground. In consequence, he made her life one long hell. Virginia told me.' For Henry's benefit he added, 'One of her children.' He'd carefully called them 'her' children not Murdock's.

Henry nodded gravely. 'Pray, continue.'

'I thought I'd settled it when I made sure that bloody interfering woman was killed. But she must have got a message through. They foiled us. Our man within couldn't stop them getting Blair elected. Pathetic. Outflanked by his own people. Someone in there knew – someone skewed the election. Never found out who.'

Henry exhaled even more loudly. 'Good God! This is absolute dynamite. This is extraordinary. This is treason! He's saying that MI5 intervened in a general election. That is sacrilege. We are not allowed to do that under any circumstances.' He stood up, then sat down heavily. 'This can't get out!'

Ben and Katy were silent. Mary put an arm round both of them and said, 'Sounds like that bloody interfering woman prevented a bloodbath. She saved thousands of lives. You should be very proud of her.'

Henry said, 'Good Grief. Of course. Yes.'

Katy's tears washed down her cheeks but she smiled through her tears. 'Yeah. I'm proud of my mum and I'm proud of my dad too.' She sniffed and reached out a hand to Ben. 'Hankie please, Dad. Got a lot to live up to, haven't I?'

Henry beamed at her. 'Well, young lady, I'd say you've done a sterling job so far. I am honoured to be acquainted with you all. Shall we continue or would you like a break.' He looked at his watch. 'Bit early for gin – even for me. Mary makes a pretty mean cup of hot chocolate – she even got me to buy one of those thingummy jiggy things that make foam. Any takers?'

* * *

As they sipped their frothy chocolate, they all looked sombre. Henry said. 'I'd never thought of Murdock as an idealogue. I knew he was a rapist. I knew he was a domineering bully and thoroughly unpleasant. And a blackmailer, of course. I suspected he was into other crooked dealings. But a fanatical Unionist? That I never suspected. He hid it well.'

'Any more in the letter?' asked Katy.

Her father held it up. 'Two more paragraphs.' He started reading again.

'Knatchbull is a lightweight. True to the cause but none too bright. He's been a useful shield but, without me, he'll eventually go under. He'll crack under pressure so I've only told him what he needs to know.'

Ben spoke. 'So this shows it was Knatchbull who protected Murdock all those years. Chris told me they couldn't touch Murdock so they had to accommodate him. He thought it was because he knew too much, stuff that MI5 couldn't allow to come out. But Murdock just knew the right person who could pull the right strings.

'Last para.' He tapped the paper.

'But he doesn't know where these are; no-one knows. Even our enforcer doesn't know. So how the hell did you find them? This will not end. The cake gets demolished and then there were Neele and the Colonel. No matter – but be warned. This battle's over but the war goes on. No surrender.'

As Ben put the paper down, Henry wiped his eyes. 'That is some confession from a person who worked for the same organisation that I was proud to be a part of. We have a history here, in Cambridge, of people working for two masters. It has made me unutterably sad that we have another to add to our list of infamy.'

Mary added, 'I'm not sad. I'm furious. It's not even a confession. A confession includes remorse. There is no remorse here.'

Ben patted his ancient friend on the shoulder. 'But, Henry, you can certainly be proud. You've helped to shatter two spy rings working against the good of our country. Of course, the difference is that the Cambridge Spies came into public consciousness. I believe that this one never will. This one will be buried and stricken from all records and perhaps that's for the best.'

Katy was stamping from foot to foot. She waved the letter around. 'Weird. What's with the cake and the Colonel? Anyway, could you oldies just stop maundering on about the past and empty that box so we can see what else that bastard had hidden!'

Chapter 44

Ben had phoned Jane and within the hour a car had arrived and they had been whisked away to the headquarters of MI5 where the four of them were awaiting a debriefing. Ben was prepared to fight their corner if there was any suggestion that they had acted illegally. And his defence would be that none of the documents that they had read were Classified. He realised, however, that they soon would be. He was under no illusions about the people they were about to meet. They hadn't risen this far in the intelligence services by being nice. One of their own, a high ranking officer like them, had been found to have been an integral part of a genocidal plot on British territory. And the finder had not been one of them but an outsider. He would need to tread carefully so as not to step on any egos.

And, of course, he was going to have to lie. He visualised his secret place in the chimney of his bedroom where lay the single piece of paper that they had removed from Murdock's box – a black-edged card with its inscription in Murdock's immaculate copperplate. They were bound to ask, and these people were trained to detect lies. That was the one part of the proceedings that he was dreading.

Jane met them and, after discussion with Security, resulting in their not having to be searched, she said in a whisper, 'I'm taking you to the crème de la crème of both Services and a man from GCHQ. They'll send me away. A pity that, I'd like to know what we've put our lives on the line for.'

They were ushered into a plush office. Four besuited men stood as one and each held out a hand. After a prolonged round of hand-shaking, one introduced himself. 'Parker – a Cambridge man myself. Shocking do, absolutely shocking.' The other three were not introduced. Ben looked at each of them in turn, faceless men, grey-beige, who would fit into any middle class, white gathering.

Jane asked if she should stay or go. After some sideways looks between the suits, Ben declared, 'Jane has been instrumental in this operation. She and Chris are a credit to your organisation. If she goes, we go.'

'Jane, come and join us.' Parker said.

Parker started by asking if Katy would be agreeable to signing the Official Secrets Act, as it would be enormously helpful to the Services if all four of them were to be signatories. That being accomplished, Parker proceeded to ask about Murdock's box.

Ben produced the box from his bag and placed it on the table. 'We've secured the site where it was found but it will need the bomb squad to deactivate the booby trap that Murdock installed to keep his secrets safe.' He passed across the table the garage key in its original envelope, with the word Tom written within a black square. He'd decided to let them try to find out where it was. If they came back to him, he would tell them. 'A puzzle for you from your ex-employee, Stanley Murdock. The key to his lock-up.' Then he continued, 'I'll go through the documents in the order they were in the box. I assume that's OK.'

'Absolutely. It is your find and we are enormously grateful to you for ensuring the contents are not being broadcast to those beyond these walls. Can I ask if you have copied any of these documents or shown them to anyone outside this room?'

'No, neither. Once we have handed these over, we want to walk away from this whole business. My one wish was to find out who had murdered my wife. I found that it was Murdock and he is dead. I buried him and now, I can bury the pain and start a new life. There is no way that any of us would want to be party to whatever has to be done now. Now, it's your problem and we wish you well with it.'

'And you have not removed anything?'

This was the question Ben had been preparing for, but before he could respond, Mary squeezed his arm. She looked straight into Parker's eyes and smiled as she replied, 'No, of course not.' She pointed to the box. 'What we need now is to pass all the information to you, because you are the professionals. Then we can move on with our lives. That's not to say that we're not proud of what we've achieved. I'm sure you'll agree that we've done well to uncover the evidence. Now it's up to you. You people have the knowledge and resources to finish the job. We want no part of it.'

Clever, thought Ben. Tell almost the truth but not quite – and stroke their egos.

'Thank you,' said Parker. 'We know that we owe you a huge debt and you will find that we are not unappreciative. We have seen the evidence you have already uncovered. Jane tells us it was found in a charity shop in Cambridge?'

Ben nodded and he saw Jane give a sly wink in his direction. Parker continued, 'And Jane has told us her part in the history. In due course, we will need to ask you to fill in gaps in our understanding. That can happen at a later date, but now we are agog to know precisely what you have found. Damning, I hope?'

'Oh yes. Decidedly damning. And shocking. These documents date back to 1996, just after Murdock returned from Northern Ireland. They show one of his murderous deeds – no doubt one of many – and the names of his conspirators. The one I think will cause you the most consternation is the list of donors to his cause. He has documented their names and the amounts they have contributed over the years. But first, you need to see his covering letter.' Ben handed over the crisp white envelope. Parker opened it and the four suits read its contents. Then they handed it to Jane. After they had all read the letter and had nodded and tutted, Ben said, 'Of course you can't confirm or deny, but Blair's landslide in '97 certainly removed any power or influence from those people recorded in Murdock's meetings. If, as Murdock suspected, someone here was involved in that change of government, then we all owe them a debt of gratitude.'

Parker nodded briefly and said, 'Of course, you know we cannot possibly comment. Shall we move on?'

But, as Parker spoke, Ben noticed a slight upward twist of his lip at one side – the sort of quarter-smile that Katy gave when she had got her own way. It arrived and then it was gone. He blinked. Maybe he'd imagined it.

Ben handed over the picture of the yacht with the yawning hole. 'You'll need to read the inscription on the back.'

One of the unintroduced men said, 'I remember this. Cabinet Minister, a Cambridge alumnus if I remember rightly. Same college as Murdock. Ethel's wasn't it?'

Parker bristled. 'As is our esteemed visitor, Professor Walpole, a Fellow of that college. Is there a point that you are making?'

Ben had no wish to intrude on private disputes and rivalries so quickly handed over the next paper. It was a single sheet with a printout of a spreadsheet. He said, 'The donors. You'll find some

Russian and Chinese names in there as well as some of the great and good of our own.'

The four suits leaned over the paper. There followed gasps of 'Holy shit', 'Christ Almighty', 'I don't believe it', 'Surely not him', 'No way' and finally from one of the suits, 'Fuck me!' followed by an apology 'to the ladies present'. Ben would not like to have been on the receiving end of the look that Parker gave him. The suit murmured a second apology.

There seemed to be some reticence in handing the donor list to Jane. Ben was becoming angry on her behalf. He said, 'If you are thinking that this information might be above Jane's pay grade, perhaps you should consider that she merits a large pay rise. After putting her life on the line and having to go into hiding from one of her superiors, don't you think that she deserves to know the truth?'

Parker cleared his throat. 'Yes. Yes, of course.' He passed the donor list to Jane but looked straight at Ben. 'We look after our own, you know. And anyone who has assisted us. But we are a secret service. That makes us wary of spreading information further than needs be. Apologies to Jane and to Chris. They have shown themselves to be exemplary in following and uncovering the truth. Do not worry on their behalf, or indeed on your own. Chris will get the very best treatment and we hope he will return to us soon. And we will look after you.'

'Hear, hear,' said Henry. 'That's the spirit. Know thine enemies and look after thy friends.' He waved his arms in a way that made Katy, sitting next to him, duck. Then he pointed to each of the suits in turn. 'I knew you all when you were in short trousers – when you were busy putting skeletons safely away in cupboards. Glad you're keeping the true spirit of the place alive. And the rivalry, I see, is still extant, showing that there's still no such thing as Oxbridge here. Never the twain shall meet, eh? Good show!'

Parker smiled. 'The same old Henry Walpole. Ebullient, affable and as sharp as a razor. You were always good so I suppose you know where all our skeletons are hidden. Your comments are noted.'

Mary brought them back to the matter in hand. 'We think the donor list will be the most shocking to you. But the army he had recruited, both serving and former soldiers, is the most shocking to me.'

Ben handed over the next list. Mary continued, 'You'll see that they had recruited quite a number of foot soldiers. There don't seem to be any officers on the list. It seems they were looking for those disillusioned with their lot. Squaddies and ex-squaddies proved to be a fertile recruiting ground. We're assuming that you will share that information with the army. John Harris will certainly be interested. And these people will all need the support and rehabilitation that appears to have been absent so far.'

Parker said, 'Noted.'

Ben handed over the next list. 'This one gives contact details of all the insurgent groups Murdock was in contact with – both here and abroad. We could not establish what they had in common with Murdock and his conspiracy.'

Parker turned to the suit to the left of him. 'Your area, I think.'

Ah, thought Ben. So that must be the man from MI6.

The suit stroked his chin. There was a rasping sound as he scratched his designer stubble. Ben thought he looked ridiculous. In his view, designer stubble was for the young and trendy – and this suit certainly could not be described as either. Ben also wondered how long it had been since he'd been in the field. His straining shirt suggested that it had been too long. 'Um. Quite a transworld party of malcontents. The first thing I can see, that several of them have in common, is that they espouse ultra-conservative religious views. The middle-eastern ones are of particular interest and the American ones are useful. We hadn't had them on our radar.' He tapped the paper. 'The British far-right groups in here are ones we already have an interest in. Thank you for this. Extremely helpful. Yes, extremely helpful.'

Ben handed over another piece of paper. 'This one is a list of his contacts in Northern Ireland. I'm sure you'll know these names.'

Parker glanced down the list and then handed it to the man on his right. 'Have we got all these?' The man drew a thin forefinger down the list of names, then he pulled a sheet from the folder in front of him. He frowned as he compared the two. Ben could see him counting silently. 'Six new to us. And confirmation of another six.' He looked up and beamed. It was the first smile they had seen since entering the room. 'This is so useful. We can get onto this straight away.'

'And, last but not least, a list of people to be contacted because they might be sympathetic to his cause. If you note, it's dated only a few weeks before his death. And some have ticks beside them.'

There were gasps from the other side of the table as the four men pointed to various names. The one who had apologised for swearing, looked up and said, 'Again, amazingly useful. This one too is dynamite but, this time…' He looked across at Mary and Katy, 'We're trying not to offend anyone by our language.'

After everyone, including Jane, had perused all the paperwork, Ben handed over the last contents of the box; four photographs. 'Two of these are old and two more recent, we think. There is nothing to say who the people are or where the pictures were taken.'

The suits studied each in turn. Parker asked of them, 'Anyone know who these are?' All shook their heads. After the four men and Jane had perused the photos and declared that they had no idea who the people were or where and when they were taken, Parker stood and proffered his hand.

Ben slid the empty box across the table. 'In case there's some secret code embedded!' Ben was pretty sure that there wasn't as Katy had examined Murdock's box thoroughly and had declared it 'clean'.

The many handshakes were repeated and Parker said, as he led them to the door, 'We'll be in touch. I'm sure you're as aware as I am that the Peace Process in Northern Ireland continues to be fragile. This information will allow us to tread our way delicately through this minefield whilst ensuring that we widen our net, if you'll forgive the mixed metaphors. Thank you again. You've given us intel of enormous importance. We have much to digest and a great deal of work to attend to. We'll be on to this straight away. Thank you again. Jane will show you out.'

Immediately they were out of the room, Ben asked her, 'You kept the provenance of the disks secret. Why?'

Jane laughed. 'Easy that – protecting your sources. You told me about Diane's informant. I thought he deserved a peaceful life.' She pointed back to the room they'd just left. 'Makes no odds to them so why involve him in more aggro.'

Ben smiled hugely at her. 'Thank you.' And he thought, a woman after my own heart. I could deal with her, and rather her than those in there.

As they approached the exit, Jane said, 'Thank you for making them include me. Could be I'll be in for a promotion as a result.'

Henry said, 'Richly deserved. Those stuffed shirts up there have forgotten what it's like to put themselves in harm's way – if they ever knew – and, believe me, some of them don't.'

And Katy added, 'About time they had a woman in that room. Go for it, Jane!'

Chapter 45

Back in Mary's kitchen, each of them was holding a glass of fizz. Ben proposed a toast. 'To the end of the pain. Oh! Hold on a minute, don't drink yet. I've forgotten the matches.'

As Ben scrabbled in a drawer, Henry said, 'We've signed his death warrant, you know.'

Katy raised her eyebrows. 'Hang on. I thought we were burning this to save him – to make his new life secure.'

Henry replied, 'I mean Knatchbull.'

'Oh! Him!' Katy gave Henry a big grin. 'I don't care a fig about him. Just like I don't care about any of them that died – Murdock, Dobson, Pedersen, Neville-Taylor. Except the nun; that was sad.' And, with what Ben considered the distance that only youth can bring, she added, 'But not so very bad, I suppose. She was ancient anyway.'

Henry said, 'Oh dear, I'm ancient too.'

Katy was immediately contrite. 'Oh, but you're adorable and I know you. I didn't know the poor nun. Sorry Henry. That was sooo insensitive. Put it down to my extreme youth and forgive me. Yes?' She gave Henry that look that she reserved for the times when she wanted something. And it worked, just as it did with her father.

Henry beamed at her. 'Of course I forgive you.'

Ben asked, 'Been meaning to ask you; did you ever find out if your rooms had been bugged?'

'Now here's the thing, dear boy. I'm so desperately disappointed. Clean as a whistle. Knatchbull obviously didn't see me as a threat. Thought I was too ancient, I expect.' And he smiled broadly at Katy.

The mention of bugs reminded Ben of another question that had been bugging him. He turned to Henry but, it seemed, Henry had read his mind. He winked at Ben and joined in with his match scrabbling, obscuring the matches that Ben had just unearthed. He whispered, 'Parker's a dark horse though, eh? Brave, foolhardy, could still get him kicked out if it became known. But I've always thought democracy to be substantially over-rated. Better keep it under our hats.'

Ben brought over the matches and Mary held out the card. Katy took it from her. 'Dad, you sort of explained what it meant, but here's my confession. I wasn't really listening. I was all revved up to meet the big suits. Scared, even. Can you just tell me again? And can we all have a drink while you're spouting?'

Ben nodded. 'Read the words out.'

Katy held up the black edged card with its few words written in Murdock's flowing script.

'Jacko, your debt repaid. RIP Tommy Mahony.'

Ben explained, 'Jacko was that paramilitary in Belfast. I'm assuming the debt was because of the incident in the pub in Belfast. Alistair says he wasn't bothered when Jacko "touched him up" but Murdock was furious. This is all conjecture on my part but I think Murdock suspected that Tommy and Margaret were lovers. After the Murdocks had upped sticks and moved to Cambridge, he arranged for Jacko to kill Tommy. Jacko somehow managed to convince Murdock that Tommy was dead. Now this is complete fantasy on my part, but the police station in Moira was bombed soon after the Murdocks came back to England. Tommy had just joined the RUC. What if Jacko was the bomber and the target was Tommy?'

Henry said, 'Not so very fanciful. I've heard of much more fantastical tales that were true in every detail. I wonder how Jacko persuaded Murdock that Tommy was dead? Surely Murdock would want some kind of proof. I suppose we'll never know. But I'm glad that poor man has been reunited with his children. Some consolation for what he's suffered.'

'So we're burning this so Tommy and Virginia and Alistair can stay out of the clutches of MI whatever number and live happily ever after.'

'That's about it.'

Katy said, 'As the youngest person here, can I light it?'

Ben handed her the matches.

* * *

A week later, Ben and Mary were having a leisurely breakfast. Mary was reading the Guardian while Ben idly listened to the Today Programme on Radio 4.

Mary smiled that slow smile that turned his heart on its head. 'Good about Chris. Dr Clare says he's progressing well. We could pop in to see him on our way to Norfolk.'

Ben nodded. 'Yeah, it'll be good to see him. They've started him on physio. He says he's knackered, wondering if they've realised their mistake and are slowly murdering him. And, do you realise, Mary Amelina, that I haven't had to visit The Friary once since you took me in hand? I'm hoping I won't need it any more.'

He tried to put on that look that Katy gave when she wanted something. Mary tilted her head to one side and looked doubtfully at him. 'You OK? Your face has gone all funny, like you've got a tooth ache or something.'

He decided he'd better practise or give up on that one. 'Mary, I was trying to look imploringly at you. I have a very big favour to ask.'

'And it is?'

'When you've finished helping Henry sort his papers, I've got six sacks full of Dobson's. You couldn't see your way to helping me wade through them, could you?'

'Wow! You do know how to give a girl a good time! Of course I will.'

'Thanks. I owe you. But why does Jane need to come to see us "with a request from on high"? Sounds ominous to me.' He looked at his watch. 'Bloody Hell, she'll be here in half an hour. Better get dressed.'

Mary tapped his hand and passed over the paper. 'Before you go...' She pointed to a small item on page 4. The headline read 'Foul play not suspected'. At the same time, a solemn voice on the radio announced, 'Jeremiah Knatchbull, an under-secretary at the Home Office, was found dead in his flat in Knightsbridge yesterday. No-one else is being sought in connection with his death.'

* * *

The visit from Jane had been brief and to the point. After they'd shown her out, Ben looked quizzically at Mary. She said, 'Well, it's good to be asked. It shows they rate us.'

'So, let's get this straight. They think we can achieve what they, with all their resources, have failed to do?'

Mary smiled that slow smile; the one that always made his heart flip over. 'But look at the great team we've got!'

He replied, 'And look at the danger we've put them in.'

'But now they know the danger, they can choose.'

He took a deep breath. 'I remember when I broke all ties with Dobson. I said I'd never get involved with him again. But I did. This time though, never means never – yes?'

'Maybe.'

He could see that she wanted to do it. Could he dissuade her – yes, probably. Did he want to dissuade her – that was a question that needed serious consideration. He knew then that life with Mary Amelina was never going to be humdrum. It was set to be 'a daring adventure or nothing'. Scared? Of course he was. But would he have it any other way?

Book 4 – Bury the Past

He had hoped to settle into domesticity. He now has Mary by his side – but she brings Russian complications.
October 2013
The conspirators in the Northern Ireland plot are being systematically murdered. Henry Walpole is the first to see the pattern. Ben informs the top man at MI5 who realises that links could be made to Murdock and Knatchbull. If their plot is uncovered, MI5 knows the Peace Process would be in grave danger. Ben is called back to do 'one last job'.

Then he is told that his first task is to talk to a dead man…

Printed in Great Britain
by Amazon